IRENE'S FALL

Ladies of Munro, Book 5

Elizabeth Donne

Dragonblade Publishing, Inc. is an imprint of Kathryn Le Veque Novels, Inc.
P.O. Box 23
Moreno Valley, CA 92556
ceo@dragonbladepublishing.com

Produced in the United States of America

First Edition December 2025
Trade Paperback Edition

ARE YOU SIGNED UP FOR DRAGONBLADE'S BLOG?

You'll get the latest news and information on exclusive giveaways, exclusive excerpts, coming releases, sales, free books, cover reveals and more.

Check out our complete list of authors, too!

No spam, no junk. That's a promise!

Sign Up Here

www.dragonbladepublishing.com

Dearest Reader;

Thank you for your support of a small press. At Dragonblade Publishing, we strive to bring you the highest quality Historical Romance from some of the best authors in the business. Without your support, there is no 'us', so we sincerely hope you adore these stories and find some new favorite authors along the way.

Happy Reading!

CEO, Dragonblade Publishing

Additional Dragonblade books by Author Elizabeth Donne

Ladies of Munro Series
Sophia's Letter (Book 1)
Ellena's Secret (Book 2)
Verity's Choice (Book 3)
Jillian's Wild Heart (Book 4)
Irene's Fall (Book 5)

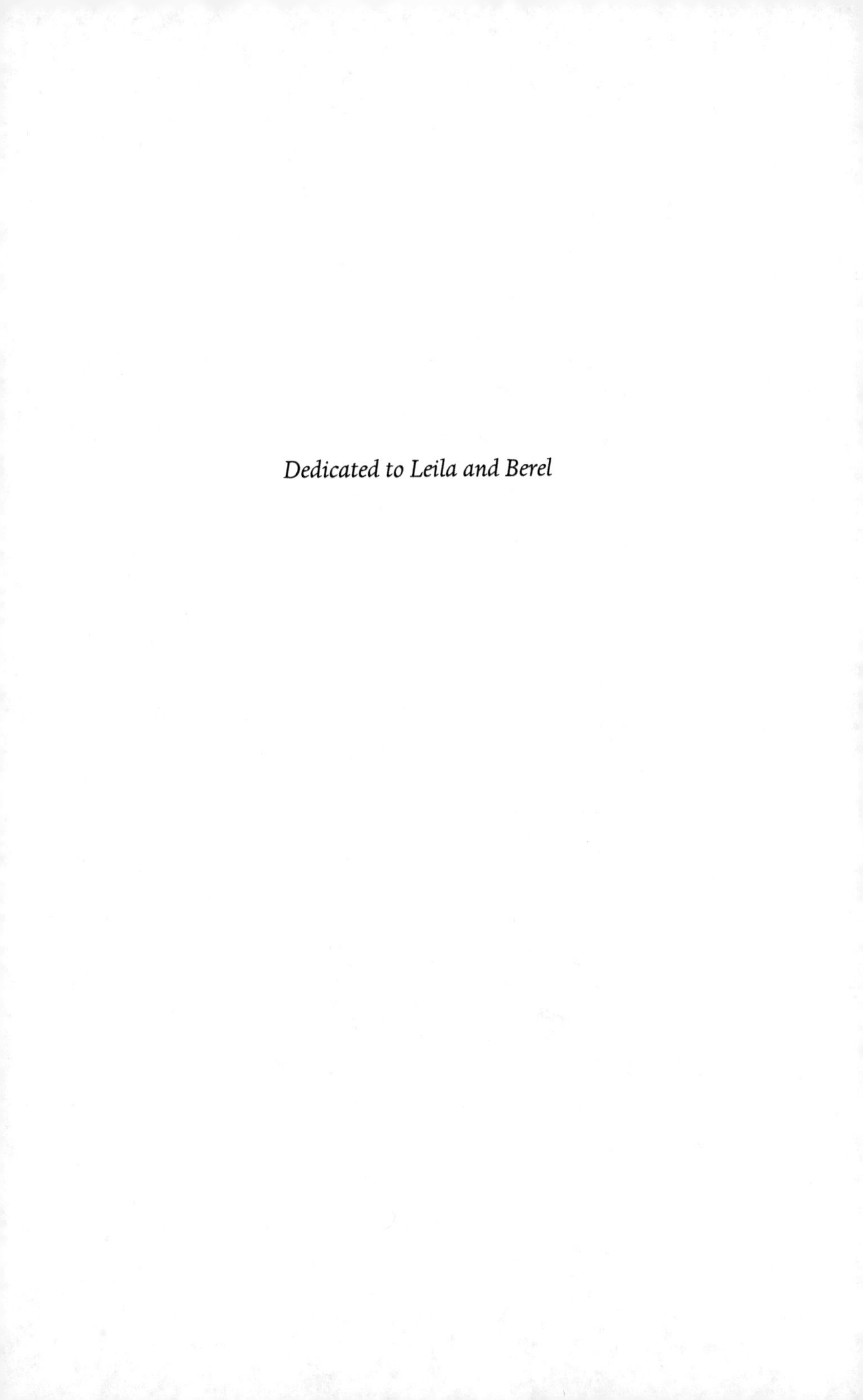

Dedicated to Leila and Berel

CHAPTER ONE

The northern city of Munro, Monday, March 10th, 1817

"Mama, Irene has *again* refused to go riding with me!"

The plaintive voice of Miss Irene Sangford's sister was followed by the young woman throwing herself upon the *chaise lounge* in a manner that should have shamed a well-bred lady of one and twenty years. Amelia, unfortunately, was used to getting her own way.

Except when it came to her sister.

Irene, two years her senior, would have been mortified to perform such a ridiculous display. Instead, she stood calm and unmoved in the doorway. She had few pleasures in life. Countering her sister was one of them.

"You only ride to be *seen*." Irene scoffed. "I have no desire to change my clothes and smell of horse merely to help you find a husband."

"Ha! You could use similar assistance," Amelia snapped back. "How many seasons has it been?" Amelia pretended ignorance, knowing full well this was Irene's sixth. "Truly, I have lost count. You are not so much 'out' as you are 'up'—on a shelf, that is. Isn't she, Mama?"

Amelia flicked her cascade of red-blonde curls over her shoulder as she tilted her perfect chin toward their mother. They often teamed up in this fashion. In both looks and temperament, the younger daughter was a youthful version of Mrs. Sangford.

Irene was not.

"You have also ridden to be seen, Irene," their mother pointed out. "I remember a time when Mr. Philip Bradford joined you on the regular. *Then* you trotted on happily enough. The prospect of marrying a baron's heir was excellent motivation. As, of course, it should be. Such a pity that didn't work out as well as hoped."

Irene repeated the phrase to herself. *"Didn't work out."* What a decidedly odd way to describe what had happened. Irene bit down on the bitterness that was always shallow in her heart. It would have been a matter of days before Philip would have proposed. She had been quite certain of that. Now she would never know. And, in the nearly eighteen months since, there had been no other suitors to ask for her hand.

It was no easy feat to net a nobleman. They were not in abundant supply. The few to whom Irene had managed an introduction were either rich in title only—as bad as having no title at all—or they showed little interest in her.

Viscount Howell, the choicest fruit of her first season, had been a bumbling mess, and she had quickly given up on trying to circumnavigate his awkwardness, which she had felt was simply rudeness in disguise.

The Earl of Carthage had been an even bigger disaster two years later. His friends and family had formed a protective circle around him, as if there could be no greater threat to his wellbeing than a connection with her.

Only a few suitable prospects had remained in Munro among those who were unmarried, wealthy, *and* with prospects of being titled—a handful of firstborn sons of barons. But none of them had given her a second glance. Philip had been the exception to her pitiful and lengthy stay in the marriage mart.

Irene was not entirely sure he had loved her. It hadn't mattered. Not really. More importantly, he had seen her as future baroness material. To the Sangfords—descendants of the Hanover *Sanfords* and (it was rumored) distant cousins to the queen—recapturing a title was *everything*.

Only… It wasn't happening, was it? Without new prospects, she was rapidly approaching spinsterhood, a fate worse than failing to secure a coveted title through marriage. Even Amelia, with her coy, cat-green eyes and a pout that made men stop and ponder her lips, had had no luck in reeling in a gentleman with the critical quality their parents demanded.

They had even attempted two seasons in London at great expense. The first two years of their debut into society should have been a resounding success. But London, with its greater supply of suitors, also boasted a greater supply of beautiful heiresses, leaving Irene and Amelia lost in the crowd. Their father had changed tack, investing his attention instead in local Munro families with meaningful connections to whom they might be introduced. This plan had been no more successful than any other. Philip had been the only exception.

Since Amelia had failed equally dismally, it couldn't have been about looks. Irene knew her sister had won first prize in that arena.

Her own features should, then, have been inherited from their father, but they seemed to belong only to her. Everything about her was elongated—her height, her neck, her narrow face, and her sharp chin. Her hair and eyes were dark, almost black, and her speech was unhurried, as if she could not be bothered with the effort. Philip Bradford had considered her elegant. But no one else had said the same, neither before nor since.

Philip had valued her willingness to approach marriage as a partnership of shared goals. He would be a baron one day, which would delight her family, bringing them back to the upper circles—something they craved, desiring it above all else. The Bradfords, in turn, had considered Irene "the right sort" to marry their son. They, too, placed the continuation of their line and the prestige of their family above love or sentiment. Both families had approved. It could have been enough. Someone had wanted her as companion. Perhaps even, to some degree, Philip had desired her. She could have been happy at last. Out from among this family, who saw her only as a bargaining tool with which to regain their status.

And children. She could have had children who wanted to be held by her, who looked up at her and thought she was the center of their universe. Was it so wrong to have hoped for a little love in the midst of bearing the heir?

Instead, she was alone.

"You should not begrudge your sister the chance of finding a good match, even if you have given up." Mrs. Sangford chastised her eldest daughter. It was a familiar refrain. Irene would like to have said she no longer paid it any mind, but it stuck in her craw and festered.

The truth was, she had always enjoyed riding. She had an excellent seat and looked very fine in her riding habit. Most of all, she savored the freedom. Besides, when she was promenading on horseback, she was potentially finding a lord. That was her sole purpose, was it not? Her parents were pleased for her to ride every day, and she had been pleased to do so. Fresh air, a little exercise, and the absence of their obvious disinterest beyond securing a noble son-in-law. Riding had been an escape.

For months, however, she had kept imagining she saw Philip. Foolish, really. He would never frequent Munro Park again. No one else awaited her arrival, drawing nearer when she appeared. The loss of such anticipation had been severe. It was not a feeling to be relished. She did not wish to go riding anymore. And a harsh winter had given her the excuse to avoid it.

"Irene, are you listening to me? I expect you to stop this pining for what you cannot have. It has been many months since you have accompanied your sister. The weather is greatly improved, and you both need to show yourselves among the riding folk, lest some other young lady draws the eye of the few noblemen available."

Irene shrugged. "There will be no one we haven't seen before. I hardly think we would suddenly capture the attention of those who have until now given us no reason to hope."

"Why, you never know! A gentleman might have a guest with him: a young lord visiting from university or a cousin who is an heir. Every day is a possibility. You must not waste it. There are enough other young women who would swoop in and grab the prize."

Their mother wasn't going to stop until Irene gave in. She knew this. It was only a matter of time before she found herself riding next to Amelia, a smug smile on her sister's stupid face.

"Fine. I will go." Irene allowed her mother to think she had won. The truth was, there might very well be a new face to consider. And she'd be darned if she let Amelia have him.

Up the curve of stairs she went, her lady's maid hastening after her moments later. The servants had learned to answer the bell at once. Mrs. Sangford tolerated nothing less than prompt obedience. Irene chewed her lip. She knew how they felt.

Dressing was a tiresome affair. Her habit included a corset, which hardly seemed necessary, given her lean proportions. Ankle boots, gloves, hair, hat—all were dealt with briskly and without conversation. There were no subtle friendships behind the scenes. Irene did not know the softness of kind words.

Sometimes she thought she had caught Finnegan, her lady's maid, looking at her with sadness. The servants had certainly, at one time or another, witnessed her loneliness and the way her mother favored Amelia. But she didn't want their pity. She had been raised to express condescension, and it was all she knew.

A supportive companion of equal status might have made a difference. Instead, she had friends whom her mother had handpicked for the connections they brought. Silly women who could be manipulated. Nasty, gossipy things.

Like herself.

Irene rose abruptly. "That's enough fussing. You may let the groom know I am ready. I will collect Amelia and meet him at the stables."

"Yes, miss." Finnegan bobbed a curtsy. Her mother would

have loved that. Anything that maintained the semblance of their link to the aristocracy pleased her. Irene could not have cared less.

She strode from the room, leaving the maid to scuttle after her in her haste to reach the groom. Finnegan needn't have worried. Amelia would not be ready.

True to form, her sister was still halfway through having her hair styled. While she typically wore her tresses in a loose pile on her head or flowing down her back, they were now being carefully shaped into twists and rolls with countless pins to look effortlessly complicated. She would likely wear only a small hat, all the better to show off the unique shine of her Venetian-blonde curls.

"Come on." Irene urged her. "By the time we reach the park, any prospects will have been claimed by ladies who worried less about their hair and more about finding a husband."

"They may do as they want." Amelia sniffed. "Once I arrive, I shall have whomever I choose. It matters little whether their interest had been momentarily held elsewhere."

Irene did not answer. She had once thought and spoken with similar confidence. She had believed any man to be like clay in her hands, hers to mold as she wished. Now she knew better.

Amelia did not yet understand the loneliness of so many unfulfilled seasons. Perhaps she would be lucky. Irene stiffened at the thought. She did not love her sister enough to wish Amelia success where she had failed.

"I'm going to the stables," she muttered. "Hurry up or I will take the groom and go without you."

"Mama will be vexed if you do," Amelia warned.

"I don't care."

Irene stalked like an angry crow across the lawn, her long skirt dragging a little on the ground. She grabbed fistfuls of it and hoisted it off the dirt. The length of it would cover her feet once astride. Such impractical fashion! Heaven forbid she should need to jump from her horse in an emergency. The demands of etiquette would rather see her stumble to her death than risk a glimpse of her ankle.

The groom stood waiting patiently, his back straight, his eyes focused ahead. Her horse's reins rested in one hand. The other touched his cap to her as she approached. A stableboy held the reins of both Amelia's mount and those of the groom's, ready to be passed along when needed.

"Hoist me up, Barton," Irene commanded, taking the reins from the groom and resting that hand on the animal's back.

The groom bent forward, his fingers interlaced to create a cradle. Irene placed her boot into it and stepped up, Barton adding momentum by pulling up into a straight-backed stance once more. Having shifted her hip into a comfortable position, Irene manipulated her right leg into the pommel, designed specifically for holding the limb in place. She rearranged her skirt, all temptation of ankle now quite hidden. Barton passed her a short riding crop. With perfect posture restored and reins in hand, Irene was ready to set off.

Amelia, who must have taken seriously her sister's threat to leave without her, arrived from the house in a rather more flustered manner than Irene had, struggling to secure a pin that was threatening to fall out.

"If my hair comes undone, it shall be your fault," she grumbled at her sister. Irene, however, sat in mute serenity.

Once again, the groom created a step to assist the young lady in mounting her horse. Amelia fussed a little longer with her attire, adjusting hat and gloves so that everything was *just so.*

"Papa wanted to know where we would be riding today," she mentioned offhandedly. "He said something about staying clear of the main road, but I was hurrying to the stables lest you leave me behind. You can be such a beast sometimes."

Irene barely bothered to control the smirk that was forming on her lips. If she had annoyed her sister before they had even left, the day looked promising indeed.

She clicked her tongue and touched her gelding lightly with

the crop. He lurched forward a little, then settled into a gentle trot. Amelia followed suit.

As the sisters rounded the corner of their private mews, the groom drew closer and motioned to her. "The master is calling you, Miss Sangford."

Irene turned to see her father waving at her. Having caught her eye, he gestured furiously for her to stop as he hurried to try to catch up with them. No doubt he was about to give them a lecture about what sort of man was worthy of their attention. And how they were, at all times, to remember they were Sangfords, of the Hanover Sanfords, and distant cousins to the queen.

They had heard it all before. There was no need to endure such a speech again.

"It will be of no consequence," she decided aloud. "We are already late for the fashionable hour. Whatever it is can wait for our return."

And she urged her mount forward, into the public road, and onward to Munro Park.

NATHANIEL MACRAE PUSHED through the small crowd outside the brothel. His horse was waiting for him and he hoisted himself into the saddle, barely pausing before tucking his heel into the animal's ribs. The stallion jolted into action, moving from a walk through a trot and straight into a gallop as Nathaniel claimed the center of the busy road in the hopes of a clear path forward.

There wasn't much time. His informant had only just confirmed what he'd suspected. The protesters would head down the main road, be scattered by the king's troops, and their leaders arrested. The air already rippled with the cries of angry coachmen as traffic on the thoroughfare was brought almost to a standstill by the approaching masses.

Nathaniel veered to the right, down the back road of butchers and tanners and other necessary enterprises that everyone used but no one wanted to see among the glamorous shopfronts of the great northern city of Munro.

The troops would not gather in such a public area, where innocent pedestrians might be hurt or members of the *ton* inconvenienced by a military confrontation. No, they would allow the weavers and other textile workers to walk calmly and (briefly) triumphantly—but most of all, unsuspecting—through the city toward the east as they headed to the crossroads and the next leg of their journey to the south, to London, to lay their appeal for relief before the Prince Regent. What followed would be a swift end to a doomed uprising and the people would soon forget it ever happened.

At least, that had been the plan.

But Nathaniel knew there was more at stake. There were those who did not think a simple dispersal of discontented voices was discouragement enough. The mills had been brought to a standstill. Such a situation—those in charge would believe—must under no circumstances be repeated. Much money was at risk. Only a deep-seated fear would prevent the rabble from rising up again and robbing their masters of their ill-gotten profits. The leadership must be incapacitated. More than that. At least one must die.

Bill O'Neal was the most charismatic and organized among them. This terrible fate would surely fall to him. The how and the who had just reached Nathaniel's ear. There was no time to lose. Already, the green acres of Munro Park rose before him. Beyond its vast grounds lay the country road that would lead to imminent confrontation.

There would be a warning from a spy posing as a supporter. A seemingly friendly hand would beckon O'Neal to safety. The shrubs and woods of the park offered refuge—the friendly deceiver would point out. A carriage, the liar would add, was waiting on the other side of the park. O'Neal could evade arrest.

Start again. This day was not a failure but a first attempt.

And O'Neal would listen. After all, was this not what they had risked everything for?

But he would never emerge from Munro Park.

Unless Nathaniel reached him in time.

The end of the fashionable hour was nearing. Ladies in attire that was honestly far too impractical for such an activity rode their mounts at a walking pace beside a friend or, if they were fortunate, beside a gentleman, a closely-following groom serving as respectable chaperone. Most of them were heading home now to change into something more pleasantly fragrant, possibly readying themselves for the daily round of social calls.

They would have greeted him in passing. Except Nathaniel was haring across the green, clods of grass spitting up behind him, so that all he received were countless cries of "Steady on!" and "Watch out!" as he left the parkgoers rapidly behind.

Any minute now, he must see the two men: O'Neal and his betrayer. Nathaniel's gaze searched the line of trees ahead, the shrubbery on the edges of his vision. The sound of approaching hooves alerted him to two ladies and their groom. And, lurching from behind the thick trunk of a holm oak, a man with a knife.

All startled in equal measure. The armed man froze for the briefest second, staring into the face of one of the riders, a tall woman with dark hair. He whirled round, eyes and mouth widening at the sight of Nathaniel before he took off into the trees. All four horses shied, their owners fighting for control. All calmed but one. One animal, more skittish than the rest, did not settle. Its owner—the tall woman with dark hair—struggled with the reins. Her mount reared, throwing her from her precarious seat down to the ground. The thud of her fall frighted the nervous creature once more. He backed up, stepping with his full weight upon her vulnerable form, the woman's scream of agony renting the air.

Nathaniel, already racing ahead, saw it all in a blur of motion but dared not stop. Already, the armed figure was weaving among the trees, forcing him to slow. The sobs of the unfortunate damsel haunted him, willed him to return and help her. But she would have to rely on her groom. Nathaniel must stay focused. There was no one else to protect Bill O'Neal.

At last, Nathaniel sighted him, hurrying unaware toward his assassin. Beside him ran his supposed friend, his face matching the description Nathaniel's informant had provided. The betrayer saw Nathaniel, hesitated, then broke away from O'Neal, fleeing in the opposite direction. The would-be victim halted momentarily at the sight of a rider bearing down on him, then froze completely when the knife flashed in the hand of the approaching assassin.

"Run!" shouted Nathaniel as his horse charged up to the two men, fewer than twenty yards between them.

O'Neal turned to find his companion gone, an armed man at his back, and made the split-second decision to obey the rider's warning. The assassin's knife missed the space between his ribs by a hair's breadth, the wielder lurching forward, stumbling a little and, in that critical moment, losing the initiative.

Nathaniel leapt from his mount, collided with the hired killer, and rolled free, jumping to his feet with fist swinging. There was no satisfying connection with hard jaw or soft throat. He ducked instinctively, evading the swish of blade through air. Tucking his head down, Nathaniel drove his shoulder into the man's chest, knocking the breath from him. He followed through with a swift knee to the groin. With a groan, the enemy sank to the ground. Nathaniel wrenched the knife from his hand.

A wild and desperate punch landed against Nathaniel's temple. A trickle of blood and sweat blinded him long enough for the stranger to get to his feet. Wiping his eye with the heel of his left hand, Nathaniel fought to get his bearings, the weapon firmly wrapped in the clenched fingers of his right hand. The enemy's focus was on the knife. Nathaniel would not be easily parted from it. Without the blade, the stranger could not complete his terrible mission. All that remained was for him to submit, escape, or die.

He chose escape. To Nathaniel's frustration, his own horse offered the criminal the opportunity. It stepped between them, nuzzling up to its master, nickering at his wound.

"I'm all right, Archer. Give over."

But the stallion would not budge.

"I'm *all right!*" Nathaniel said again, pushing at the solid muscle of the horse's shoulder.

Archer shifted one leg and planted it solidly.

Nathaniel tried to step around, but the stallion simply shifted his impossible size to block his owner.

If not around, it would have to be up. Archer stood firm as Nathaniel hauled his athletic frame up and into the saddle. But it was too late. There was no sign of the attacker. Nor Bill O'Neal, for that matter.

He urged his horse in the direction in which O'Neal had gone. A few broken twigs marked his passage, but the man himself had disappeared. Nathaniel reined Archer in, stopping to listen and look about. Not so much as a leaf stirred. No footfalls sounded in the distance. Not of man or murderer.

Instead, Nathaniel heard a strained voice. "Get *help*, Barton!" it said. "I think it's broken."

He steered Archer back through the trees. O'Neal was safe, for now. The assassin had escaped, but Nathaniel had seen his face. It was only a matter of time before his network of spies ferreted the man out.

At this moment, he could lay down his covert responsibilities. A young lady needed him more.

CHAPTER TWO

THE SCENE WAS unexpected in every way.

To begin with, the injured party was the only one who had kept her head.

"Talk some sense into him, will you?" She grimaced while she spoke, appealing to Nathaniel in the absence of the groom's helpfulness. The fellow was kneeling at his mistress's side, his legs apparently so weakened with shock that he could not get himself up to ride for help.

"Your mistress needs you," Nathaniel urged. "Get up and be off with you. What will your master say if he hears you have not done your duty?"

The subtle threat had the desired effect. The groom found a sudden burst of strength, though his knees buckled as he stepped toward his horse. Nathaniel gave him a boost, telling the man to send for a doctor and bring a stretcher and enough helpers to carry the lady with care. Then he slapped the horse's rump and sent the hapless groom on his way.

"I think it's broken," said the injured party, who was leaning back and away from her left leg as if she wished to be as far from the pain as possible.

"With your permission, Miss…?"

"Sangford," she answered through gritted teeth. "Irene Sangford."

Oh. The Sangford sisters. Nathaniel looked up at the other young woman, who must have been Miss Amelia. He was ready to dislike them both. The family had quite the reputation.

"Miss Amelia Sangford," said the vision, extending a gloved hand over her sister's prone form and allowing him to touch the tips of her fingers.

Nathaniel's heart caught in his throat. She was exquisite. From her strawberry-blonde tresses that were starting to come undone in a very alluring way to the yellow-green eyes that watched him with interest, not to mention the full pout that begged to be kissed. Nathaniel forgot himself completely. And poor Miss Irene Sangford too.

"Perhaps you could lift me from the wet grass," said the injured party, her voice laden with pain and not a little rebuke.

Nathaniel managed to draw his gaze from one sister to the other. "I was about to ask for your leave to examine your leg," he said. "I should not like to move you if the injury is too severe."

"You may," agreed what must have been the elder Miss Sangford, for it was clear she lacked the same degree of youthfulness as her sister. "I feel the worst of it at my shin." Without any hesitation, she threw her skirt aside to reveal her leg up to her knee, swelling already forming in the middle of its length.

"You can't just toss your modesty away like that!" Miss Amelia exclaimed a little more indignantly than necessary. Was she concerned for her sister's decorum, or might there be some jealousy at play? Nathaniel savored the knowledge that the angelic creature that was Miss Amelia Sangford should feel envy for the innocent attention her sister received from him. As he gently pressed around the swollen area, he couldn't help but think what a waste it was to touch this slim leg instead of the succulent shape of a different calf.

"I suspect a fracture, but no displacement," he announced, trying to keep his mind on where he was needed. But what he wanted was very distracting and only a few feet away.

"You see," said Miss Amelia pleasantly, "it's not so bad, Irene.

There is no need to fuss so."

Nathaniel was a bit taken aback at the lack of sisterly love. Then again, the Sangfords were not known for their sentiment.

"I warrant that even a simple fracture is exceedingly painful," he gently corrected her. He half-expected her to express dismay that she had not fully understood her sister's discomfort. Instead, she pursed her full lips and withdrew her coy gaze from him.

"So, I can be moved?" Miss Sangford wanted to know. She did not seem in the least bit bothered by her sister's lack of empathy. Almost as though she had come to expect it. Nathaniel thought that unlikely. *Surely, so rare a beauty as Miss Amelia must have a matching warm heart?*

"If you trust me to do so," he answered, "I will carry you to that bench. We could tie the horses to it also. We have been lucky they have been grazing quietly after their shoddy behavior earlier. However, I don't think we need to add runaway horses to our list of problems."

Miss Sangford attempted a smile, but it was clear that pain robbed her of much humor. "I ask that you do so swiftly," she said. "I would far rather reach the seat quickly, for there shall be misery in the movement no matter how careful you are. Better for it to be brief." She reached her arms up to encircle his neck as he bent down and slid his hands beneath her thighs and back. She winced as he lifted her but did not complain. Miss Sangford, Nathaniel had to admit, was made of strong stuff.

Despite her urging him to move quickly, Nathaniel took great care to mind his step. If he should stumble, the jerking motion would be excruciating for the young lady, not to mention the risk of dropping her entirely. The bench was not as close as he might have liked for her sake, but it did not add to his burden. Miss Sangford weighed little and did not wriggle at all. He was able to lower her with a good degree of control onto the seat of the bench so that she sat along the length of it, the injured leg straight out and the healthy one supporting her with her foot on the ground. Nathaniel politely rearranged her skirt to fall as it should, covering both feet with its excessive length. He tutted to himself at the ridiculous design. How was a woman supposed to manage a fall with such cumbersome constraints? Small wonder she had suffered injury!

"Thank you," murmured Miss Sangford. Was that a blush on her cheeks? Perhaps it was simply exertion. She did not seem the sort to easily show feeling. Possibly she viewed it as a form of weakness. No, it must have been the effort at composure that flushed the color to her face. He was certain of it. And the fact that she now lowered her lashes in a way one might consider demure was only the result of her resting her eyes as the constant pain fatigued her.

"I have brought the horses," Miss Amelia said behind him.

Nathaniel turned to see the young lady holding a set of reins in each hand and looking rather pleased with herself. Now *she* was an open book. "Much obliged," he said as he watched her preen a little.

"Of course," she answered, her shoulder lifting nonchalantly to her rosy cheek. "Who else would do it? You have had your hands full with my sister."

It was a simple statement on the surface of it, but, *heavens*, what undercurrents ran beneath!

Nathaniel ran his fingers through his thick, dark-blond hair, which already lay in combed-back fashion from his brow to the base of his collar. Miss Amelia would be quite the handful if he should pursue her. But he was not so easily frightened. If he were, he would never have managed the tasks Viscount Howell had put before him.

"Perhaps you would like to introduce yourself now that the situation is in hand," the younger Miss Sangford said blandly.

There it was again. The mild rebuke. This time from Miss Amelia. But it was deserved. He had blundered the introductions, his thoughts focused on rendering assistance and not on formalities.

He rendered a stiff bow to make up for it. "My apologies,

ladies. Nathaniel Macrae, at your service."

"Oh," said both women at once. Was that the sound of disappointment? Ah, yes, he remembered now: the two Misses Sangford would only consider a man with a title. A strange expectation when they had no connections of their own, save vague and distant ones. There was, however, tremendous wealth and no son to inherit it, the allure of which they no doubt counted on to attract a suitable match.

Nathaniel recalled, with a pang of guilt at his hardness of thought, that Miss Sangford had, indeed, come very close to finding a most suitable match. Mr. Philip Bradford, eldest son of Baron Bradford, had paid her exactly the sort of attention that one might expect would lead to an engagement. There was every reason to believe—according to the gossipmongers—that such an engagement was imminent. The abrupt death of Philip Bradford had been a terrible blow to both families. Miss Sangford had gradually disappeared from the fashionable riding hour in Munro Park, where she and Mr. Bradford had enjoyed much of their courtship. Nathaniel looked at her now, carrying what must have been agonizing pain with as much dignity as she could. Perhaps it had been the same with the loss of her beau.

Mr. Albert Sangford, however, would have wanted his daughter to seek another ambitious match. He was notoriously driven in this pursuit. To this purpose, he had taken great care to keep his name unsullied. He lived the life of a gentleman of the first order. Even his finances were reliant only upon rentals and investments. No drudgery touched his hands. Not like the…

Hang on. Mr. Sangford had shares in several of the local mills, did he not? What were *his* thoughts on today's march? If business had been hurt by the protests, he would have a very strong motive to stop such uprisings. Perhaps even more than most. A gentleman on the face of it—cold ambition at the heart of him. His only chance of marrying his daughters to lords was through wealth. It that were at risk…

"Thank you… for your kind… assistance, Mr. Macrae." Miss

Sangford's words came forth with some struggle. Her face had grown pale. Rather, he should say, *even paler*, as her alabaster skin was turning a worrying shade of gray.

"Perhaps you should lie down," he said. "The bench is long enough. Here, let me put my coat under your head."

Nathaniel shrugged off his brown tailcoat and folded it into something resembling the shape of a pillow. "Allow me." With his hands at her back, he lowered her onto the seat and its makeshift pillow. She shuddered slightly, probably from delayed shock.

"We need a blanket," he said, looking about as if one should materialize when required. "The horses! We can take the blankets from beneath their saddles." He made to loosen the girth of the first animal, but Miss Amelia immediately voiced her displeasure.

"You should first tie them to the bench as you suggested. What if this gelding rears again and strikes me down? You shan't have enough hands to care for us both."

Nathaniel had the distinct impression Miss Amelia would like very much to see to whom he would tend if he had to choose. The attention from her, which he had considered so flattering but ten minutes before, now seemed out of place. Did she not grasp the severity of her sister's injury? At best, a fracture would require months of healing and learning to walk properly again. At worst, infection could cost her the limb. Nay, even her life.

"You are right," he told her, keeping his disappointment to himself. "If the gelding is so unreliable, we do not want it dragging at the bench upon which your sister lies. We shall tie the horses to the lower branch of that oak," he decided, and he began at once to do just that. Having tethered the two mounts securely, he removed their saddles and claimed the soft blankets beneath, carrying them to Miss Sangford. He lifted her gently and wrapped one of the rugs about her shoulders. The other he lay with infinite care over her lap, determined not to cause her further suffering.

"It might help if you sat with her," he suggested to Miss Amelia. *Mercy!* Did she not have an ounce of pity or nurturing sympathy to give her sister? Must he guide her to perform even the smallest of kindnesses? The beauty of the young lady was fast receding in his eyes. What worth did it have if not blended with warmth and compassion?

To add to his disenchantment, Miss Amelia turned up her nose and moved even farther from the bench. "Ugh! I'd rather not. Such a strong smell of the stables is not meant for a young lady's delicate senses." She pressed the back of her gloved fingers beneath her nose. "I thank my stars it is not I who must endure it. Those blankets are intended for animals, not a woman of sophistication." She threw a disdainful glance at her sister, whose trembling had mercifully stopped. "But I suppose beggars can't be choosers."

So, it was true, after all. The Sangfords were a heartless bunch. He had hoped, upon meeting the lovely Miss Amelia, that she was the exception. Misunderstood somehow. But no, she was an empty bauble, and Nathaniel was no longer entranced by her. The veil had been thoroughly wrenched from his eyes.

The cut near his left eye now began to smart. It hadn't bothered him until now, focused as he'd been on helping where he could. The wound felt tender and sponge-like to the touch, a bruise having risen around the cut. It must have already been a nasty shade of purple. And yet Miss Amelia had not commented on it, had shown no alarm or concern. Nathaniel was beginning to wonder if she had *any* emotion to show.

He considered the elder Miss Sangford for a moment. He could not blame *her* for her lack of attention to his minor injury when her own must torture her continually. She had said little and complained even less. Perhaps her pride would not allow her to show herself as frail. Be that as it may, her fortitude made a pleasant change from the callous expressions volunteered by her younger sister. For now, she was resting as peacefully as the constant hurt would allow. A little color had returned to her cheeks, but the sooner her leg was tended to and some form of pain relief was administered, the sooner it would put his mind at ease. As far as Miss Amelia was concerned, she could entertain herself.

With nothing further within his power to do, Nathaniel allowed himself to shut out all other thoughts and review the case that had brought him to Munro Park in the first place.

As far as he could tell, Bill O'Neal was safe. That, at least, was something. Half of Nathaniel's mission was complete. And he had identified the betrayer. Since the rogue had committed no actual crime against the law except that which governed personal integrity, he could not be apprehended. But men like him had a way of drawing trouble to themselves. It was just a matter of time before their paths crossed again. When he broke the law—and he would—Nathaniel would take great pleasure in bringing him to justice.

Of far greater concern was the escape of the assassin. He might very well try again. Odds were his payment depended upon it. It was helpful Nathaniel had seen his face, but it had rung no bells. Nathaniel would have to rely on his underground network to assist him once more—the dockworkers, gaming hell owners, ladies of ill repute—anyone who moved freely within the underbelly of society or where information passed easily and unnoticed.

To move naturally among his informants had meant to become as one of them—a frequenter of all things lewd and secretive. As a consequence, Nathaniel had earned a blistering reputation among the *ton* as a degenerate rake, a title that offered him useful inroads into venues and inner circles where his presence might otherwise have been questioned.

It had not been as helpful in finding him a wife.

When Viscount Howell had asked for his help two years ago, Nathaniel had been more than willing. Howell cared about the city, invested generously, and used his own infamous network of informants to great effect in weeding out corruption. If Nathaniel could contribute to such a worthwhile cause, he was all for it.

What he had not expected was the addictive thrill of the chase. Until then, he had occupied his time with the usual activities deemed suitable for a gentleman of good standing: riding, dancing, hunting, attending suitably approved gentlemen's clubs. He had been considered a fine catch for any young woman with matching excellence of character.

It was just as well he had not followed through on the many hopeful introductions that had been made. He could never have brought such shame upon his bride as his name now invoked. In truth, Howell would never have asked for Nathaniel's help if he had had a wife to consider. But he didn't. And so, instead of married bliss and the relatively dull existence it would have allowed, Nathaniel had discovered the excitement of covert investigation and quite forgotten that wedded life could hold any allure.

Howell's informants had been steadily added to with his own paid eyes and ears. At times, criminals revealed themselves to Nathaniel directly, viewing him as nefarious as themselves. It was not uncommon for him to be seen exiting a building in which a true gentleman would never have set foot. And yet he was well liked. Not only by his informants, whom he treated with decency no matter what their fallen state, but even by many of good society. After all, what he did in his own time was none of their concern, provided he did not try to marry one of their daughters or sisters.

Ladies sighed heavily when he entered a room. What a waste, that such a fine and charming gentleman should have put himself out of reach for the sake of low habits!

Nathaniel had been compelled to tell his distraught parents the truth of his behavior. It did little to appease their sorrow that their only son—indeed, their only child—should deprive them of a daughter-in-law, grandchildren, and the public satisfaction of their offspring's sound reputation. Still, they were proud of him. Quite possibly, if he had let them, they would have boasted of his sacrifice to all and sundry. *"Did you know? Such a clever lad! While the elite sleep in their comfortable beds, one of our own is keeping harm at bay."* Yes, Nathaniel could imagine it all too well. And he loved them for it.

Sometimes, however, the elite were the ones to watch out for. Nathaniel's thoughts wheeled back to Mr. Albert Sangford. Much as it pained him, he knew it would be a gentleman—at least, one who could be called such by status and breeding—who had put the bounty on Bill O'Neal's head. And Mr. Sangford was a likely suspect. Nathaniel's usual spies would not have access to the world of gentlemen's clubs where the meetings of such plotters might occur. It would be even more challenging if the conspirators gathered in one or more of their own genteel homes. Greater still, if one highly motivated individual had acted on his own. A man with shares in multiple mills would be just such a candidate.

Nathaniel threw a thoughtful glance at Miss Sangford. It would be well within the bounds of propriety to accompany the injured party he had assisted safely back to her home, making certain she received the care she urgently needed. Introductions would follow naturally. And if he called on the young lady a few days later to see how she was faring, it would be nothing but good neighborliness. His presence would be no threat. Not to Mr. Sangford, the suspect. Not to the daughters of the house.

Since his fall into disrepute, Nathaniel had known his place— a welcome partner at the card table, but not in the domestic sanctuary of the drawing room or at the dinner table. He might have been the finest dancer in all of Munro and led many a young debutante by the hand in a reel, but he would never call on her afterward. The maidens of Munro were quite safe from his attentions. No father would consider him husband material. And he did not dare counter their opinion.

A grin spread across Nathaniel's face, and he turned away to hide it. His way into the Sangfords' good graces could be managed with ease. If he should happen to drop the name of an eligible marquess of his acquaintance, Mr. Sangford would at once welcome him into his home as an old friend. A simple plan, but those were often the best. If Nathaniel was lucky, he would catch the assassin sneaking a meeting with the guilty party. Even if Sangford were innocent—a broad term, and unlikely to apply to him fully—he might carry information about who should be investigated instead. It was a starting point.

The heavy sound of a coach upon the compacted mud of the riding lane caused Nathaniel to twist in that direction. The groom, Barton, was at the reins, looking considerably calmer now that he had brought rescue for his mistress. He drew the vehicle to a stop as close to Miss Sangford as he dared. From beside him on the driver's seat, a young stablehand jumped down, heading straight to the horses tied to the oak. A footman—more muscular than the usually lean young men chosen for the position— descended from the back and approached the bench.

"Mr. Sangford sent the carriage, miss," he told her. "He said it would take too long to carry you home on a stretcher. He has sent for the doctor and expects he will be waiting for you when we get you back to the house. If you permit, miss, I will carry you to the carriage."

Once again, Nathaniel was struck by the stiffness in the communication. A servant who loved his mistress would express concern, even show alarm at seeing her wrapped up, supine and silenced by pain. This fellow, however, barely hesitated before unceremoniously scooping Miss Sangford up and transporting her to the carriage, where she whimpered as he manipulated her damaged body through the door and onto the seat.

Miss Amelia, meanwhile, was protesting a great deal more loudly than her injured sibling. "What do you mean, I have to ride back? I should be in the carriage with Irene. If you think I'm getting back on a horse after what just happened to her, you are gravely mistaken!"

"Duchess is much calmer than Prince, miss," said the stable-boy. "I will ride him and accompany you. You will be safe, miss. Do not worry."

Nathaniel's grin threatened to return. Even the horses had been given titles. The Sangfords' obsession extended farther than he could have imagined. It would serve him all the better in inserting himself into their lives.

"I shall worry as much as I see fit," Miss Amelia continued. "I have no desire to spend the season confined to a settee, as my sister must be. Lead Prince home by the reins if you must. Or walk them both. They are not my concern." And with that, she glared at the footman, who hastily extended a hand to help her into the carriage.

The stableboy stood with saddle in hand, the rugs that had covered Miss Sangford having been left on the bench in favor of more comfortable blankets inside the coach. He considered Prince rather dubiously. It was a long walk back to the Sangford residence, but the alternative was no more encouraging.

"Why don't we tie them to the back of the carriage?" Nathaniel suggested. "Or, at least, just Prince? You could ride behind on Duchess and keep an eye on him. I doubt he will misbehave again. But I shall ride with you if that will help. I would like to know Miss Sangford is delivered safely after all she has been through."

This seemed to satisfy the unfortunate lad. Nathaniel lent a hand with saddling them up again. Once Prince was settled behind the carriage, Nathaniel and the stablehand mounted up and filed in, side by side, behind what had now become a small procession.

The little convoy moved forward slowly, Barton likely nervous of putting his mistress through unnecessary torture. Nathaniel wondered whether this was a sign that at least one servant felt compassion for Miss Sangford, or whether he simply did not want to be reprimanded by his master.

Thus, with thoughts of the curious Miss Sangford intermingled with his plans to catch a killer, Nathaniel rode on in silence. The day was far from over. He must keep his wits about him. And pray that no further incidents distracted him from his purpose.

CHAPTER THREE

THE LAUDANUM HAD begun its work. Irene unclenched her jaw and breathed out. Doctor Matthews, having done what little he could, stepped back and let the surgeon get to the more difficult task of setting the bone.

"Good news, Miss Sangford," Mr. Sunderland said from where he knelt to assess the break. "The tibia is still in place, so no unpleasant traction is needed to adjust it. And I have studied William Cowper's methods of immobilization. We shall not have you weighed down by a block of gypsum or any cumbersome contraption to stabilize the leg. You see here, I have sent for some clean rags and egg white and wheat flour. I shall wrap the leg with a layer of cloth. Thusly, you see?" He deftly folded the material around her lower left leg.

"Now, if someone could hold it in place so I may free my hands…"

A small maid—possibly recently employed, though Irene seldom bothered to learn their names—stepped forward from among the curious onlookers.

"Thank you. Yes. Just so. Do not press upon the leg. Just prevent the cloth from coming loose. Right. Now we dip each rag that follows into this mixture." He indicated the bowl with the watery paste of egg and flour. "Once it is thoroughly soaked, we allow the excess to drip from it. So. Yes, that is good enough. And we place the soaked cloth about the dry inner layer."

His hands worked lightly and with confidence. The mild weight of the wet cloth hardly added to Irene's discomfort. Or perhaps that was the laudanum numbing her senses. Either way, after a few short minutes and multiple layers of treated rags, her injury had been encased in a sort of *papier mâché*. The surgeon stood and admired his own work.

"Very good. Yes, indeed. Now, it is absolutely imperative that Miss Sangford does not move for the next hour. It will take a week for the cast to cure completely, but after an hour, it should be dry to the touch. I shall return after two months to remove it and we can discuss the reintroduction of weight-bearing movement. Until then, the patient is to rest the leg completely. Understood?"

Even through her medically induced haze, Irene did not appreciate being spoken of as if she were not there.

"The advantage of this method," Mr. Sunderland continued, oblivious to her affront, "is that Miss Sangford can be moved with relative ease and will not be confined to her room. I think you will agree that is a welcome bit of news. Not so, my dear?"

It took Irene a moment to realize he was addressing her directly. "Oh. Yes. I believe I would go quite mad if I had to spend two months in bed."

"But you will be careful, dear lady, will you not?" He shifted his spectacles so that they sat straighter upon his nose. "The disadvantage of this technique is that it offers less protection if caution is not applied. You may use crutches if you feel you could manage them without falling. Under no circumstances must you put any pressure on that leg or foot. Not yet, at any rate. If you wish to ride again eventually…" Irene pulled a face. "Or perhaps dance?" She nodded. "Well, if you wish to dance again, you shall have to be patient for the time being. Trust me. I have seen many an injury heal poorly thanks to the patient's lack of discretion, deciding for themselves when to resume walking. If you follow my advice, I believe you may know a full recovery toward the year's end."

Oh, good, thought Irene, *in time for winter and the indoors once again. Another season gone. Would there even be a point in trying again next year?*

"I shall put your name on my dance card as soon as you are able," said Mr. Macrae pleasantly, his gray eyes creasing into an encouraging smile.

"Oh!" Irene was quite taken aback at the noble offer. "That is very… thoughtful." She had, in fact, never danced with Mr. Macrae before. They hadn't even met until this day. The Macraes, her parents believed, were rather too progressive in their thinking, welcoming *all sorts* to their balls. Since this usually meant there were no suitably titled bachelors to be had, there was therefore no point in exerting oneself at such an event. A pity, really. The talk about town was that Nathaniel Macrae was famously good at any dance, often being asked to call the steps, which he did with enthusiasm, grace, and, occasionally, too much complexity. She could believe him capable of all of the above. He was certainly built for it—not so tall as to be gangly, with lean muscle that hinted at both agility and strength. She had also seen his mouth—its upper lip shaped like the curve of a butterfly— break open into a broad smile, his eyes almost shutting to accommodate the rise in his cheeks.

In short, he was handsome, even captivating, and well beyond her reach. Unless he suddenly inherited some hitherto unknown title, of course. Even then, he was more likely to choose Amelia.

And then there was the unfortunate matter of their ancestors, who had stood on opposite sides of the Jacobite rebellion. That would have been fifty years before either she or Mr. Macrae had even been born. But some people were silly about such things. Her parents, famously proud of their Hanoverian heritage, were hard-pressed not to spit upon the ground where the great-grandson of a Jacobite now stood.

Nevertheless, Mr. Nathaniel Macrae had been invited into

their home for his gentlemanly service to their daughter. Perhaps, on a rare occasion, that was all it took. A personal connection. Gratitude. Such things could change minds that had been set too long in foolish ways. At least, so it appeared today.

"Perhaps, sir, you will allow me to call upon Miss Sangford in a few days?" Mr. Macrae asked her father. "It would give me great peace of mind to know she is recovering well from both the injury and the shock of it all. It has been quite the ordeal."

There it was again. Irene would never get used to it. The way he worried about her—a woman he had never met before. A woman he had every reason to disapprove of. And yet he wished her well, as if she deserved it. Perhaps all people did, at some basic level. But that was not how Irene had been taught to think.

"That is very kind of you," her father answered. "I am certain my daughter would welcome a little company. Her lady friends have the terrible habit of nattering like common fishwives. A calmer presence might be what is called for instead. Her sister can attend as chaperone."

Amelia's eyes lit up at once, but, to Irene's immense satisfaction, Mr. Macrae did not turn his head toward her to acknowledge the mention of her name. How wonderful! She was to have a gentleman's company. One who was coming for her alone. A gentleman, she couldn't help thinking, who was a feast for the eyes. And, as far as she could tell, he would make intelligent conversation. Better and better.

What good fortune that Mr. Macrae had been in Munro Park when she had needed a sensible man. Although the way his horse's hooves had been tearing up the lawn, one might wonder how sensible he truly was. Some men did enjoy a race. Competitiveness seemed to be a hallmark of the male of the species. But no one had been with him. And he had gone after the knife-wielding thug as if he had taken the fellow's frightening of the ladies personally.

"What happened to the man you were chasing down?" Irene asked suddenly. "Did he give you that nasty cut? We should ask

Dr. Matthews to look at it while he's here."

"Thank you, but that won't be necessary. I've had worse."

"But it might need stitches!"

"Stitches will lessen the scar. And a man needs a good scar to frighten off the competition." He flashed one of those smiles that filled his entire face.

"'The competition'?" Amelia wanted to know. "You think ladies prefer a man who cares nothing for his looks?"

"The ladies whose company I frequent don't seem to mind," Mr. Macrae answered carelessly.

Amelia wrinkled her nose. Small wonder. She seemed to have forgotten that this delightful Adonis chose to associate with such low society. Nor did he hesitate to remind them of it. Yet his manner toward Irene had been every inch the gentleman. He was quite a puzzle.

"The man you chased… He had a scar," Irene pondered aloud. "Not a big one. But he looked directly at me, so I noticed it clearly. It was through his eyebrow, as if a bald line had been shaved there. I think… Yes, it was the left eye facing me, so it was *his* right eye. Did you notice it too, Mr. Macrae?"

Irene could have sworn the gentleman had turned a shade whiter.

"He looked at you?"

"Well, yes. What is wrong with that?"

"And he saw that you looked at him?"

"It would have been impossible not to. We were both frozen with shock. Then I fell and noticed nothing further than an overwhelming sense of pain."

Mr. Macrae's head swung round to her father. "Miss Sangford is a witness. Do you realize what danger that puts her in?"

His words, uttered with such intense concern, sent a chill down Irene's spine. "What sort of danger?" she asked, afraid to know the answer.

Mr. Macrae's frown melted away as he turned to her. "You are perfectly safe here." His eyes flicked back to her father, as if to confirm that with him. "I would recommend, however, that, should you leave the house for any reason, you do not go far and that a strong, alert servant remains in your company."

"You don't think…?" Irene's mother, who had said little thus far—not even to fret and worry at her daughter's injury like any *real* mother would—finally raised an iota of concern.

"I'm sorry to cause you alarm." Mr. Macrae appeared to be genuinely so, his hands reaching toward Irene as if to placate her fears. "Whatever mischief the scoundrel was up to, it was no good. Not if he had a weapon at the ready. And I was unable to apprehend him."

He paused. His eyes twitched toward her father once more. But there was no response forthcoming. Her father—a man not shy to make his opinions known—was surprisingly still.

Having waited fruitlessly for her father to make comment, Mr. Macrae closed his eyes, shaking his head almost imperceptibly. Irene envied him. The Sangford callousness was still new and disconcerting to him.

"Perhaps," he said, "that is the end of it. A chance meeting. An unfortunate accident. You should never encounter him again." His words were meant to reassure, but his clenched jaw said otherwise.

"But?" Irene pressed him.

Mr. Macrae took a while to answer. He seemed to be weighing up how much he should say. "The thing is…" he began.

"Yes?"

"If he did not want his identity known…"

"And I saw him," Irene said solemnly, "as clear as day."

"What would he want with Irene?" Amelia asked, her green eyes flashing—impossibly jealous, even when the only reason Irene was receiving attention was because she might be at risk.

"Hopefully, nothing." Mr. Macrae chewed on his lip. If she hadn't been so unsettled by the talk of a threat, Irene might well have found the action pleasantly distracting.

"And if it is not nothing?" Her father's words, slow to arrive as they were, only served to push the thought of danger deeper into everyone's minds.

Mr. Macrae considered his host with some gravity. "Sir, perhaps we can discuss this privately? Miss Sangford has endured enough today. I would not see her further upset by something I have mentioned carelessly. I am sorry I have done any harm at all. I would prefer not to make it worse."

But Irene wasn't having it. "Do you really think that leaving me out of the discussion is going to prevent me from thinking about it?" she asked. "I assure you, it is better to inform me of all I might face than to leave it to my imagination."

"I'm sure you'll be *fine*." Amelia pooh-poohed her sister's appeal, stepping a little closer to Mr. Macrae and touching him on the arm, all the while keeping her eyes focused on Irene. "You agree, don't you, Mr. Macrae? After all, just because the bad man saw my sister does not mean he has any idea who she is. Nor would he expect her to know who he is. Their paths crossed unexpectedly. There is no reason they should again. Am I not speaking soundly and reasonably? I believe that is what this situation requires. A level head. We don't want any hysteria. Very unattractive, that," said the absolute hussy that was Irene's sister.

The most annoying thing about Amelia was that she would counter Irene just for the sake of it, to rile her up, knowing there was no one in the family who would take her side. Irene was not the golden child. She was not the pretty princess. Amelia wasn't even trying to get on Mr. Macrae's good side anymore. Now that she knew he carried no title, he was of no interest to her other than as a means to vex her sister. Every time their guest showed Irene any kindness or took her feelings into consideration, Amelia was ready to undo the gesture with the insinuation that Irene did not deserve it.

On any other occasion, Irene would have fought back. She could match Amelia, snide comment for snide comment. It was a favorite entertainment between the sisters. But today, the pain—though greatly lessened—ate away at Irene's reserve. It was all she could do to keep her composure. Possibly, where Mr. Macrae was concerned, that was the best revenge. He did not appear to have much tolerance for manipulative speech. And Irene's composure at such talk would likely win his sympathy. Indeed, at this very moment, he was looking at the fingers upon his arm as if they were made of dung. He dropped his hand into his pocket, forcing Amelia to release him.

Irene swallowed a satisfied smirk. In the past year, she had considered… No, she had *feared* the possibility that Amelia might be wed before her. As the older sister, that would be the ultimate insult and humiliation. Still, she felt could say with absolute certainly that her sister's triumph would *not* be with Mr. Nathaniel Macrae. For some strange reason, this mattered greatly.

"Your reasoning has merit, Miss Amelia," Mr. Macrae conceded, "up to a point. One can certainly hope that the man whom Miss Sangford can identify will think as you do—that they are unlikely to meet again and that he can forget all about the incident. As for hysteria, however, your sister has given no indication that she has a tendency to express her nerves with such lack of control. She has borne the horror of today—both mental and physical—with remarkable fortitude. I am sure you will agree."

Irene could no longer hide her satisfaction at seeing Amelia put in her place. Mr. Macrae had not only paid *her* a compliment when Amelia had been trying to curry favor for herself, but the gentleman now expected Amelia to concur! No fan was within reach with which to conceal her amusement. She was unable to turn away sufficiently, for her leg must stay still. Her hand might cover her mouth, but not the twinkle in her eyes, making a pretense at yawning a meaningless disguise. There was nothing for it but to grant freedom to the smile that rippled upward from heart to lips to cheeks and beyond.

And then Mr. Macrae pinned his gaze on her. It wasn't stern as such. There may have been a slightly raised eyebrow. Perhaps a small twitch to the lip that suggested he was even a little amused at her expression.

All at once, he swung his head down and away, breaking the contact they had shared. Irene was astonished at how much it hurt. The loss of his gaze. The brief, almost intimate, connection... gone.

The grin of glee fell from her face. She felt oddly abandoned. For the last two hours, Nathaniel Macrae had been her champion. No one had paid her any attention since Philip. None had thought her deserving of their loyal defense. She wanted his face upon her once more. She needed to be seen.

"Mr. Macrae..." Her speech, usually so unhurried and confident, now carried a note of urgency.

His neck twisted toward her, his gray orbs focusing tightly on its target. Irene shuddered at the way he held her, for that moment, at the center of his universe.

"Yes?" It was only one word, but it demanded an answer. And Irene had nothing to say.

"Er... thank you." It was ready at the tip of her tongue, anyway—the immense gratitude she felt toward him. "For everything."

"'Everything'?" A slow grin eased across his features. "My dear Miss Sangford, I have barely scratched the surface of 'everything.' Perhaps, in time, I will do more than the small 'something' of today. Until then, I am at your service."

He made a chivalrous bow, though the formality of it was tempered by a sensual rush of fingers through his hair when he straightened, so that the dark-blond mass lay back as neatly as before.

Irene considered her own long, almost-bony fingers. How would it feel to tidy a strand from his cheek around the shell of his ear, the sensation of skin and stubble, hair and heat beneath her touch?

"Excellent!" said her father.

"What?" Irene nearly choked on her own thoughts.

Mr. Sangford looked at his daughter with some perplexity. "Why, Mr. Macrae's kind offer, of course. What else?" He narrowed his eyes a fraction, considering the flustered state of his usually indomitable daughter. "Dorothea," he said, addressing his wife, "I think it is time to bid our guest adieu and let Irene rest. You understand, don't you, Mr. Macrae? I do not wish to seem ungrateful."

"Not at all, sir. Not at all," Mr. Macrae assured him. "I shall take my leave at once. In a few days, I shall call again, with your kind permission. And, er… I hope to find Miss Sangford *safe…*" He paused and gave Irene's father an oddly intentional stare. "And her health greatly improved," he finished.

"Yes, indeed. As you say," her father answered, his arm extended and his gaze indicating the direction of the front door. "Hutchins will see you out."

And with that, Mr. Macrae gave a friendly sweep of the room with his eyes, turned smartly on his heel, and was gone, the light diminishing as his presence was lost, the gloom of her existence and the pulsing ache of her injury descending upon Irene once more.

"The gentleman certainly does not lack any charm," said their mother, "but, then again, it is too easily given, and, sadly, in all the wrong places."

"Oh, *yes*, Mama," cried the treasonous Amelia, "he is not our sort at all!"

"It didn't stop you from fawning all over him," muttered Irene.

Amelia touched the tips of her fingers to her neck. "I'm sure I don't know what you mean. Perhaps it is your own feeling that you assign to me. Wouldn't you agree, Mama?"

Mrs. Sangford opened her mouth to answer.

"Don't bother." Irene cut her short. "You will only echo whatever Amelia says. *Wouldn't you agree, Mother?*" She pulled a face as she copied her sister's words, her voice rising to a childlike rendition of Amelia's own.

"That is uncalled for," Mrs. Sangford declared. "I suppose I should be grateful you did not behave thus while Mr. Macrae was here. He may not be a man of subtle habits, but—despite his sins—he still moves in important circles. It would be wise to remember should he visit."

"So, you would not object if I married him?" Irene could not help herself. The words had slipped out before she'd had time to amend them. She was just so tired of the hypocrisy.

"Oh, don't be ridiculous, Irene! There is a world of difference between showing common courtesy and marriage! And well you know it. Honestly, it seems not even a grievous accident can startle you from your habitual causticism."

"Ah, yes." Irene sat back as best she could without disturbing her leg. She could feel that the cast had begun to lose its flexibility. It had shrunk ever so slightly, fitting snugly without constricting the limb. "Me and my terrible habits. Small wonder you can't get rid of me."

Irene bit down to silence herself. There was truth to what she had said. She had meant to implicate her family and their unrealistic expectations of seeking a title for the next generation as the real reason for her failure. But such facts were incomplete. There was more to it.

She was not a nice person. Whether she was so by design, by choice, or by circumstance, Irene had made no effort to change. She did not hold her tongue when thinking unkind thoughts. What were the feelings of others to her? Rather, she sought out their weaknesses, played games with them. Why should they not all carry pain as she did? Long before today and the damage inflicted upon her body, she had been broken inside.

Why had nobody loved her? She didn't mean *now*, of course, when she had strived to *make* herself unlovable, but all those years ago, when she had been little and sought a lap to crawl onto, a hand to lay gently upon her head, a kind word. It was not that her parents were incapable of affection. Amelia had known the experience of it well. Irene, however, had only been there to witness it and to wonder why she had not been allowed to know the same.

"I see you are in one of your moods again," said her mother. "Amelia and I will remove ourselves so as not to be targets for your entertainment." Mrs. Sangford rose abruptly, caught sight of the cast on Irene's extended leg, and paused, softening her voice just the tiniest amount. "I will have tea brought in for you. You will likely want to eat something too. Laudanum can be strong on an empty stomach. I will see to it." And then the shutters came down again.

Amelia and their mother swept from the room, an option currently denied Irene. It was one of her favorite things to do—removing herself with dignity and a hint of offense. Irene tapped a short devil's tattoo on the arm of her chair with the tips of her nails. It was going to be a long and tiresome two months. Worse yet, she would be entirely dependent on others, people—family and servants alike—who did not hold much sympathy for her. She hated being beholden unto any of them.

She could have her friends—such as they were—call upon her. At least they always provided her with a pleasant (if false) sense of superiority. They all had two things in common. They moved in circles with eligible lords. And they lacked the ability to think for themselves. They hung on Irene's every word, allowing her to decide for them what they should do, how they should choose. It was akin to a life-sized puppet show with Irene as the puppet master. Ah, yes, they would certainly alleviate some of the boredom in the weeks that lay ahead.

Her usual patter of thought stuttered to a halt.

What about Mr. Macrae? Might he call upon her *more* than once? Did she want him to?

Her heart mocked the foolishness of this last question with an ache that rose within it. It was pointless denying her feelings. Seeing him again mattered greatly.

He knew what she was. He must. She had carefully assured that everyone who was not a potential suitor should taste her scorn. Arrogance was a common quality of the upper echelons. Claiming it for herself was another means of ingratiating herself with the people among whom she must, through marriage, belong.

She had seen Mr. Macrae's expression when they had introduced themselves in the park. He had tried to strip the disapproval from his face—an attempt that had only made her like him more. These small but significant gestures were the hallmark of a true gentleman. And she had not been allowed to know many.

Mr. Macrae had chased the danger from her. She shuddered at what might have happened if he had not chanced by. And he had returned to check on her, dealing with Amelia (she rolled her eyes with pity), taking charge of Irene's needs. He had done so with exceeding thoughtfulness, despite any personal reservations he surely bore toward them.

She felt herself curiously drawn to him. She would know him better, understand the workings of his mind... and heart. She felt—it was ridiculous, really—a previously unknown desire to be found pleasing. It mattered that he liked her. Why his opinion should be of such importance, she could not say. Irene only knew that is was.

Below the knee, her leg complained at its broken state. Irene ignored the steady torment of it. Instead, she focused her mind on Mr. Macrae, a worthwhile distraction. He had touched her upon that bruised skin, gently, without any intended intimacy. Much like Mr. Sunderland had done. Only, Irene did not recall the presence of the surgeon's hands upon her uncovered limb with the same degree of thrill creeping up into her entire body, stirring her blood.

One of the nameless maids brought tea and a sandwich. A reminder that her mother was not entirely cold toward her needs. She nibbled and sipped a little, but the laudanum had taken root fully now, drawing her eyes closed. Irene sat back against the plush chair, its deep cushioning the closest thing to a tender touch she had received since returning home. With a tired sigh, she gave herself up to the small gift of its embrace, imagining, as she fell asleep, the arms of a Jacobite's great-grandson lulling her to rest.

CHAPTER FOUR

Munro House, home of Viscount Howell, Thursday, March 13th, 1817

"I TOOK YOUR advice," Lord Howell told Nathaniel, "and had Albert Sangford followed. Simmons here has the full report. I thought you might like to hear it."

Nathaniel had never grown used to the reasonableness of Munro's most powerful resident. Powerful in both rank and physical build, he was nevertheless soft-spoken and sensible, which made their working arrangement a most satisfying one.

"Thank you, your lordship," Nathaniel replied. "My own informants have not seen any visitors to the Sangford home who might have a vested interest in the Bill O'Neal business. If Sangford *is* involved, he is either keeping his head down until the worst of it blows over, or he is meeting with his accomplices outside of his home."

"There is the possibility that he has merely been making simple business or social calls, but the man has certainly been active," said the viscount. "Let's hear what you've got, Simmons."

The diminutive size of George Howell's top informant contributed much to his success in his job. His short stature, dark looks, and the natural ease with which he moved helped him blend into his environment, allowing him to observe without being noticed, to hear conversations intended to be private. Simmons could be relied on to ferret out the facts of a matter, and his daily reports to the viscount were invaluable.

Currently, he was standing with feet slightly apart, hands folded together behind his back, his eyes focused on a random point on the ground some distance in front of him. As he spoke, he stood quite still, as though he were reading the details of his account from an invisible page on that random spot on the floor.

"On Tuesday, March 11th," he began, "the day after the Munro Park incident, Mr. Sangford departed the house at ten in the morning. He traveled on horseback and did so alone. He first stopped at the house of Mr. Phineas Pratt, where he stayed for a full hour, suggesting it was a matter of business and not a quick social call. From there, he proceeded to the home of Mr. Harry Bligh, where a meeting of similar length took place. Finally, he called on Elias Upton, Baron Cranbourn. His stay there was much briefer, and his departure an unhappy one, as was apparent from the haste with which he left and the lack of civil niceties."

Simmons blinked, as if turning a mental page. "Subsequent investigation has revealed that all three men are either owners of or shareholders in weaving mills about the Munro area, sometimes even beyond. Lord Cranbourn, specifically, has suffered recent financial losses in his other investments, necessitating him to rely more heavily on his income from the mills."

Another blink. Another page. "Since Tuesday, there have been no further visits, nor has there been written communication between the four gentlemen in question. If they *are* fellow conspiracists, they are being careful not to put anything incriminating in writing. However, all four are members of the same gentleman's club—Shelby's, on Riverside—where a more clandestine meeting could be held. I have no access to such places. Perhaps Mr. Macrae is better suited to explore this avenue."

And, with that, Mr. Simmons closed his mental book and looked up. "Would you like me to keep my eye on anyone in particular, sir, or should I move on to a different assignment?"

Lord Howell tilted his head toward Nathaniel. "What do you

think? Any suggestions? I imagine Lord Cranbourn might be made a priority."

"I would like to believe, first and foremost," answered Nathaniel, "that this is a good indication Miss Sangford is not in any danger. If her father is involved, or knows who is involved, he would ensure that the would-be assassin steers clear of his daughter. There is no reason to harm her if she cannot identify the man. And if she never sees him again, it will be impossible to identify him."

"Certainly," agreed the viscount, "that is reassuring. However, we cannot be as certain of the safety of Mr. O'Neal. He is still in hiding somewhere. Even Simmons has been unable to discover where. The man poses a double threat to his enemy. He verges on being a martyr for his cause. And he has seen the face of his attacker. Of course, so have you, but you can take care of yourself."

"Yes, sir." Nathaniel nodded. Lord Howell's blunt statement was a compliment to Nathaniel's skill of self-preservation, which hadn't let him down yet.

"Unfortunately," Howell continued, "everything is conjecture at this point. "These gentlemen could be discussing the challenges of the millworkers' uprising without actually being involved in the attempted murder of Mr. O'Neal. We need more information. And we need it soon. There is talk of another protest in the works. Such rumor will push desperate men toward action. We must be ready. Our fine city of Munro cannot be a place where so-called gentlemen take the fate of honest laborers into their own hands. Not more than usual, at any rate."

"Just as you say, your lordship. I will have my watchers inform me should any of these four men head to Shelby's so that I, too, may seek a convenient evening's entertainment at the club. Meanwhile, I am due to call on Miss Sangford to see how her recovery fares. Perhaps I shall glean some subtle hint of her father's involvement. Young women often know more than they realize."

"Hmph!" The viscount threw Nathaniel a sidelong glance. "Miss Sangford more than most!"

"Your lordship?"

"Nothing. Pay no attention to my comment."

"Is there something I should know about Miss Sangford?"

"Nothing pertinent to the case." Lord Howell returned his attention to Simmons, hesitated, then looked back at Nathaniel. "Just be careful. She is dangerous in her own right."

Nathaniel's brow gathered into a frown. "I'm sorry. I don't follow."

His lordship sighed. "No, I suppose you don't. Despite your line of work, you continue to see the best in people. Nothing wrong with that, of course. Except you'll be hard-pressed to find anything good in Miss Irene Sangford."

Nathaniel shrugged. "I've heard they are an ambitious family."

Howell squeezed one eye shut. "That is one word for it. There is an excessive arrogance that fuels their ambition. It is unpleasant enough to see such woeful behavior in those who have the power to support their hubris, but the Sangfords have no such claim. The Sangford daughters have been raised to expect society to kneel to them. They seek husbands who will turn this expectation into a reality. In short, they are shiny, empty shells, without charm, without soul."

Nathaniel considered the viscount's words. His lordship was a very private man, protective of his wife and very young son. Their conversations until now had chiefly been focused on the business at hand, seldom going beyond what was merely civil or useful. This unusually strong expression of feeling from the taciturn Lord Howell gave Nathaniel pause.

He had heard the talk. In general terms, he knew what these ladies were: socially ambitious, with little more than money to promote them. Then again, that was very often enough to achieve their goals. The marriage of bankrupted land and title to an infusion of wealth was as old as time.

Nathaniel was also cognizant of the Sangford family's chilly treatment of all whom they felt would one day be beneath them if they succeeded in their aspirations. They had no qualms in ostracizing the vast majority of Munro's citizenry. His own family included. Miss Amelia had certainly shown herself capable of coy manipulation when it suited her. But the elder Miss Sangford? She had been quiet. Reserved, even. Certainly, she had been managing a great degree of discomfort. But she had done so with grace and self-control. Nothing about Miss Sangford had appeared false. Indeed, if anyone were guilty of such a nomenclature, it would be her sister. Yet it was Miss Irene Sangford whom Lord Howell had singled out.

"If you will forgive my asking, has there been a particular incident to create such a strong distaste for the elder Miss Sangford over the younger?" It was a fair question, and Nathaniel hoped that his lordship would not mind answering it, despite his natural inclination to speak only of what was relevant to the task at hand.

"It has been several years," Howell admitted. "But the memory of her evil intent has not dulled with time."

Evil. A strong word, especially from the viscount. Nathaniel could not marry such a word with his brief experience of the young lady. "Would I benefit from knowing the details?" he wondered aloud.

"Probably not, unless you were expecting to start a real friendship with any of them. Suffice it to say, extortion is not beneath her. She would ruin an entire family if she stood to gain from it."

It was a monstrous accusation. Nathaniel was momentarily at a loss for words. "Extortion? As in, for money? But they are exceedingly well off, as I understand."

"No, not for money. For the one thing that family wants most in the world."

"A title?"

"Correct."

"I am afraid to ask."

"She had designs on a good friend of mine, whom I shall not name out of respect to him. She threatened to reveal a secret that would harm an already suffering family if his nephew did not assist her with an introduction to this friend. Fortunately, when she discovered that I would be her quarry's protector, she withdrew the claws she would have tried to sink into him."

Nathaniel was taken aback. "That is an excessive choice of action for a mere introduction."

"You underestimate the extent of the arrogance I mentioned before. From what I was told, she had complete faith that an introduction would be all she needed to secure her attachment to the gentleman in question. I am sorry to say, some gentlemen are not immune to feminine wiles. Of course, it wouldn't have worked on my friend, but I am grateful she had no opportunity to explore that possibility."

Nathaniel tried to overlay his limited knowledge of Miss Sangford with the new information the viscount had shared. It was a jarring mismatch. Then again, Miss Sangford had had nothing to gain by behaving in such a Machiavellian fashion with him, which did not disprove that she was capable of it. She was certainly intelligent. And the family was infamous for its raging desire to grab a title. Had the achievement of this goal been sufficient motivation for her to have acted with such extreme malice? If so, that would be no excuse. To the contrary, it would be a grave disappointment to picture the young lady in such a dim moral light.

"I have taken note of your warning," he assured Lord Howell. "Fortunately, Miss Sangford's conniving nature should in no way hamper my investigation. Besides, though she be as wicked as you say, she still deserves protection from a roaming assassin."

"You are a better man than I, Macrae," the viscount confessed. "I have no patience for people who draw trouble to themselves and then squawk at the outcome."

"Ah, now, you do not mean that. I have seen your work

within the community. It is born from a generous heart. If Miss Sangford stood before you, the assassin's knife at her throat, I wager you would not let her die. After all, in *this* matter, she is entirely innocent."

"No, I would not see her physically harmed," Lord Howell conceded. "But it would give me great satisfaction if her father were indeed a part of the conspiracy against the millworkers. If he were to be found guilty, the lasting shame upon that household would prevent any further attempts to claim a title through marriage. I cannot think of a more suitable punishment for Miss Sangford's actions."

"Was this... I'm sorry to suggest it is not enough on its own... Was this Miss Sangford's only foray into such devious behavior?" Nathaniel asked.

"You mean, other than general spitefulness and unnecessary condescension? This was the worst of it—a singular event, perhaps, but not one to ignore by any means."

"Certainly. Unless, of course, in the years that have passed, she has grown a little wiser?"

Lord Howell cocked a disbelieving eye at Nathaniel. "You would write off such willful villainy merely because it was an isolated occurrence? I knew you to be of sanguine nature, Macrae, but you *cannot* be as idealistic as that! She is a viper. Do not be drawn in by any charms she has learned. For, I assure you, they are not natural."

Nathaniel nodded curtly, keen to bring this uncomfortable topic to a close. "Duly noted. My time in her company will be purely functional. I wish to guarantee her safety and, in finding out what I can about her father, to also guarantee the safety of Bill O'Neal and any other targets certain powerful men may have their sights on."

"Hmm. We shall see. I shall assign one of my men to investigate if Miss Sangford has been up to any of her old tricks, just to be sure. You have a soft heart, Macrae. I would not see it taken advantage of."

Nathaniel could not help but laugh. "And me the fool, thinking how tough and manly I am!"

"But woefully inexperienced when it comes to women."

"Ha! Most of Munro would disagree with you!"

"You and I both know that is an act," said Howell, looking hard at Nathaniel. "You wear that unfounded reputation like a shroud to keep eyes from seeing what you're really up to. I hope you do not come to regret the doors it has closed for you."

"If you mean marriage and a family, no, not at all." Nathaniel shoved his hands in his pockets to reflect the ease of his existence. "I am having the time of my life as I am. And I have you to thank for it."

His answer did not seem to please Lord Howell. "If you lose your heart one day, I fear you will hold it against me when the object of your affection will not have you. You have ultimately barred yourself from a suitable match."

"Then it shall have to be an *unsuitable* one." Nathaniel winked good-naturedly.

His employer remained solemn.

"Come on, Simmons," Nathaniel said, as if he had any power to dismiss one of Howell's personal informants. "Let's get to business. I've got a fascinating young lady to visit, and you, well, only you know what it is you do."

Mr. Simmons raised his eyebrow by the merest sliver, received a nod from the viscount, and made his silent exit. Nathaniel followed with a lighthearted finger to his non-existent forelock, shooting the digit forward in an informal salute. "Wish me luck," he said.

"You will need more than luck," came the sober response. "Keep your head about you. There is much at stake."

"You have my word," Nathaniel answered, though he did not match Howell's serious tone. He had already begun to prepare himself for the role he must play—that of a charming rogue. If Miss Sangford was as clever and calculating as Lord Howell had said, she would see through his pretense unless he fully embodied it.

And so, all the way down the viscount's marbled passageway, through the heavy doors at the entrance to Munro House, and throughout the ride to the home of the Sangfords, Nathaniel sank deeper into the mindset of the concerned visitor and lovable rake.

In the background of this mental theater, the machinations of his investigative brain were equally busy, exploring the tricks he might use to enter Albert Sangford's study unnoticed…

CHAPTER FIVE

"I CAME AS soon as I heard!" lied the once Miss Mary Dunbar, now Mrs. John Fane.

It had been a full three days since the incident at Munro Park. Irene knew the rumor mill worked a lot more quickly than that. Servants talked. The cook would have told the butcher's boy when he made his delivery at the kitchen door. The lad would have mentioned it to his employer, who would have shared the gossip with every single customer as he tried to sell them day-old off-cuts at a promisingly reduced price. From there, it would have been a matter of hours before the ladies of Munro had completed the distribution of the news.

As it was, Mary had waited two days to be the "first" at her friend's side. And Olivia Bathurst had therefore beat her to it. As Irene's supposed best friend, one would have expected nothing less from Olivia. This was her second visit, her shrill voice competing with the pain in Irene's leg, her annoyingly perfect blonde ringlets bouncing in doll-like fashion as she spoke in animated fashion. If only her parents had had the wisdom to teach her to modify her pitch, she could have found a husband by now—and spared many a companion the urge to complete her sentences for her.

"Do have a seat, Mary," Irene bade her new guest.

"Oh, you poor thing!"

"It is not so bad," said Irene. "As long as I keep the leg still, it does not hurt too much."

"Irene told me she is to wear the cast a full two months," said Olivia sadly. "And just as the spring dances are coming up!"

She opened her mouth to comment further, but Mary was quicker on the draw. "Such a pity. Of course, as a married woman, *I* no longer attend the balls for the same reasons I once did. But I could have been a chaperone for you, Irene dearest. Perhaps even arranged an introduction to my sister-in-law's cousin. He has no title himself, but, being in finance, he regularly circulates among those who do. It seems I shall have to offer the advantage of such an introduction to Amelia instead. As I said, such a pity."

"Oh, but Irene can still attend the dances," Olivia trilled loyally. "She will have to stay seated, but she can still be introduced and, dare I say, admired. She is such a beauty. If only she could meet someone worthy of her."

Irene felt as if she need hardly be there. The two women were carrying on the conversation without any need of her presence. They had already begun the usual dance of rivals. Who was the better friend? Who had the most to offer a future lady of the aristocracy? It didn't help that her leg had begun to ache again, either.

"*Of course*," the dowdier Mary replied, syrup dripping from her words, "there is no accounting for gentlemen's tastes. Why— when they could choose someone as *brilliant* as our own dear Irene—they look elsewhere at all is beyond comprehension. The fault is certainly with them. Do you not recall our first season together? We were all so certain that Lord Howell would pick Irene. None among us could claim better breeding or carry herself with such finesse. And yet he hardly looked at our friend."

"He hardly looked at anyone at all," chirruped Olivia. "A singularly rude fellow, he was."

"And then he married that merchant's daughter…"

"Although she *is* very beautiful…"

"Olivia Bathurst! How can you compare her to our Irene?"

Olivia did not seem bothered by the censure. "There are many lovely women in the world. And I wasn't comparing them. I was just saying…"

Mary winced as one sentence followed another from Olivia's lips. "Yes, well, never mind what you were saying. I'm sure Irene doesn't need to…" The words died on her lips as the butler ushered in a gentleman who took the young lady's breath away and allowed his introduction to occur in completed, awed silence.

"Mr. Macrae has come, Miss Sangford," said Hutchins before withdrawing from the room.

No! Irene wailed soundlessly. *Why did he have to come when these silly women are here?* She had so looked forward to his visit. Then again, if she had been alone, Amelia would have been sent for as chaperone, and she would have gone out of her way to spoil it for her older sister. Perhaps, then, it was better that she had her friends with her, women who would at least sing her praises before going off and gossiping about her visitor.

"Mr. Macrae," Irene said, "may I introduce my friends, Miss Olivia Bathurst and Mrs. John Fane? Olivia, Mary, this is Mr. Nathaniel Macrae, my gallant rescuer."

Irene thought she had handled the formalities smoothly, but something must have shown in her face, something the two ladies had not seen there before, because they slipped each other a knowing look, as if to say, *"We will* definitely *be discussing this later!"*

It would be easy to deny any insinuations about her interest in him. Both Mary and Olivia knew all too well Mr. Macrae did not meet the mark for a Sangford husband. However, there was nothing wrong with admiring a handsome vision of a man, was there? They did not need to know how much he meant to her, especially since she herself could not explain her strange and lingering attachment to him.

Mr. Macrae offered a warm and genial smile. Not the kind that rippled up into his eyes. Irene was glad of it. She did not want to have him share such a bountiful smile with present company.

"Won't you take a seat, Mr. Macrae?" she offered, watching every detail of his movements as he carried them out. He flicked his coattails back, revealing a strong thigh and perfectly tailored trousers that rounded his, ahem, *back form* precisely until he sat on it and hid it from view. He stretched out his long, shapely legs in front of him, crossing one ankle over the other. Irene's heartbeat quickened as her gaze trailed back up his torso and followed his hand as it tidied his hair with a quick sweep of his fingers through his dark-blond mane.

She snapped out of her delicious observations a moment sooner than her companions, catching sight of their unrestrained stares. Had she, too, been that obvious? To his credit, Mr. Macrae made no issue of having noticed their conspicuous salivations. Or maybe it was simply because he had grown used to such looks and they no longer warranted his attention.

"I am pleased to find you comfortable enough to receive me," he said, lowering his sea-gray eyes upon her person. "It matches the impression you created when we met: that you are someone who takes such challenges on the chin."

Irene felt a treacherous blush creep into her cheeks. Honestly! It was bad enough she had developed this girlish crush. She certainly did not need for him to know it!

As if a distraction had been called for, Olivia Bathurst obliged by introducing Mr. Macrae to the singular experience that was her voice.

"Oh, yes! Irene is an inspiration to us all!" She beamed proudly at her inspiring friend, pausing just long enough for Mr. Macrae to regain his bearings and fall back on the defense all used who had suffered such an onslaught: he began to talk before *she* could.

"It is to your credit that you have secured such admiration from your friends," he said, his eyes watering ever-so-slightly. Olivia opened her mouth to add further comment, and he continued hastily, "And I am so pleased that you are able to enjoy their company here in this sunny drawing room. I seem to remember that the thought of an extended period in bed"—he winked knowingly at Mary, the only married person in the room, causing her to titter and touch her earlobe self-consciously—"was a thought beyond bearing."

Irene scowled at Mary. Really! She ought not to flirt with a man who was not her husband, especially one carrying the weight of such a sordid reputation as Mr. Macrae's. The fact that Irene was also wildly jealous that he had not flirted with *her* did nothing to calm her feelings.

"I would have been even happier if I could sit outside on that bench," she said, not a little sulkily. "It is a waste of a beautiful morning to be cooped up indoors."

Mr. Macrae turned his head to see the bench in question. It was just outside the large window, with easy access through ornate French doors barely fifteen feet away. He stood abruptly. "That is no challenge at all," he declared. "I will have you there in a jiffy." His long legs brought him to her in two strides. Just enough time for her to fully understand his intentions.

"Oh!" she said. And then, again, "Oh! Mr. Macrae, no, no, you can't. I should ring for a footman."

Seeing her friend in such distress, Olivia jumped up from her chair and ran toward the bell pull.

Mr. Macrae did not move. "The footmen have their hands full with other duties. Come now, Miss Sangford, you would not deny a gentleman the satisfaction of playing the hero once more. And it is barely any distance at all. Surely, you do not believe me so brazen as to have my wanton way with you while your friends are here to watch my every move?"

Irene was not at all sure she *didn't* want him to have his wanton way with her. Here or anywhere. A rush of desire convinced her she must be blushing *all over*. For once, she was grateful her friends were here. Mr. Macrae would only take such liberties with them present as guarantors of her reputation. And she was looking forward to this liberty very much.

"Very well," she said as prudely as possible. After all, she could not appear too eager. "I shall allow it because you mean it as a kindness. Come, Mary, hold open the door for Mr. Macrae. Here, Olivia, put this rug upon the bench in case it is still a little damp."

Her obliging lackeys obeyed at once, being provided with enough distraction so that Irene could savor the moment with no eyes upon her except Mr. Macrae's.

He reached down and put one muscular arm around her back. Irene sensed the power in his movement, remembering how he had carried her as if she were mere air to the bench in Munro Park. Trusting him completely, she wrapped her arms about his neck, relaxing her head onto his shoulder, his cologne sending forth notes of musk and leather, which rapidly unraveled her inhibitions. She could picture herself nuzzling into the space beneath his chin, the softness of her cheek nestling into Mr. Macrae's manly warmth.

His other arm slid beneath her, its sensual rush against her legs stirring strange, electric feelings Irene had never experienced before. In one deft, effortless motion, he lifted her and drew her toward his chest. They were wrapped within each other's embrace, their exhaled heat mingling as he looked down to make sure that she was not in pain. If she had been, it was certainly not currently in the forefront of her mind!

What followed was the merest intake of breath. Mr. Macrae's lips parted, and the smallest sound drew into his mouth. Irene knew that sound. Something had touched a chord within him. Something entirely unexpected. She had experienced exactly such a moment with Philip, many a moon ago. Where she had thought they would have only mutual understanding and respect, she had suddenly tripped over a sensation of *more*. She had drawn in her breath, small and sharp, just so. And she had never told Philip what she had felt.

Irene raised her eyes to meet Mr. Macrae's. He swiftly looked away, tightened his hold on her, and began to walk toward the door, which Olivia had thrown open and now stood against like a human doorstop.

Outside, the sun was high and unhindered by cloud. Irene shielded her eyes as they grew accustomed to the sharp light.

Having lowered her onto the bench, Mr. Macrae set about collecting chairs from a garden set a little way off and arranging them in a cheerful arc for companiable conversation with Irene facing her guests. Olivia and Mary seated themselves, hands upon their laps in a demure fashion, while their expressions spoke entire volumes about what had just transpired.

"This is so much better," declared Mr. Macrae as he placed the third chair and seated himself upon it. "An excellent suggestion, Miss Sangford. Would your family want to join us, perhaps? There are enough chairs. I could let them know we—"

"My mother and sister have gone on their daily round of social calls. My father is at the stables, making sure the horses are getting enough exercise now that Amelia and I are not riding. You will have to make do with our company, I'm afraid."

"In that case, I shall organize some tea and we shall make a proper visit of it," he announced as if it were his home and he were playing the host. "I'm sure you ladies would not say 'no' to a pot of tea and whatever else the Sangfords' cook can rustle up on short notice. Unless you were about to leave, in which case I would have to excuse myself, having brought no chaperone. I suppose we could send for Miss Sangford's lady's maid. Or I could impose upon the friends of Miss Sangford to tarry awhile and allow me more time in this picturesque garden."

He flashed an irresistibly hopeful smile and was answered with a duet of "But of course!" and "It would be our pleasure!" in mismatched timbre.

"Excellent! I shall just pop down to the kitchen and have a word with Cook."

"That won't be necessary," said Irene. "You simply need to ring the bell pull in the drawing room and one of the servants will come and take a message to the kitchen."

"Ah, my dear Miss Sangford," said Mr. Macrae, shaking his

head sadly, "you underestimate the power of my charming personality. We do not want just any dry biscuits that Cook will rummage around and find in a tin somewhere. We want the little cakes she has just baked and is saving as dessert for the family dinner." He winked. "I am certain I can persuade her to be parted from them."

Irene wished with all her heart she could be Cook. To be teased and flirted with for the sake of a few small cakes. All three ladies sat in silent anticipation of the treats in question, the thought of Mr. Macrae's tantalizing acquisition of the delectables leaving no room for speech.

Having met with no further opposition, the gentleman stepped around his chair and disappeared through the French doors to complete his mission.

CHAPTER SIX

"Oh, my sainted aunt!" cried Mary Fane as Mr. Macrae headed toward the kitchen. "If I weren't already married…"

"It wouldn't make any difference," Irene reminded her. "Dashing good looks and irrepressible charisma cannot mend the taint of notoriety."

"So you *have* noticed his fine qualities, then?" Mary quipped in response, her lips twitched into a playful pout.

"I have noticed it all," Irene answered dispassionately. "But there is nothing to be done with it. Attractive gentleman may exist without me throwing myself at them. I have standards, you know."

"Of course!" Olivia shrilled. "Mary could not possibly have meant for you to take any serious interest in the gentleman. But he *is* a delight. Such a pity he has wasted himself on inferior company."

"It wouldn't have mattered, Olivia," said Mary. "The man may have many fine qualities, but possessing a title is not one of them. And our Irene deserves nothing less."

Irene let the two women battle out among themselves who was the more supportive friend.

To be honest, she was growing exceptionally weary of the whole title business. It wasn't just because Mr. Macrae had none.

It was that almost no one did. Having depleted the available pool of suitable candidates, she had not been allowed to consider anyone else. Not even a second son of high nobility whose title could not be passed on to their children, nor a gentleman of good character from a family who carried longstanding approval from the elite.

Worse yet was the hole she had dug for herself. Having snubbed any man or woman who could not bring her nearer to her parents' relentless goal, there were now no prospects to be had among the regular gentry, either. As a result, it was no surprise that Mr. Macrae had been the only person of any reasonable status who had shown her genuine kindness without having anything to gain from it. If he had had any siblings, no doubt they would have discouraged him from doing so. As for friends, his acquaintances were of such dubious reputation that they likely did not care where he cast his thoughtfulness.

"That's an ugly wound he has to his temple," Olivia commented, free to do so since Irene had not filled the silence. "Did Prince do that to him when he came to your rescue?"

Just in time, Irene remembered not to mention any details of the man who had caused her horse to rear. "No, er... perhaps it was a low-hanging branch. He was going rather fast."

"Is that when he was chasing the man with the knife?"

Irene's blood chilled. "What man? What are you talking about?"

"The one who frightened your horse. Did Mr. Macrae not chase after him?"

"It was in this morning's paper," added Mary, not to be left out of the conversation. "Papa read it out to us at breakfast. It's no wonder Amelia fainted with fear. Who can blame her? To think you have seen the face of this mysterious criminal, for a criminal he must be. What sort of law-abiding man hides in the bushes and jumps out with a knife? What horrible things he might have done if Mr. Macrae had not happened upon you at that exact moment! One shudders at the very idea."

"How can it be in the newspaper?" Irene asked of the general universe. There had been no witnesses other than Barton, Amelia, and Mr. Macrae. Which of these three had betrayed her identity for a story? Surely not Mr. Macrae! He had been most concerned for her safety. Could Barton have wanted to earn a few shillings for his information? Or did Amelia hate her sister so much that she would risk Irene's life to draw this sort of attention to herself?

No, *hate* was too strong a word. It would have been done to draw public sympathy. *"Poor Amelia,"* they would say. *"She may not have been hurt, but what a terrifying ordeal! Is she not the pretty thing we met last summer? I did not realize what a brave creature she was. If it had not been in the paper, she would never have spoken of it. So humble. I should call on her. Make sure she is recovered from the shock of it all. And I will take my friend the marquess to cheer her up."*

It was all too clear it had been Amelia. Irene would have laughed at her sister's conniving attempts to gain favor if it had not also put her at risk. Even those who could not read would hear this juicy piece of gossip. It would be the talk of Munro. And the assailant in the park would know who she was. If he wanted to tie up loose ends…

Irene shuddered.

"Are you cold, Miss Sangford?" came the reassuring tones of Nathaniel Macrae as he stepped back into the garden. "The tea should be here shortly. It will warm you up from within. Or would you prefer it if I brought you back inside?"

"Tell him," Irene instructed Mary. "Tell him about the news story."

Mr. Macrae twisted 'round to face Mary, his friendly frown deepening to one of greater concern.

"Well, it wasn't exactly on the front page. That's been reserved for all this talk about the millworkers' strike. But someone has given the details of what happened to Irene to the editors, including her name, and they have printed it. I don't suppose it was you, sir?"

The gentleman stiffened at the news. By the time Mary had made her less-than-subtle accusation, he had already turned to Irene, seen the worry in her face, and sat down heavily.

"This is not good. I cannot think who would benefit from revealing the incident to the press and having your name dragged into it. Could it be one of the servants? Was there somebody else at Munro Park who went unnoticed?"

"These are all possibilities," said Irene. What did it matter who it was? The damage was done. "The question is: what is the likely outcome?" She shivered again, rubbing her arms to warm herself.

At once, Mr. Macrae was up again, stripping off his coat and placing it about Irene's shoulders. He remained next to her, a vigilant guard.

"Your father will need to be told," he said, his voice trailing down from where he stood. "He should talk to any contacts he has about assuring your wellbeing."

"Then there is a risk?"

He put a firm hand upon her shoulder. "Not if I can help it." His expression was grim, his jaw tight, his gray eyes staring ahead as he pondered a solution.

Sure enough, mere moments later, he announced, "I have an idea. It will mean a lie. One that your family, your friends, and the servants will all have to agree to. We can arrange with the editor for a follow-up article. One that speaks of the shock you have endured. How it has affected your memory of the day. You recall nothing after leaving your home. You only remember waking up again in your bed with your leg bound and your worried family gathered around you. We will have Dr. Matthews call it by some clever medical name. If you remember nothing, you cannot be a witness to anything. That should do the trick. Our villain has enough to deal with without trying to access a witness that no longer knows what she saw."

As lies went, it was clever and sound. Except for the part about her worried family gathering by her bedside. But that was irrelevant to the greater picture.

"Ladies," Mr. Macrae said, leaning forward as if to appeal to them, "would you consider the merits of telling a lie for the safety of your friend? I have heard you speak so highly of her. I must assume you carry her wellbeing close to your heart."

"Of course!" they cried in unison. Or, at least, their words were as one. Even in this trying time, Olivia's particular pitch could not harmonize with any other. Irene had the urge to scratch the itch that had developed in her ear. She was grateful that her friends had made no longer pledge than these two simple words.

"You shall be our witnesses," Mr. Macrae told the two young women. "You have called on Miss Sangford and observed for yourselves that her mind is a blank as far as the incident is concerned."

Willing nods followed from Olivia and Mary.

"Ah! And here is our tea!" Mr. Macrae stepped forward and received the tray from the footman. If it had been one of the maids, she would doubtless have grown flustered at the handsome gentleman's proximity. As it happened, however, this particular footman was a decidedly vain fellow and likely fancied himself fair competition for the ladies' attention. He was, of course, mistaken.

The footman fetched the table from the garden set, which had now been brought almost in its entirety to its new position near the bench where Irene sat as if she were holding court. Mr. Macrae placed the tray upon the table and Irene was wondering how, as hostess, she was going to manage the niceties of pouring for her guests, when her father found them in the garden.

"Ah, Mr. Macrae! I am glad you have found your way to us. I suppose you have seen this morning's paper?" His eyes flitted to Irene.

"The ladies have told me all about it," Irene informed him. "You do not need to protect me from the truth."

Her father looked strangely tired. Dark patches beneath his

eyes suggested he had not been sleeping well. He was not a man easily brought low. Irene would have liked to think he was worried about her. But the cause of his concern was probably the mills. Their family's entire position in society hinged on their abundant wealth. And her father's status within the *ton* of Munro was everything to him.

"If you will permit," said Mr. Macrae, "I have a possible solution for the difficulty the news article has created. Shall we leave the ladies to their tea and discuss it privately?"

Mr. Sangford's weary droop shifted to action. His spine lengthened and his eyes shone with hope. "Yes. Yes, indeed. I am grateful for your assistance. If you will follow me." He dipped his head to the rest of the guests. "Ladies."

Irene's father and Mr. Macrae duly disappeared into the depths of the house to discuss the latest developments. The two men had barely removed themselves from earshot when Olivia leaned forward and said with great glee, "You like him! You should have seen your face when he carried you out to this bench. You can't be in love with him, Irene. He's a scoundrel!"

"I am *not* in love with him," Irene replied hotly. "Your imagination has run wild."

"I saw it too," Mary chimed in. "You were definitely all doe-eyed."

Irene glared at her friends.

"Don't misunderstand me," continued Mary. "The gentleman is as dreamy as they come. But you have never allowed that to lead where your future cannot follow. You wouldn't want Mr. Macrae to think you can be toyed with. You are much too good for him."

Am I? Irene was not convinced. Nothing in her character gave her the right to claim superiority over him. More importantly, would she want to? What if she wished for a man who was good for *her*, someone her parents would never approve of? With her prospects looking slim indeed, could she... *dared* she choose someone who might love her, just a little?

Irene's thoughts drifted back to that intake of breath. That tiny moment in which Mr. Macrae saw her differently. She would give anything, *everything*, to have that moment back. For it to linger, stretching out in time until all else was forgotten and the connection between them became their only reality.

Something clawed at her ear.

"Irene? *Irene!*" Olivia's voice chiseled at the image of Mr. Macrae that Irene was trying to hold on to. "I was saying, we must be going."

Irene's gaze fell automatically to the plate of little cakes. Unsurprisingly, it was empty. Olivia's sweet tooth had been satisfied. She had done her duty in visiting her friend. And had the surprise of meeting Mr. Macrae, to boot. Moreover, she was now part of a secret pact to carry a lie for a noble purpose. It was not often Olivia's day was so utterly perfect in every way.

Irene felt a pang of pity.

What was this? A hint of human kindness? What was happening to her? Caring was for people with a heart. Weak people. Those who relied on others for their happiness. Irene had learned to carve her own destiny. Without the love of family. Without friends who cared more for her than the influence she would wield when her title was won.

Olivia is a simpleton, Irene thought rather uncharitably. A wiser woman would have adjusted her speech to make it more palatable. Olivia didn't even notice that she was constantly being talked over! She hung on to Irene's every word, slavishly obeying her every command. Such a foolish creature! Why should she pity her?

And yet... she did. The hard crust around Irene's heart had cracked open, and it was warm inside. A wisp of pity had slipped out. Irene grumbled to herself. What would be next?

This was all Mr. Macrae's fault. She, who had made herself immune to the gentler emotions, was discovering that she was not, in fact, impervious to them when they were offered freely and sincerely. The sensation was new and unsettling. Her world was too unbearable without her armor.

And so she hardened herself, resorting to her characteristic cynicism.

"I see." She folded her arms, then immediately freed one again to wave it about irritably. "Do you just intend to abandon me out here? You could at least fetch someone to take me inside."

"We will ring for a footman on our way out," said Mary. "But we really must be going now. We have so many people still to see. You know how it is."

Irene understood all too well. They had stopped by her home first, knowing they would be collecting news about her condition that no one else would have had access to. Mr. Macrae had slowed their progress to the next house, but his addition to their morning had been worthwhile. How much more did they not have to share with their other friends now! Not that it should have mattered. If these women had not been handpicked by her mother, they were clearly of no consequence to Irene. Still, the thought of being fodder for gossip irked her.

So that was it. Her visits done for the day. Perhaps even the week. Irene's only two friends had paid their respects. Mr. Macrae would not come again, now that he knew she was recovering as hoped. It was back to reading all day.

Perhaps, instead of going indoors, she could have the footman bring her easel and paints outside. But someone would have to stay with her in case it turned cold or the pain in her leg grew unbearable. Her sister would not want to keep her company. And her mother would do whatever Amelia wanted. It would have to be a servant. It couldn't be Finnegan. This was her one day off. No, it would be someone else who, as Mr. Macrae had pointed out, had enough to do without being given extra errands.

Bother Mr. Macrae! Why should she care what he thought? But she did. Far too much.

Olivia and Mary said their goodbyes. The footman came. Irene considered the fact that she really should learn their names. Especially this one, who held her with a confidence born of surprising self-assurance. He was a servant, and not Mr. Macrae, and had no business tucking her so firmly in his arms. Yes, she would very much like to know the man's name to have Hutchins scold him. He carried the quietly fuming Irene back to her chair in the drawing room, collected the tray from the garden, and deposited a small silver bell on the side table next to her. "Mr. Sangford's orders," he explained, "since you cannot reach the bell pull." And then he left, but not before affronting Irene with a casual wink.

Irene considered the lonely room. She was tempted to ring the little bell just to see if anyone could actually hear it. There was always a maid about, dusting or polishing or doing whatever it was they were supposed to do. She knew she hadn't really been abandoned. Her needs would be met. Well, most of them.

A dark-blond head peered around the door. "Ah, you are here!"

Why did it matter so much that he seemed pleased to see her?

Mr. Macrae's full length appeared as he rounded the doorway and approached Irene. "I thought I should say goodbye properly. Your father and I have spoken at length. We are of one mind in dealing with the issue of your safety. Please do not waste even a second concerning yourself with it any longer."

The crack in the hard shell of her heart eased open a little further. It was strange and wonderful to receive so much thoughtfulness. Even when she had done nothing to earn it. Then again, that was how thoughtfulness worked, wasn't it? She wasn't sure. It was not a familiar theme in their home.

"Thank you," she said, and she meant it with her whole being. "You have given much of your time when it is not your responsibility. I am profoundly grateful."

"It is nothing. Any man in my shoes would have done the same."

It was an outrageous lie. He must realize that. And yet. Perhaps that was just the sort of man he was. Chivalry came naturally to him. He really was fundamentally a true gentleman.

The realization deeply wounded Irene's ego. He had not done anything special for her. It was merely his excellent nature.

"I think you will find, Mr. Macrae," she said, trying not to sound sorry for herself, "that you are not like other men at all. That is certainly my experience, anyway."

His smile fell away. "I am sorry to hear that. I must insist, then, that your experience is sorely limited. For there are a multitude of good men in the world."

Irene did not want to argue. Not with him. "I will take your word for it. As for me, I am grateful to have met at least one such man."

"And there is your father, too," he coaxed, seemingly determined to lift her mood.

"He does his duty," was all she replied.

Mr. Macrae pushed no further. "I see you are reading Voltaire." He picked up the volume from the side table. *"Letters on the English.* Not the usual romantic novels most young ladies prefer."

"I am not partial to romantic ideas," Irene answered, then wished she hadn't. She didn't want him to think her churlish. Even if it was true.

Her companion, however, was sympathetic to her point of view. "I suppose romance is not practical. Finding an appropriate match is many a young woman's priority. And those who are led by the notions of romance are often sorely disappointed by reality."

"Just so," Irene said gratefully. "Whereas Voltaire"—she tipped her hand toward the book he was holding—"broadens the mind. And it gives me something to do in the long afternoon."

Mr. Macrae looked about the room, noting all the distractions that were beyond her reach. "At least your sister will be home soon. Then you shall have the enjoyment of her company."

Irene tried to keep her face from showing her opinion on that comment. Not because she cared what Mr. Macrae thought of her sister, but because she would not have him see her bitterness. He thought well of her. When he was with her, she wanted to be her best self, whatever that was. She had certainly had enough practice at being her worst self.

"I miss being able to choose where I go," she complained as quietly as possible. "Your visit was the first time I have been out of doors since the accident. I know I should be thankful it was not worse. And Mr. Sunderland has wrapped my leg expertly. But I am not accustomed to relying on others."

The gentleman did not respond with some light quip about how lucky she was or how she was in good hands. Rather, he stood in solemn contemplation for several seconds before his face lit up and he said excitedly, "I believe I have just the thing to improve your circumstance. But let me make sure of my facts before I make empty promises. If I am right, I will be back tomorrow with a surprise."

Irene could not help herself. The hope of seeing him was balancing on a precipice. "And if you are wrong... Does that mean you will not come?"

He tipped his head askew, as if contemplating the intention behind her question. "If you wish it," he said solemnly, "I will come regardless."

Irene's pulse beat in her ears like a drum. "I wish it."

Mr. Macrae pointed a foot forward, lowered his head, and drew one hand to his heart, the other flying back in an old-fashioned bow as was once the style in the royal court. "It shall be done." Then his eyes lifted to her and his mouth widened as a smile crept onto his face. "Do not miss me too much until then." He twitched his eye into a wink before dropping into a bow once more, this time with a touch of drama, his hand twirling at the wrist to keep the mood light and playful. "Adieu, fair lady. We shall meet again on the morrow."

Irene laughed in spite of herself. The sound was alien to her ears. It startled her. Then the joy of it settled upon her. "Go away, you scoundrel," she said in jest. She laughed again, savoring the thrill of the sound bubbling up from her chest.

"I live to obey," answered Mr. Macrae, spinning around and

departing so suddenly that the breath was knocked clean from Irene's throat. Just as he'd reached the doorway, however, he looked back over his shoulder and added, "But only until tomorrow." Then he was gone.

Emotions tumbled within Irene, a wild somersault of shock, happiness, and anticipation. Fun! She was having fun! The only pleasure she had known before was what she had created for her own amusement. Cruel, selfish acts that she had believed in her power to achieve. But this had been easy! Irene felt light and carefree.

And there was the promise of more tomorrow.

Perhaps it was this thought that kept her buoyant. Even when Amelia came home and tried to resume their usual bickering. Despite the fact that her mother hardly looked in on her. Voltaire's heavy subject matter could not deter her from her new optimism. In fact, she imagined discussing the themes with her visitor the next day. Real conversation. How exquisite!

Irene sighed contentedly, hugging the image of another visit with Mr. Macrae to herself.

Until she realized Amelia would have to chaperone her this time.

She fought back valiantly to sustain her excitement. It wavered, dropped several rungs on the ladder of enthusiasm, then held. Mr. Macrae could make even Amelia's company bearable. She would rather have both than neither.

Irene hummed a little tune to soothe herself after the brief disappointment. A passing maid stopped, stuck her head in the door and saw who it was, a momentary shadow of confusion shifting across her features before she resumed her task elsewhere.

I am a woman of mystery, Irene thought to herself, grinning, alone but not lonely, before dipping her head and focusing once more on the pages of her book.

CHAPTER SEVEN

Friday, March 14th, 1817

A SCRUFFY MAN in a patched jacket and corduroy trousers padded down the road at a steady pace. Nathaniel saw him approach from some distance. He stepped back from the lush shrubbery he had been using as concealment and walked to the wagon that was parked partially hidden in shadow down an alley. An oddly-shaped object was tied onto the bed of the wagon beneath a tarpaulin. Nathaniel hopped up and slipped in under the cover.

The footfalls drew closer. The wagon suspension dipped on its axle as the man hopped up into the driver's seat.

"Ready, Mr. Macrae? I don't know how long Mr. Sangford will be from home, but he has only just left. We'd best be moving right along."

Nathaniel's voice, muffled beneath the thick cloth, called out, "Ready. And let's make absolutely sure no one is about when you let me out."

"Yes, sir," came the reply. A snap of the reins sounded, and the wagon began to move.

Nathaniel could feel the heavy wheels turn into the main residential road, trundle on a short distance, then rumble down the mews toward the Sangford stables. It lurched to an abrupt stop.

"We are behind the house now, sir, said the man in a low

voice. "You can slip into the back garden from here."

"Right," said Nathaniel, crawling out from beneath the musty space he had occupied. He dusted himself off, looked about quickly, then walked through the shrubbery that hid the kitchen from the rest of the grounds. He narrowly avoided the gardener, who was thankfully pushing a wheelbarrow and focusing on the ground in front of him as he went.

Nathaniel tried to be inconspicuous, but he maintained his composure. It would be much easier to explain his presence if he were found strolling like a gentleman and not lurking like some vagrant.

Across the lawn sat the partial garden set, still arranged in a half-circle around the bench. The seats were empty, and the table held no tray. The French doors stood open and the sound of a piano drifted up into the morning air.

Nathaniel ducked down the side of the house, away from the music and the people who might have been listening to it. He counted silently as he went. Two. Three. At the fourth window, he gingerly tested to see whether the frame would lift. If the latch he had undone the day before on his way back from the kitchen had been locked again, his plan was foiled. The heavy sash window budged a little. Then with a mighty push from Na-thaniel, it glided upward, allowing him ample room to heave himself through and into Albert Sangford's study.

In the few minutes he had had to search the room the day before, nothing obvious had revealed itself. The drawers of the desk had been locked, however, with no sign of the key. Today, he had come prepared.

One of the advantages of keeping company with the more illicit members of society was that he had acquired an unusual set of skills. From his pocket, Nathaniel drew a small pouch, which he rolled open onto the desk. From the collection of strange, curved pins he selected two that looked promising, inserting them into the lock of the first drawer. Careful maneuvering produced a satisfying "click." He pulled the drawer open, slowly and quietly, casting a quick glance toward the door to make sure no one was approaching.

A perusal of the stack of papers revealed several contracts, a deed to the property, and letters from Sangford's solicitor confirming that assigned tasks had been completed. Nothing looked suspicious or even vaguely out of the ordinary.

Nathaniel shifted his attention to the other drawer. It proved considerably more challenging to release the second lock. A film of perspiration formed on his back. He paused, pulled off his coat, and folded it neatly over the chair before tackling the fiddly mechanism once more. A draft from the window cooled his dampened shirt and, with his concentration renewed, the lock at last gave up its guardianship of the drawer. Nathaniel pulled it open with greater haste than the first, all too aware that time was running out before he would be discovered.

The drawer was empty.

Why on earth had Albert Sangford locked an empty drawer? Was it force of habit? Nathaniel stuck his head almost right into the cavity, probing with his fingertips. Nothing.

Hang on…

One of the corners of the base had a worn patch, as if something had touched that single corner many times. Nathaniel pressed down with two fingers. A click sounded. Nothing else happened. The base of the drawer did not suddenly lift to reveal a hidden compartment. In fact, everything looked exactly as before. It made no sense at all.

He sat down in exasperation. What had he missed? It must have been something important to be both locked up and concealed in this way. He took one more look, feeling his way across the base of the drawer. Nothing new revealed itself.

Frustrated, Nathaniel pushed the drawer shut. Or tried to. It was stuck. He wiggled it, but it would not budge. As if something was in the way.

Getting down on his hands and knees, he peered under the desk. There, on the farthest side of the drawer, a narrow, hinged strip of wood had fallen open. Nathaniel had to hand it to the carpenter: it was clever work.

His hand could only just slide in up to the wrist, but it was enough for his fingers to feel the distinctive shape of a book within the hidden compartment. Using his fingertips for traction, he coaxed the object out of hiding and crawled backward out of the awkward space beneath the desk.

He placed the book, which appeared very much like a ledger, onto the surface of the desk and sat down to have a good look at it.

At first glance, everything seemed as it should. Household accounts. Returns on investments. No once-off payment to an unidentified assassin. Nothing out of the ordinary. Most descriptions were predictable. Wages. Repairs. Rent. Taxes.

Wait a minute. Now, *that* was interesting. Here was a name Nathaniel knew all too well. Madame Dubois. But why was she receiving a fixed monthly stipend from Mr. Sangford? His mouth dropped open as realization dawned. The old goat! He must have a mistress! And him being such a self-satisfied prig and all! What a hypocrite, putting on a great show of superiority, only to have a little something on the side...

This was a world Nathaniel understood all too well. Many of his female informants worked for Madame Dubois. Their male customers liked to talk. After all, who were these women going to repeat their secrets to? And who would believe them? As it happened, the answer to both questions was "Nathaniel Macrae."

With a worthwhile lead established, he slid the ledger back into its secret compartment, closed the hinged panel, and pushed the drawer shut. He quickly slipped his coat back on, eased himself down from the window, and pulled its frame down to close it.

Nathaniel stepped away from the wall and took his bearings. Experience had taught him that this was not the time to grow careless. Being caught now was just as risky as it had been when he had first entered the garden. His vigilance allowed him to evade the maid who had come out to hang up the washing, her presence made known by the song she was singing to cheer herself during an otherwise dull task. He looked back as he moved on, making sure she was out of his line of sight.

"Oof!"

The gardener, who had just backed into him, straightened at once and dropped the long branch he had been dragging. "Sorry, sir. Clumsy of me. I've only gone and stood on your finely polished shoes. Let me fix that for you." He loosed the rag that was tied about his neck and knelt to clean the mostly-shiny leather of Nathaniel's footwear.

"No need to worry, my good fellow. No harm done. I had actually just come looking for you." Lying smoothly at a moment's notice had become one of Nathaniel's strong suits.

"How can I help?" asked the man, using the same rag to wipe the sweat from his neck before tying it into a small knot again.

"It occurs to me that Miss Sangford is largely confined to one chair in one room. If she had a cheerful bouquet, perhaps one that also carried a pleasing scent, it could help her feel that she is, in a sense, out of doors. I gather she has always been active. Being unable to take herself into the sunlight must be a grievous loss. Between us, I would like to rectify the situation. But," he added hastily, "*you* should take all the credit. It would be suggestive of certain intentions on my part if it was said to have come from me."

"That is a very kind thought, sir. I am happy to oblige." The gardener looked toward the house. "And you are right. Miss Sangford does like to ride and walk. She prefers her own company. Her current limitations must be driving her 'round the bend." He rubbed the back of his neck with his calloused fingers. "I am only sorry I did not consider such a kindness myself. One does not always think of the Sangfords as... well..."

"Human?"

The gardener raised startled eyes to Nathaniel. "I didn't mean... They are just a little..."

Nathaniel laughed lightly. "I understand perfectly. They are not a warm and endearing family. You do your duty—with great pride, I am sure—but have never imagined a world in which they think of *you* as a person, either. You are their gardener. They are your employers. It is not a sentimental relationship. Nevertheless, Miss Sangford will appreciate your gesture."

"Yes, sir. I will certainly do my best."

"Excellent. I shall be on my way, then. I have a surprise of my own for the stricken lady."

"Yes, sir. I shall be along shortly with the flowers."

"Good man."

Nathaniel would have tipped his hat to him, but he had left the bothersome thing behind in his secret space under the tarpaulin.

The remainder of his escape was mercifully uneventful. However, as he approached the side of the property where the wagon would be waiting, he heard voices. They were not arguing as such, but there was a definite tone of agitation.

"I'm telling you, Mr. Macrae said he would be along shortly. I was to wait."

"But you can't leave this lumbering vehicle here without Mr. Sangford's permission. Mr. Macrae has made no such arrangement." The voice was Barton's, the groom whom Nathaniel had needed to address sternly in the park.

"Miss Sangford knows about the delivery," countered the driver. "And I can hardly wait in the main road. I will get in everyone's way."

Barton responded with some notion of it not being his problem. But the driver in the corduroy trousers wasn't listening. He had caught sight of Nathaniel and realized that the groom was blocking his only escape. Throwing his arms up in a pretended huff, he climbed down from the wagon and walked round to the front of it so that Barton was forced to turn and face him.

"Fine," he said, "if you want the wagon gone so badly, *you* move it. I will not disobey Mr. Macrae. He told me to wait, and that's exactly what I'm doing." He folded his arms to put a point to his statement.

Using the opportunity created for him, Nathaniel edged past the wagon, reaching in under the canopy to grab his hat before briskly walking away and off the Sangford property. He rounded the corner onto the main residential street, walking along its pavement before turning up the pretty garden path to the Sangfords' front door. A quick slicking back of his hair and his hat was donned, his cravat tidied, and the creases in his trousers smoothed. He pulled back the knocker on the door before giving it three sharp taps that echoed into the spacious entrance beyond.

CHAPTER EIGHT

"**G**OOD DAY, HUTCHINS," he greeted the butler, passing his hat to a footman. "I am expected."

"That you are, sir," Hutchins answered pleasantly. "If Miss Sangford could pace the floor, I believe she would be doing so."

Nathaniel liked the Sangfords' butler. He was not the usual epitome of formality. Not with Nathaniel, at any rate.

He happened to know that Hutchins had a good eye for a winning bet and a subscription to the horse racing almanac, both of which aided him in setting up a fine retirement fund for the day when his tired legs and sore back would no longer allow him to run a household. Hutchins, in turn, knew that Nathanial carried this incriminating knowledge yet said nothing of it to his employer. Hence, the friendly demeanor.

"I suppose she is in the drawing room again?" Nathaniel confirmed.

"Yes, sir. With her mother and sister. Your presence will bring welcome relief to all, sir."

And with that, he led the way, despite Nathaniel already knowing the route through the house, because that was what butlers did.

Hutchins had not exaggerated. The moment Nathaniel was announced and entered the room, Miss Sangford all but levitated from her chair. Miss Amelia's hand immediately went to her hair, and Mrs. Sangford likewise sat a little straighter.

"I see I am spoiled for company today," Nathaniel said, for that was expected of a man with his reputation. Mrs. Sangford and her younger daughter smiled, confident in their right to such a compliment. But the dark-haired Miss Sangford lowered her eyes as if such a claim saddened her. Did she feel underserving of flattery, or was it that she did not wish to share it?

"I will need the help of one or two of your stronger footmen so that your surprise may be delivered to you," he said directly to Miss Sangford. "The wagon that brought it is causing some disturbance near your stables, and I should not like to be the originator of unpleasantness."

"I will see to it at once, sir," said Hutchins, without being asked.

"Have them bring it in here, will you?" asked Nathaniel.

Hutchins nodded and disappeared to complete his task.

"Won't you have a seat, Mr. Macrae?" Mrs. Sangford offered.

"Thank you," answered Nathaniel. He could feel their eyes upon him as he lowered himself into the chair nearest Miss Sangford. He had become accustomed to the hungry look of ladies who deemed him below their standards yet wanted him all the same. At least Miss Sangford had the decency to look embarrassed at her own blatant desire.

He was struggling to see in her any of the elements suggested by her damning reputation. Miss Amelia matched perfectly with all he had heard about the sisters. She was aloof, arrogant, mean-spirited. According to Lord Howell, the elder Miss Sangford was even worse—downright dangerous and evil. To be honest, Nathaniel thought she looked rather lost.

In the end, he supposed, it didn't really matter. He was not here to befriend her. After all, if her father was involved in attempted murder, friendship with her would be impossible. However, he would willingly protect her from the same man who threatened the life of Bill O'Neal.

Still, she intrigued him. It was not often a woman had this

effect on him. Miss Sangford might well have a manipulative streak, but she had had no motive to exercise it over him. Meanwhile, she had been hamstrung by her injury, cut off from society, her chance for marriage this season slipping through her fingers. It was a sorry situation, and he pitied her.

But there was something more. A fundamental sadness. His covert lifestyle had made him observant, and he could pick up on those signals the body sent that the owner of said body would rather keep to themselves. Miss Sangford was profoundly unhappy. Possibly due to her own doing. Likely made worse by the burden of a broken leg. The way the sadness sat on her was like the wearing of an old coat. She hardly seemed to know it was there. But to the person seeing the coat for the first time, it was obvious. This sorrow had not originated with her accident. It was part of her, as though she had carried it her whole life.

Nathaniel had learned something interesting through his many interactions with people from all walks of life: those who carried the weight of such heavy feeling without the power to change their circumstances very often chose a different emotion to show to the world, one that suggested power and control because, in fact, they had none. What was Miss Sangford's disguise? Anger? Disconnection? Meanness?

Whatever it was, her disguise was slipping. Perhaps she had grown tired of wearing it. Maybe she no longer cared what people saw.

And if the disguise was falling free, it was possible she was also shedding the skin of her past.

It was clear to Nathaniel that she was intelligent and capable of whatever she put her mind to. What if the things she had once wished to put her mind to had changed? Lord Howell had painted a very bleak picture of her indeed. Nathaniel had accordingly done a little digging of his own. The incident the viscount had referred to had happened nearly three years ago. And, from what Nathaniel could tell, it was the only such scheme she had concocted. Other than that, the anecdotes collected had not painted her so much a schemer as consistently cold, condescending, and strangely bitter for a woman of very comfortable means.

There had been talk of an engagement more than a year ago. But that had ended rather tragically. Since then, it was as though Miss Sangford had stopped trying. And a woman who no longer cared about securing a husband had a very deep wound indeed.

Nathaniel was pondering the cause of such far-reaching hurt when he realized the room had grown quiet. Mrs. Sangford had been talking incessantly, mostly praising the talents of her younger daughter, but she had stopped and was now waiting for a reply which he had no idea how to give.

He was rescued from his embarrassment by a curfuffle in the room adjacent. A familiar squeaking sound, as of ancient wheels needing oiling, preceded two footmen and a strange-looking wicker chair that resembled a small, open carriage.

"Good grief!" cried Mrs. Sangford. "What sort of contraption is that?"

"It was my great-grandfather's," said Nathaniel, crossing the floor to take ownership of the fangled thing. "He lost the use of his legs during the Jaco… *ahem*, in battle. But he was not the sort to sit around and bewail his misfortune. So, he had this wheeled chair constructed. He could be pushed from behind or, with some effort, maneuver the large wheels himself. I had someone fish it out of our attic yesterday and then asked our carpenter to add these handles onto the rim of the wooden wheels so that Miss Sangford could manage the push and pull of the chair more easily herself. Within the confines of a room, she might now, for example, be able to take herself to the piano or the lower shelf of the library without needing to call on others to facilitate her needs. She might even manage to exit the French doors into the garden, provided the route is unencumbered by debris or a challenging slope. A meander through Munro Park could be managed with a footman providing the push-power. The world—and the weather, for that matter—is far too beautiful to be avoided for two whole months. Don't you agree, Miss Sangford?"

He turned to the lady in question, fully expecting to see her beaming at the anticipated freedom this gift would allow. He had not envisaged a scene where she would be sitting absolutely motionless except for a single tear that trailed down her cheek. She wiped it away vigorously, staring at her wet fingers as if they had betrayed her.

Nathaniel looked away quickly to give her an opportunity to recover herself. To draw all other eyes from her also, he sat himself down in the wheeled chair and began to tug at the handles that had been recently attached.

"See, if you pull them toward you *so*, the chair reverses at a steady pace. Or, you could push to go forward, turning in the desired direction by moving only one wheel."

He proceeded to take the vehicle across to the piano, where he maneuvered himself next to the light, wooden bench that was more typically used. "Perhaps this piano seat could be moved when no one else is playing to give Miss Sangford access to the entire keyboard. Else she will be confined to only the high notes." He promptly played a jaunty tune that tinkled within the last three octaves.

"Oh, Mr. Macrae," said his hostess, completely ignoring the gift and the daughter for whom it was intended. "You *must* hear Amelia play! She is in great demand at dinner parties. We have held many a recital for her, which have been enthusiastically attended. Such a shame that there are so many gentlemen with a good ear, yet none have asked for her talented hand."

"Yes, sister dear," said Miss Sangford, sounding a lot more perky. "Play *Rondo alla Turca*. Mr. Macrae will be *so* impressed."

Miss Amelia shot a barely suppressed glare at her sister. "You *will* continue to mock me for the rare occasion where I have played a false note. I should like to see *you* manage Mozart as well as I do."

"No, thank you," replied Miss Sangford sweetly. "We all know no one plays *nearly* as well as you do. But I shall now have a means of escaping your endless practice. Mr. Macrae, will you allow me to take your place in this glorious vehicle? I should like to see how easily I may emulate your agile steering."

"But of course! That is why it is here." Nathaniel climbed out of the wicker nest and was about to lift Miss Sangford into its comfortable space when a footman stepped forward and received her ivory arms about his neck. Nathaniel remembered him. A presumptuous fellow. All too ready to receive the young lady's willowy body against his chest. And far too handsome for his own good, even by footmen's standards. No doubt he considered himself charming and Miss Sangford blessed by his proximity.

For the first time in ages, Nathaniel found himself a trifle flustered. Collecting Miss Sangford in his arms had become almost second nature. Even from a distance, he could pick up the lavender wisps of her perfume. He could feel, as if it were actually happening, her releasing all fear to him, relaxing into his shoulder with full trust.

In the care of this footman, her head was up and stiff, looking to both sides to ensure that she did not bump her leg into an obstacle. Even safely in the chair, when the footman had stepped back, she quickly tidied her skirts. She had not been as prudish with him, Nathaniel remembered.

"That will do, Cedric," Miss Sangford said curtly and at once began to experiment with the handles of the wheeled chair, tugging and leaning this way and that. "It's heavier than I imagined," she said, a little out of breath. "You made it look so easy, Mr. Macrae. I am not as strong as you."

"No, but you have a strong will, Miss Sangford. That will be all you need. That, and a little practice." He offered what he hoped was an encouraging smile, and she returned to her efforts. Before long, she was at the French doors, facing the garden.

"I don't think I can manage the grass," she said. "It will drag at the wheels. But I can feel the breeze from here and look all the way across the lawn to the bottom hedge. And when I feel it get chilly, I can simply shift myself away from the draft. How absolutely wonderful!"

She smiled up at him. And there it was. The beam of joy he had expected earlier. Her eyes were sparkling. He had not seen them do that before. The effect was particularly fetching. It lit up her whole face with a childlike glee that softened her angular features with a tint of pure delight. It must have been a rare experience for everyone else, too, because both her mother and sister stared at her as if they had seen her sprout an extra head.

"I am so pleased you find it useful," Nathaniel said smoothly. But really, he wanted to grab the handles at the back of the chair and race down the garden with her until she shrieked for him to stop, laughing helplessly. He pictured himself shaking a branch of tree blossoms over her so that they fell like a sweet-scented shower of color all around her. Then he would collect a fresh bloom from the garden and tuck it gently behind her ear. And later, much later, when she was alone in her room, she would silently remove the flower, twirling its stem thoughtfully between thumb and forefinger as she recalled the happy hours they had spent together.

Nathaniel jerked from his reverie. What was happening to him? He couldn't have feelings for Miss Sangford! He hardly knew her! And what he knew was far from encouraging. Not to mention the fact that her father was very likely involved in a murderous plot! It was ridiculous. He spent much of his days—and nights—in the company of women who were beautiful, uncomplicated, and willing to please him even without their usual fee. Not that he ever mixed business with pleasure. But he knew he could if he wanted to. Why, then, would he want Miss Sangford—quite possibly a nasty, manipulative daughter of a dangerous man?

And yet... he was finding to his own amazement that he liked her. *Really* liked her. She was a unique challenge, nothing like anyone he had met before. He had endured the company of many women who were peacocks: self-involved and only outwardly beautiful. Others were like doves: sweet, tame, and all too much alike. But Miss Sangford... Miss Sangford was a hawk.

Her mind was sharp and her talons apparently no less so. But her wing was broken. And, from what he could tell, had always been. So she bit and fought to keep everyone from her, lest she be hurt again. Only… for some reason he could not guess, she sat quite still for him.

It made him want to care for her. Since she could not fly, he wished to let her ride upon his shoulder while he ran and let the wind rush through her outspread feathers, that she might feel all that she had been denied until now. He could not mend what had hurt her so deeply, but he could help her experience tenderness and full-throated joy.

"You are so very kind," she said, drawing his thoughts back to the room. "How can I ever thank you?"

Miss Amelia's eyes narrowed. Her hand reached surreptitiously to the side and she nudged her mother. Mrs. Sangford looked down at the hand, then up to her younger daughter's face, following its pointed stare to the newly-contented sister. A quick glance at Nathaniel, and Mrs. Sangford turned her eyes upon her younger daughter once more, a question mark lodged within her rippled brow. Miss Amelia nodded slowly. Her mother's mouth formed an "o" of disbelief. They had seen her vulnerability. They had connected it to him.

A warning pricked at Nathaniel's spine. Here they came. To clip her other wing.

Nathaniel felt sick to his stomach. Why would a mother choose one daughter and not another? He had seen enough of this family to guess at the wound that had grounded his hawk.

His hawk…

What right had he to such a claim? She was nothing of his. They had barely begun their acquaintance. Yet he felt absurdly protective over her. It was more than just offering a watchful eye to keep would-be assassins from her. She had snuck into his heart when he hadn't been paying attention. And he could sense her seeking refuge there, as though he were a mighty oak whose branches gave sanctuary to the flight-robbed bird.

But he should not, *could* not be that person for her. He was mid-investigation into her father's possible involvement in a terrible crime. And her sister, heaven help her, had spotted a weakness with which to torment her. It was him. *He* was her weakness. The realization was flattering and unsettling all in one.

"Please, Miss Sangford," he said, "no thanks are needed. The contraption was simply gathering dust in our attic, and you are giving it purpose again. Now that I know you can manage moving about in it, I shall take my leave. I hope you continue to heal quickly."

He had tried to distance himself from her with these words, but it now appeared he had been all too successful in his attempt. The glow evaporated from Miss Sangford's face as if she had been struck. Nathaniel watched as she fought to regain her composure. He noticed that her mother and sister were watching too, but with a sort of hunger that was completely out of place. How he wanted to reassure her! But he dared not. Better she be disappointed now. Soon her odious family would forget seeing this chink in her armor. The best way to protect her from them was to stay away.

"You will return soon, Mr. Macrae, won't you?" coaxed Miss Amelia, her motive all too obvious. "My sister so looks forward to these visits. We are such dull company for her. Do say you will come again."

Bile rose in Nathaniel's throat. *Vile woman!* To think he had considered her beautiful. All he could see now were the deep-green hues of jealousy and undertones of malice.

"I'm afraid my duties will keep me occupied for some time," he said. "I do not know when I shall have the opportunity for a social call again."

"'Duties'?" inquired Mrs. Sangford. "What duties does a young man of leisure have?"

Nathaniel wanted to bite his tongue. He should have bitten it a moment sooner, fool that he was! He posted what he hoped was a gleam of mischief upon his face. "Ah, you know how it is,

Mrs. Sangford. Mothers sometimes like to think up tasks for their wayward sons to conjure up the mark of respectability. For all my faults, I adore my mother. I shall not say 'no' to a few weeks of her reasonable demands."

His hostess nodded sagely, his words seemingly making absolute sense to her under the circumstances. Or, at least, the circumstances as she understood them.

"Well, then, we bid you success in pleasing your patient mother," she replied. "For who else endures one's faults better than one's mother? You should not disappoint her."

She did not have to look at her elder daughter for the aim of her gibe to be clear.

Nathaniel had had enough. "Not all mothers are equal. I only know I am blessed with mine."

He turned his back to the cold-hearted duo and bowed to Miss Sangford. "I look forward to that dance when your leg is whole again."

A fine shade of color returned to her cheeks. He did not dare infuse more. "Ladies," he said to the room in general, touching his finger to his brow, "if you will excuse me."

As luck would have it, the obnoxiously charming footman appeared at that moment, vase in hand. "Compliments of the gardener, Miss Sangford," said Cedric. "He thought you could use a bit of cheering up, being stuck indoors and all. Where shall I put them?" he asked, indicating the profusion of flowers.

"Oh!" cried Miss Sangford. "How lovely! Perhaps put them up on the shelf where I can see them from anywhere in the room."

"Er… they smell rather good," remarked the footman.

"Do they?"

"Yes, miss. See?" He brought the arrangement closer and dipped it forward to just beneath her chin.

Miss Sangford lowered her head so that she could breathe deeply from the bouquet as a whole. She closed her eyes and savored the scent. "You were right to point it out to me. I would have hated to waste such a feast for the senses on a high shelf. Put it here, on the sideboard, where I can reach it with my wonderful new traveling chair. And tell Mr. Corbett I say, 'Thank you.' It was incredibly thoughtful."

Nathaniel slipped from the room while all the attention was on the new gift. Miss Sangford would know he was not the only person who could be kind to her. If such happy events were less of a novelty, she would cease to associate them with him. It was for the best.

"Well, I never!" Miss Amelia said as he withdrew through the library. "Since when does Mr. Corbett care about the state of our mood? *I* have certainly not been considered in this fashion. Have you, Mama?"

"Indeed, I have not. I suppose we must make drama with a broken leg before such effort is made on our behalf."

Nathaniel grinned to himself. He had struck a blow to their weakest point: their pride. Miss Sangford, he knew, would calmly ignore their outrage, knowing it made her the victor. He imagined her serenely tilting her head—her elegant silhouette angled down—as she drew in another breath of floral bliss. And in the background, her mother and sister blustered on like so much wind.

He whistled as he approached the front door.

"A good visit, sir?" asked the butler.

"I would say so," Nathaniel answered.

"Shall we be seeing you again soon then, sir?"

"Not for a while, I think, Hutchins."

"That is a pity, sir."

Nathaniel half-turned. "Is it?"

"Yes, sir. Miss Sangford… She… Well, it seems she benefits greatly from your calls, sir."

"She has other friends, I understand."

"Not really, sir."

Nathaniel grew quiet. "I see."

"Do you, sir?"

The words gave Nathaniel pause. "You are a tad impertinent today, Hutchins."

"Sorry, sir."

Nathaniel flicked a non-existent spot of dust from the top of his hat before lifting it to his head and pressing it down firmly. He continued on his way rather more soberly.

He shoved thoughts of Miss Sangford aside. For now. He had business to attend to. Madame Dubois was first on his list. And he needed to have another meeting with Viscount Howell. Duty called. But not as loudly as before. Nor was its voice alone. For in the background, a whisper had joined it. It spoke of hawks and broken wings. And the way they might be mended. He did not chase the whisper away, instead letting it nest gently in his mind.

He strode on, across town and into a less savory corner of its great, rambling streets. It was only when he stood at the door of the bordello that he shut the whispers down. They did not belong here. Not only because they were too precious for such a seedy place. But here he would find a witness who may very well destroy Miss Sangford's father. He could not think of her now. He must do what was right.

Only… what was right had become a complicated matter.

Nathaniel shook himself like a dog trying to release water after a swim. He must free himself of these thoughts. They were getting in the way of his responsibilities. But, as he knocked on the door and waited for answer, Nathaniel knew it was hopeless. He would never be free of Miss Sangford again.

CHAPTER NINE

THE WHEELS OF the mobile chair moved almost soundlessly across the carpeted hallway. Irene tugged at the handles extending from the wooden rims, pushing and pulling as one set of handles slipped around and down and out of reach, the next circling round to be gripped and used.

She had managed to take herself all the way to her father's study, an achievement she was well proud of. Hutchins had assured her that her father was back and had gone to his sanctuary, but as she maneuvered her way through the door, there was no sign of him. Instead, a discontented muttering arose from beneath his desk.

"I'm getting too old for this," Mr. Sangford grumbled as he stood, one hand pushing against a knee for leverage, the other holding what appeared to be a ledger.

Low in her modified chair, Irene must have been less conspicuous, for her father did not acknowledge her. Instead, he opened the volume of records before him, found the page he wanted, and sucked in his breath. He looked abruptly to his left and right, then down to the floor, staring at something that caught his attention before reaching down to claim it. It was—as far as Irene could make out—a single thread.

Her father's faced blanched. He placed the thread within the spine of the opened pages, snapped the ledger shut, and waggled it about, the thread staying put. This seemed to upset her father further.

"Hutchins!" he thundered, standing up abruptly, only to catch sight of his eldest daughter watching him.

"Irene…" His voice was tense, her odd contrivance remaining unacknowledged. "What are you doing here? How long have you been there?" And then, as more detail entered his senses, "What is that thing you are sitting on?"

Hutchins appeared, a little out of breath, one hand tucked behind his back. Irene, who was near the door, could see a folded booklet hidden in his fist. She could just make out the word "Almanac" and nothing more. It wasn't important to guess the full title, although Irene did wonder what Hutchins had been busy with when her father had shouted for him. It had never before occurred to her that the servants had lives beyond what they did for the family. The realization came as something of a shock.

"Who has been in this room today?" her father demanded of the butler.

"No one, sir," Hutchins replied, "save perhaps a maid come to dust. Is something wrong?"

"Someone has been at my desk."

"Possibly, sir, to dust."

"No, I mean *in* my desk. Rifling in these drawers." Mr. Sangford indicated downward irritably.

"I shall speak to the staff about it at once, sir," said Hutchins, his manner stiff and formal, but a nervous glance to the floor suggesting he smelled trouble.

"See that you do. And if there is any indication of someone having touched my personal documents…"

"I shall release them from your employ immediately." Hutchins nodded.

"No, you will bring the guilty party to me. I want to know what they were looking for."

"As you wish, sir."

"And Hutchins…"

"Yes, sir?"

"From now on, I will be locking this room when I am out. The maid will have to clean while I am present."

"Of course, sir." Hutchins performed a small bow, then turned and hastily went to call a meeting of the staff.

Irene—quite forgotten in the midst of her father's alarm at the intrusion into his personal affairs—waited to be acknowledged.

Mr. Sangford had sunk back down into his chair, his palms on the re-opened pages of the ledger, his eyes on the simple thread that still rested between them.

"It's a wheeled chair," said Irene in answer to the question he no longer seemed to remember he had asked.

"What?" Her father lifted his head, appearing astonished that she was still there. His mouth fell open and he stared at her without seeming to understand.

"Mr. Macrae has kindly lent it to me. It was his great-grandfather's. Such a clever design. Do you see?" She began to twist the little carriage this way and that to show her father its ease of movement. "I was able to come all the way to your study by myself without disturbing my leg at all."

Mr. Sangford blinked. "Macrae was here?"

"Yes, he had promised yesterday that he had a surprise for me and that he would deliver it today. He has been a man of his word. And so thoughtful. Are you not happy for me? Is this chair not a marvel?"

"Did our guest ever come into my study on some pretense?"

Irene cocked her head. "No, of course not. Why would he? Hutchins showed him in. He talked with Mother and Amelia and me, showed me how to work this mechanism, and then he left."

"And there was no one else who visited?"

"No one." Irene felt the exploration of this topic had now been worn out. Her father was being neurotic. So what if the silly thread had fallen free of the ledger? It could have happened easily without being noticed. Why did he have this security check in the first place? What could possibly be so important among those stuffy records? Who would care how many shillings were being spent on bread and milk?

"And how was this contraption delivered?" her father continued, his investigation apparently incomplete. "Mr. Macrae surely did not push it through the streets of Munro."

Irene shrugged. "He mentioned a wagon that he had waiting near the stables, so there must have been a driver, I imagine."

"And this driver was left unattended?"

"Well, no. Mr. Macrae said the presence of the wagon was upsetting somebody. You could ask Barton. It is likely he would have taken umbrage at a stranger in the mews."

"And rightly so." Mr. Sangford tapped an irate finger on the desk. "I shall wait to hear what Hutchins discovers and then speak to the groom. Somebody must have seen something."

"Our staff have been with us for years," Irene pointed out. "Why would they start snooping now? And a stranger could hardly walk through the house unnoticed. Is it not possible the little thread simply slipped out when you last closed your ledger?"

Mr. Sangford's head jerked up. "What do you know of it?"

"Of what? The thread? I came into the room while you were looking for and found it. I assumed you have been using it to see if someone has been tampering with your accounts. If they were careless, the thread would fall from the book. But why would anyone bother? What's so special about our household expenses?"

"Nothing," her father said curtly. "I just don't like the servants being nosy."

"But you as much as accused Mr. Macrae of being the guilty party! I struggle to fathom what motive he would have to snoop about in your study. If anything, he'd be loitering in the kitchen to charm the maids."

"You are right, of course," her father conceded. But his eyes did not clear and his mouth did not soften. "I'm overreacting. Let's see this chair of yours." He stood and walked around the desk, then circled the wheeled chair before coming to a halt in front of Irene. "It is certainly ingenious. Mr. Macrae has been very kind to think of your comfort. Perhaps we should have him to dinner of an evening. Some time in the next week or two. He might not be our usual cup of tea, but he is still a gentleman and has been a godsend in your time of need. It would be remiss of us not to acknowledge that. Perhaps, if we invited his parents too, it would raise the tenor of the gathering."

The switch between paranoid suspicion and grateful hospitality was so quick that Irene was a little startled. "You want to invite to dinner a man whom you believe capable of sneaking into your study and rifling through your documents?"

"I told you, I overreacted."

Irene, of course, thought the idea of having Mr. Macrae to dinner a particularly welcome one. But her father's behavior did not sit well with her. It distracted her from what should be an undiluted delight at having Mr. Macrae invited by her father, a man who handpicked everyone with whom he allowed his daughters to mingle. She should have been hugging herself at the thought of the gentleman's imminent return. After all, he only stayed away to perform duties his mother had thought up to occupy him. Surely, an invitation to dinner at the Sangford home would take precedence over such obscure tasks?

And yet her father's earlier actions niggled at her. Irene had a good mind to have a look at this precious ledger herself. Something important must have been hidden within its pages. Something her father would not share with her.

It lay upon the desk, open, inviting. In a little while, it would no doubt be locked away in one of the drawers, the key safely upon her father's person. If she was to discover its secrets, she would have to access the volume now.

But how to do so with her father in the room?

As luck would have it, her mother arrived, flustered and annoyed. "Where is Hutchins? Someone is at the door. They have already knocked twice. And there is no footman in sight, either.

What is happening in this house today?"

"I have asked Hutchins to call the staff together for a brief-ing," her husband explained. "They must all be gathered in the kitchen. He might be a while. I suppose I shall have to see to the door myself. It is hardly a job for a lady. There is no knowing who waits outside. Bother!"

"My dear!" cried Mrs. Sangford. "It is most inappropriate! I shall ring the bell for a servant. If they are all in the kitchen, they will hear it."

"No, they are busy with a serious matter. *I* shall attend to the visitor, just this once."

Mrs. Sangford's hand remained at her bosom in a show of indignation as she followed her husband down the corridor.

Irene wasted no time. The chair rode smoothly across the floor. Some careful negotiation around the desk and a tenuous reach from her disadvantaged position was needed before the book slipped down into her lap, the thread floating down and landing mercifully on the ledger rather than the floor. Irene took firm hold of it, for it was vital evidence to prove that no one had tampered with the pages.

The ledger was, predictably, open on the last page that con-tained any writing. Irene ran her finger down the entries. Repairs to a garden wall. Oats for the horses. The butcher's bill. The amounts did not mean much to Irene, as she had never needed to make such purchases. But all looked in order as far as she could make out.

She turned to the previous page. More of the same. No, wait, here was the account for Amelia's most recent shopping spree. My, it was a fair expense! There was an asterisk next to the total. Did that mean it was not yet paid? Or, perhaps, it was an amount her father did not wish to see repeated.

Her gaze now shifted to the column on the left. It was, as intrigue went, decidedly dull. Some income now became apparent. Rent from tenants. A return on the investment in the mill.

Irene's finger halted its downward course. Who was Madame Dubois? The Sangfords had no French acquaintances. The war had seen to that. If they looked down upon a man who carried Jacobite connections from decades before, they certainly weren't going to befriend those who had been enemies to the Crown less than two years ago.

It was a payment of ten pounds. Perhaps a purchase of high-quality clothing for her mother? French fashion remained popular, even if the French themselves did not.

The note beside the amount was blank. That in and of itself was strange. Every other entry had been fastidiously recorded with a description of what it was for. Why was this the exception?

Unable to solve the mystery, and knowing her time with the ledger was limited, Irene quickly glanced over the pages of the previous two months, ignoring expenses and income that seemed both reasonable and regular.

There she was again. Madame Dubois. Ten pounds. No note. And again the month before. Irene now flipped through the pages. Month after month of similar payments. Nothing else looked out of place. But Madame Dubois certainly was.

Irene placed the thread gingerly back into its groove, her fingers trembling slightly. She tipped the ledger back onto the desk, sliding it across to the position she had found it in.

Several sets of footfalls in the corridor made her throw her wheeled chair into reverse and swing it around to face the window.

Her father entered the room, with Messrs. Phineas Pratt and Harry Bligh close behind. All three looked at Irene with surprise.

"You're still here," her father said, his tone pitching a little.

"You left your… er, documents… unattended. I stayed to keep an eye on them. And to enjoy the view." Irene indicated the garden on the other side of the window. "Besides, we were not done talking about our dinner invitation to the Macraes."

Mr. Sangford marched across to his desk and slammed his ledger shut, the little thread wagging like a tiny tail before hanging limp once more. "Thank you," he said to Irene. "That was very considerate of you. However, I'm afraid we'll have to resume our conversation later. These gentlemen and I have business to discuss."

"Perhaps you could help me to the door?" Irene asked. "I will see myself the rest of the way."

Mr. Sangford obliged, steering the chair to the passage before closing the door unceremoniously to his daughter's back.

Irene immediately repositioned herself so that she might place her ear against said door. The sounds within were a bit muffled, but she could make out the name Cranbourn. All three voices were agitated. Then her father's voice rang out. "He is putting my daughter at risk. I won't have it!"

Mr. Bligh, a short, stout man with gruff voice to match, now mumbled something. This was followed by the menacing tones of Mr. Pratt—who always sounded as if he were threatening someone even when he was merely giving them the time of day—saying something very much like, "It's too late now." The usual hint of a threat hung in the air, but Mr. Pratt's words suggested it was more than a mere hint this time.

Irene did not like the implications of any of it. Which daughter was at risk? What did Elias Upton, Baron Cranbourn have to do with it? More importantly, how was her father involved? Mr. Pratt's threat did not sound friendly at all. Not that threats ever did. How had her father found himself in this situation?

Someone behind her cleared his throat.

Irene twisted around to see Hutchins looking at the floor. It was not his place to say anything accusatory, despite finding her ear pressed to the door of his master's study.

"What do you want?" she demanded to know, quick to be on the offensive, though she had the good sense to keep her voice low.

"Mr. Sangford is waiting to hear the results of my meeting with the staff," he explained.

"He has two gentleman with him on matters of business."

And goodness knows what else, Irene thought grimly. "He will send for you when he is done."

Hutchins nodded. "Of course." He glanced at the closed door. No doubt he imagined her resuming her earlier eavesdropping pose. "Would you like me to help you back to the drawing room?"

"No, thank you, Hutchins. I can manage well enough on my own."

He hesitated, possibly torn between loyalty to his master's privacy and respect for Irene's wishes. "Yes, miss." He turned to leave.

He had barely taken a step when Irene called him back in an urgent whisper.

"Hutchins…"

He swung around to face her. "Yes, miss?"

"Have you ever heard my father mention a Madame Dubois?"

If the butler had been eating something, he would have choked on it. His eyes bulged. His body stiffened. A second later, he had gathered himself and resumed his butlerish formality. "No, miss," he said, his manner cool and dismissive.

"But you know the name." It was not a question.

There was a long pause.

"Oh, spit it out, man! I am not a child. How bad can it be?"

Apparently, Hutchins felt the answer to that question to be *"very bad indeed,"* for he remained silent.

Irene crossed her arms. "Very well, then. I shall simply have to ask my father."

The butler's shoulders slumped. "You put me in a very awkward position, Miss Sangford."

"I am sorry for it, Hutchins. But it is important that I know."

Another pause. A relenting sigh. Then, "She is what many would call an 'abbess,' the ladies whom she is in charge of being referred to as 'nuns.'"

"What are they really?"

"Er… the opposite of nuns."

The truth dawned slowly and with some discomfort.

"She is *that* sort of madame?"

"I'm afraid so."

"I see."

"Will that be all, Miss Sangford?"

"Yes. Actually, no. How does one go about making contact with such a person without actually visiting the… er… 'nunnery'?"

"Miss Sangford," protested the poor fellow, "you cannot expect me to be complicit in such an introduction!"

"Fine. I will ask Mr. Macrae. He moves in those circles."

Hutchins was sweating now. "Please, miss, that is even worse. You must not ask a gentleman such a question. Even if he does have a reputation."

"You are right. Perhaps Barton will have fewer scruples. You may go."

But Hutchins remained.

"Was there something else?" Irene knew she was putting the butler in a terrible position. A week ago, she would not have cared. Now a twinge of guilt sat ill upon her. But there was something happening with her father. And it involved at least one secret. Hutchins would *have* to help her, even if she regretted the steps she needed to take.

"You could write to her," the butler said miserably. "I would see that it gets to her."

"Would you do that for me? Or would you be pleased with the opportunity to seize the letter and burn it?" Irene asked.

Hutchins hid the guilt in his eyes by lowering his gaze to his immaculately-polished shoes. "I would ensure that you receive a reply, miss."

"In your own hand? Come now, Hutchins, you take me for a fool. It would require a more calculating mind to best mine."

"What would you have me do?"

"I would have you deliver an invitation for her to meet me.

Perhaps in a tea room. Somewhere respectable."

"But your leg, miss…"

"I can sit just as quietly in a tea room as I do at home."

"Surely, the journey would be uncomfortable…"

"I shall put my leg up on the carriage seat and manage well enough."

If Hutchins had not been expected to maintain a formal stance, he would no doubt have scratched his head at the whole idea. "Would you have a footman carry you into the tea room?"

"Don't be ridiculous, man! We will take Mr. Macrae's wheeled chair. Between Barton and the footman, it can be lifted onto the carriage roof and secured. I will enter the tea room with dignity or not at all."

"And what if Finnigan speaks of this meeting to Mr. Sangford?"

"I shall arrange for my own chaperone and discard them at the appropriate time. Do not fret so, Hutchins. It will be someone of sound reputation. Of course, Madame Dubois will have to dress the part of a proper lady. Yes, that will do nicely." Irene pinned the butler with her gaze. "If she does not turn up, I will know you have not done your part."

"This is most irregular," the butler complained. "If Mr. Sangford discovers my role in this, he will dismiss me, and rightly so. Not to mention the shame if anyone recognizes the 'abbess' at the tea room with you."

"Well, if they do, they certainly wouldn't confess to it."

"Won't you reconsider, Miss Sangford? No good can come of this."

"No," Irene answered sourly, "I suppose not. But there are secrets I wish to unravel. I will deal with the consequences once I know exactly what they are." Before he could protest further, Irene added, "Have a footman fetch me to my room, where I can write the letter in private. I will slip it to you at dinner. I expect to have it delivered within the week. That is all."

Hutchins bowed in obedience, but he pursed his lips tightly, unable to mask his displeasure at the task that lay ahead.

Inside the study, the discussion raged on. From what Irene could make out, they were debating the situation at the mills. Boring business, then. Nothing else worth listening to. She gripped the handles of the wheels and rolled herself a short distance before turning in at the library. It was best she was found in a more neutral space when the footman came to collect her.

So, a letter to "Abbess" Dubois. And an invitation to tea for Miss Bathurst. Olivia did love a good cake. And she was easy enough to manipulate out of the way when the time came.

Despite having a plan of action, Irene was not happy. Strange things were happening under this very roof. Dealings with "madams" and threats against family, perhaps even herself. Well, she was about to tackle the former. The latter was going to have to wait until her father was less paranoid about the staff. She needed to speak to him calmly. But she would be keeping her eyes and ears open. If either Amelia or herself were in danger, she did not want to be caught off-guard.

The last time her life had been at risk, Mr. Macrae had come to her rescue. She wished she could confide in him now. His cool, gray eyes would rest upon her in that way of his that made her blush right down to her toes. It wasn't intended to be seductive, but it seduced her nonetheless. It was an honest gaze. Behind his eyes, his bright mind would seek solutions. And while he did so, she would be thinking of the softness of his curved lips and how good it would feel to kiss them.

Her moment of bliss evaporated as a new image entered her mind. Had those lips kissed Madame Dubois? Or one of her "nuns"? Irene shuddered. Why did he have to be such a scoundrel?!

She cast her desire for him forcibly aside. He was not for her. And she had more important matters to attend to.

Soon she was at her desk, quill in hand, her fingers poised over a blank page. The little bell her father had provided sat next to the inkpot. She strained to put her thoughts to paper. Mr.

Macrae was ever at the edge of them.

"Focus!" Irene scolded herself. She pushed her feelings down. But they were not gone. It was most frustrating.

"All right, then, if you won't leave, Mr. Macrae, you're going to help me."

Irene let her mind summon his smooth, blond hair combed back from his bold forehead, his nose, thin and straight like hers, his jaw strong but not brutish. She allowed the handsome specter's hand to fold around hers, guiding the quill as, together, they arranged a meeting with the disreputable woman.

She shivered a little, doubt creeping in. The phantom-Macrae pressed in close behind, offering reassurance. Irene resumed her writing, her hand within his, her confidence returning.

When the task was complete, she left the sheet to dry and sat back, resting her head against the illusion of Mr. Macrae's chest. She remained like this for some time. At peace. Until there came a knock at the door.

"May I come in, Miss Sangford? I need to dress you for dinner."

"Just a moment." Irene hastily folded the letter and then called for Finnegan to enter. The moment the lady's maid did so, the room felt strangely emptier. Irene looked down at her hand. It was quite alone.

And, possibly, she thought with some regret, *always will be.*

CHAPTER TEN

"MR. MACRAE, YOU know I only *manage* the girls. I am not one of them. Asking for an hour of my time is most unusual. I'm sure Sally told you that. Did your session with her not exhaust your needs?"

Madame Dubois was an exception to her type. Most abbesses took clients, but only from the most discerning members of society. They had often started out as beginners in their field, earning their way up through the ranks with skill and shrewdness. They were also typically bosomy women with excessive paint on their cheeks, dressed in satin and lace to show the success of their trade.

Madame Dubois, however, who was slender and wore modest attire, had skin that had remained youthful despite her graying hair, which she made no effort to disguise, and was famously discreet. No lonely sailors or roaring drunkards entered her establishment. None of her girls sat around looking eager as customers entered. Rather, Madame Dubois interviewed each hopeful gentleman and selected with whom he would spend his time—and money.

In short, Madame Dubois appeared more like a neat housekeeper than the owner of a brothel. And her sternness with her clientele was legendary. She was the one woman Nathaniel had been unable to charm.

"I have a private matter to discuss with you," Nathaniel explained. "I would offer to pay for your time if I did not think you would take it as an insult."

"I know what you are, Mr. Macrae," she said bluntly. "If the men who visit us choose to be loose-lipped about their dealings beyond these walls, and you invest your coin here to gain information rather than pleasure, I have no qualms about that. They know what they risk if they share their domestic or business secrets with my employees. But *I* do not divulge secrets about their identity or activities here. Not for any price. The men we entertain rely on my ability to keep their business here confidential. You are wasting your time if you are hoping I will reveal anything of that sort."

"Understood. Let us say it is more a monetary sort of question I would like to ask."

Madame Dubois, whose French alias did not match her very English, very aristocratic speech and manners, looked at him over her nose. If she had been wearing actual spectacles, they would have suited her very well.

"Very well," she agreed. "You may ask one question. If I am satisfied there is no harm in answering it, you may ask another."

Nathaniel nodded. Wasting no time, he inquired, "Do the gentlemen always pay you in cash?"

Madame Dubois lifted an eyebrow, the only part of her no-nonsense expression that shifted. "Not the sort of question I was expecting. And I shall answer it. Yes, I expect payment up front. I run no tab, not even for men of the *ton.* The type who come here are already engaged in secretive behavior, which means they are liars from the start. I do not trust them any further than their open purses."

"Do any of your clientele visit so regularly that they spend precisely the same amount here every month for months on end?" asked Nathaniel, quickly adding, "I will not need any names."

The other eyebrow lifted to join the first. "Are you looking to enter the business, Mr. Macrae? I don't recommend it. Gentlemen are oddly distrusting of other men. That sort of arrangement is usually left to the streets. It is not my cup of tea."

"Answer the question, if you please."

"Very well. I suppose there is no harm in it. No, I recall no one who attends with such extreme regularity. Even if they can be relied on for a weekly visit in a general way, something often comes up that disturbs their plans. A dinner with guests their wives have planned, for instance. Or a trip to London."

"And that is the only service you offer?"

Her eyebrows plummeted into a scowl. "I don't know what you mean, Mr. Macrae."

"I am simply wondering if there is any other reason a gentleman might make a regular payment to this establishment."

"No."

"Not to book a certain lady of his choosing in advance?"

"No."

"Not to receive preferential treatment?"

"No. Look here, Mr. Macrae…"

"Why would a man set aside ten pounds every month without fail to pay you, then?"

Madame Dubois's healthy complexion paled. "Your questions are no longer simple to answer, sir," she said stiffly. "And so I choose not to."

Nathaniel leaned forward and steepled his fingers upon the desk. "If you know what I am, madame, you will also know that my investigation will not end here. It is better to explain yourself to *me* than to have others reveal your secrets in a less, shall we say, *careful* way."

She narrowed her eyes. "Are you threatening me, sir? If you are, I would say your days of visiting my establishment are over, along with the easy access to information which you gather here."

"I have no intention of threatening you, madam. I am merely being open with you. Let me be even more plain-speaking, then.

We both know which man is involved in this arrangement."

He waited to study her reaction.

"I admit to nothing," she answered through tight lips.

Nathaniel sat back, his hands sliding backward to his hips. "Is it possible there is more than one gentleman with whom you have such an arrangement?"

"I think you should leave." Madame Dubois stood to indicate the finality of her words.

Nathaniel remained unmoving. "I find it odd that you are comfortable with your chosen form of business, even though it is not what one might call *morally pleasing*, and yet there is an element of it that you wish to keep hidden. What can be worse for someone to know?"

"What concern is it of yours?"

"It affects the life of a friend of mine. I would not see her hurt."

A flicker of uncertainty crossed Madame Dubois's face. Her typically poised manner slipped for a moment and she broke eye contact with Nathaniel.

He tilted his head quizzically. "You know who I am talking about, don't you?"

Silence.

He took a chance, hoping to catch the woman off-guard. "Mr. Sangford is busy with dealings that are putting his daughter at risk. Is that something that you care about?"

She stared at him defiantly, then her gaze fell to the floor and she sat down abruptly. Her voice grew soft. "No, I would not want any harm to come to her."

"Then you will tell me the truth so that I can protect her."

Madame Dubois lifted her chin. Her eyes searched his face, a question shallow within them. Then a knowing smile warmed her normally brusque manner. "Why, Mr. Macrae, you are in love with her!"

Nathaniel was not one to bluster. His work called for a calm demeanor under pressure. Yet he found himself blurting out rather emphatically, "I hardly know Miss Sangford! Our friendship is a fledgling one. It is quite a stretch to infer anything more."

"And yet…" She waved a hand as if presenting a dish. "There it is. Plain as day. Does she know?"

"Of course not. You are imagining things."

"But you have been to see her. More than once."

"A mere courtesy. And to ensure her safety."

"And to bring her a gift, I understand." She smiled as Nathaniel jolted with surprise. "I, too, have my spies, Mr. Macrae."

He tried to shrug it off as a matter of little consequence. "I have given her the use of my great-grandfather's wheeled chair. Someone of her usual independence should not be confined to a single room all day."

"I see." The smile lingered. "And did she like it?"

"She appears to have mastered the maneuvering of it very quickly." Nathaniel's mouth quirked as he pictured Miss Sangford getting stronger and bolder. "It won't be long before she's bumping into the shins of servants who do not jump out of the way fast enough."

Madame Dubois's smile twitched and she tilted her head meaningfully, forcing Nathaniel to fight the urge to blush. "That was very considerate of you, sir. I imagine she will get good use from this mechanism. Few men show their affection in such practical ways. I wonder, though… It does not bother you that her manners are not what one might expect from a lady of her standing?"

"Why should it? As I have said, we have no romantic understanding." Nathaniel wanted to bite his tongue. He should have defended Miss Sangford instead of himself. Should have said that her manners lacked nothing. That she was every inch a lady. But he had not. He had been more concerned about maintaining his neutral role. Even though he knew his feelings could no longer be described as *detached*.

"But you are not disinclined to the notion."

Nathaniel hesitated.

"You know my reputation, madame. I would not be considered suitable. Nor am I blessed with a title."

The woman tapped the tip of a forefinger upon the desk. "Some might say that is a blessing in and of itself. A title can get in the way of things."

He shrugged. "I certainly have no use for one."

Her eyes lifted to his. "Miss Sangford is of age. She could choose whom she wants."

"What is the point of aggravating her already tenuous position with her mother?"

Madame Dubois pursed her lips. "If it is so fragile, perhaps she is best rid of it."

Nathaniel arched both brows sharply. "That is quite a mercenary position, madame."

"Am I wrong?"

Nathaniel remembered the hunger with which mother and younger daughter had pounced on Miss Irene's weakness for him. "No, you are not wrong."

The abbess tapped her finger on the hard, wooden surface of the desk once more. "I suppose you think she must be grateful to have a life of comfort, where she has prospects and security."

"I would certainly be happy to know she is safe."

"And loved."

"I do not believe Miss Sangford shares your opinion of my feelings," he told her.

The abbess grew solemn. "No, she would not assume a man loves her. She has not been raised to think like that."

The intimacy of the statement gave Nathaniel pause. "You seem to know her well. I did not think you would move in the same circles."

"We do not."

"And yet…"

"And yet I know enough, Mr. Macrae."

"Perhaps through her father, with whom you are having an affair?"

Madame Dubois froze for several seconds, then her normally-austere expression fell away as a broad smile bloomed into full-throated laughter. "Oh, Mr. Macrae," she said, wiping tears of mirth from her eyes, "you couldn't be more wrong. And here I thought you such a talented spy!"

A little *ping* of hurt ego was followed by a solid *thump* of disappointment. "But," he said, genuinely confused, "why does he pay you ten pounds a month, then? Is there another secret of his that you keep? And why do you know such intimate details about his daughter?"

Madame Dubois gathered her composure, putting the invisible spectacles back upon her nose. This time, however, some of the earlier reserve had not returned. She considered Nathaniel carefully and seemed to reach a decision.

"You say Miss Sangford's father is involved with something that is putting her at risk? Tell me your concerns and I will tell you why I care."

It was an odd bargain. Still, Madame Dubois was a useful ally to have. She knew how to keep secrets and had sensitive information on men at every level of Munro's upper society. He could see no harm in drawing her into his investigation. Especially since he was making such slow progress on his own. "Very well. You have a bargain."

"Excellent," answered the abbess. "Let us begin. We neither of us have time to waste."

Nathaniel began to lay out the details of the case thus far. The situation with the protest march was public knowledge, and the description of the assassination attempt merely drew a nod as she listened with concentration. He explained how the Sangford sisters had come to be involved in the case, and the danger that the newspapers had put Miss Sangford in by speaking of it, forcing the family to publish a lie about her loss of memory.

"We have yet to identify who arranged for the attempt on the life of Bill O'Neal," he said. "Mill owners are the logical candidates. Mr. Sangford meets regularly with Mr. Pratt, Mr. Bligh, and

Lord Cranbourn, all of whom have significant shares in the affected mills. From what I can gather, all four stand to lose a considerable portion of their wealth if work at the mills continues to be disrupted. Of course, it is possible they are meeting merely to discuss business…"

"But you suspect they might be involved in the plot?"

"I cannot rule that out."

The abbess spread her palms upon her desk. "I do not like the sound of this. If Miss Sangford's father is innocent, and the guilty party wants to remove the witness, he cannot protect her. Not truly. And if he is guilty, I have no doubt you will find him out. He will be arrested. Her future will be ruined. These are not good alternatives."

"No, madame, they are not."

"And yet you waste your time trying to determine whether Mr. Sangford has a mistress?"

"If he did, it would speak to his character. And whether such a secret could be used against him."

"I see. Well, he does not. At least, not to my knowledge."

"And you are likely to know?"

"I have made it my business to know."

"Why is that, Madame Dubois? Does he have other secrets which he pays you not to tell?"

A less experienced eye might have missed it. But Nathaniel saw the tiny flicker of fear.

"Would it matter if he did?" she asked with feigned calm.

"Certainly. If Sangford carries secrets, he could be manipulated by those who share them. He might be used by other powerful men to take care of the unpleasant matters they want seeing to without rolling up their own, very expensive sleeves. Suppose the man is involved against his will? He could be both guilty and innocent to varying degrees."

"Are you suggesting *I* am manipulating him? Why on earth would I want Bill O'Neal dead?"

"Oh, I am not saying *you* are the mastermind in this case. But you might not be the only one who shares his confidence."

"I assure you, Mr. Macrae, I protect only one secret where Mr. Albert Sangford is concerned. And it has been shared with no one. But I will share it with you because you clearly care about Miss Sangford. And because, heaven help me, I trust you. However…" She interlocked her fingers and lay her folded hands, with knuckles facing him, upon the surface of the desk. Leaning forward, her eyes unflinchingly focused upon him, her voice thick with warning, she added, "I will know if you betray me."

Nathaniel ignored the threat. He had no intention of divulging secrets unless it was to prevent a crime or bring a perpetrator to justice. Even then, he would simply use the information to solve the case and not embarrass the innocents involved by making the facts public.

The lady—for she looked every inch the part—drew her hands into her lap and sighed deeply. "Do you know, I have not spoken of this for so many years, I had almost forgotten how it felt to do so."

Nathaniel did not rush her. He waited until she was ready to begin and then listened in silence. No questions. No comments. He observed the emotions that stormed across her face, strangely wild and unshackled. He did not judge. Oh, no, *she* was not the one to be judged. He only knew that this secret was nothing like what he had expected.

The story was not long, yet it felt as if it stretched through time. In a way, it was ageless, eternal. And the burden of the secret, finally revealed, was heavy and cumbersome, sitting ill upon Nathaniel's shoulders.

"And you say Mrs. Sangford is aware of it all?" he asked at last.

"Oh, yes," the woman answered bitterly. "She has known almost from the start."

"So, this is the reason for the ten-pound payments?"
She nodded.

It all made sense now. How different life would have been for his broken-winged hawk if…

"You should tell her," he urged.

Madame Dubois stared at him. "Are you quite mad?"

"She needs to know."

A wry smile twisted her mouth. "Does she indeed? And how will that solve anything?"

"She deserves the truth."

"For what possible purpose? Will it improve her life in any way?"

"The truth has its own power. And she has too little of it."

Madame Dubois grew quiet.

"You know I am right," Nathaniel said.

"I think it is time for you to go, Mr. Macrae. Our bargain has been fulfilled. You will not speak of what you have learned. Good day to you, sir."

"But…"

"I said, 'Good day.'"

Nathaniel rose reluctantly. "I will keep my promise, even if it pains me. But I would ask you to reconsider your silence on the matter."

"I will do as I see fit," Madame Dubois answered, her stern voice and posture reestablished. "We will not talk of this again."

Nathaniel departed with a heavy heart. He was no closer to knowing who had put a price on Bill O'Neal's head or whether Mr. Sangford was involved in any capacity. Instead, he had learned why his hawk's wing was broken.

And he could not mend it.

CHAPTER ELEVEN

Friday, March 28th, 1817

TWO AGONIZING WEEKS went by before Irene could meet with Madame Dubois. Olivia *would* choose this exact time to be visiting her aunt in Steeples. Without her gullible, pastry-loving friend, Irene knew her arrangement would never work. She would not be able to convince her father to let her go to the tea room with a footman's assistance if she had no chaperone. And she would not be able to have a private conversation with Madame Dubois if she couldn't shake off her friend for a while with a flimsy excuse. Olivia was the perfect candidate for the role.

Getting the "abbess" to agree to the meeting had also been a tricky matter. Irene's first attempt at an invitation had been returned with a footnote on her own letter, simply stating "Unavailable to meet."

A second letter had followed with the promise of a payment to make it worth the woman's while. It had been summarily returned with another short comment: "Not for sale." Irene thought this rich coming from the madame of a brothel.

A third letter took the gloves off. Irene made mention of the ten-pound payments and suggested that a meeting between them would be all that stood in the way of her going to her mother with the information. This time, Madame Dubois complied.

And then Olivia had been away for ten days. To Irene's enormous surprise, Madame Dubois had written to her during this time, asking why there was a delay and wanting to know if Irene had discussed the payments with anyone else. The woman was clearly nervous after the threat in the third letter.

Hutchins, now thoroughly wretched at having so much covert correspondence to courier to and fro, had complained that he would not deliver a single one more. And yet he found himself doing so, anyway. Much to his relief, it had been the last one. Upon Olivia's return, arrangements to meet had been finalized at once. Which was why, at this very moment, Irene found herself seated comfortably in her wheeled chair at the Café Bon Bon with Olivia and the owner of a brothel.

She hadn't quite known what to expect. Madame Dubois had been advised to dress as a regular patron, and she had done just that. The woman fitted in perfectly with the crowd partaking in their afternoon tea and sweet treats. She was simply a lady enjoying an outing among her peers. The difficulty came in picturing her as anything else.

Madame Dubois was slender and graceful, even regal, her hair coiffed in a manner that was both stylish and uncomplicated. Her clothing matched those of a woman of society, though the colors were muted. In short, she looked the part without drawing any attention to herself.

The same could not be said of Olivia Bathurst. The moment Olivia had opened her mouth, guests at the closest tables turned to see who was making that awful sound, tilting their heads down toward each other to comment on it in hushed tones.

"I never knew Irene had a cousin who lived in Belgium, Mrs. D'Arby," Olivia said politely, her intentions less jarring than the sound she made expressing them. "The war must have been hard for you."

"Mrs. D'Arby" raised a quizzical brow at the assault upon her ears that emanated from Olivia's mouth. "Is that your natural voice, Miss Bathurst?" she asked, to Irene's horror. "Or do you mock me?"

"Oh, goodness, no!" Olivia replied. "I would never want to

offend anyone of Irene's acquaintance. This is indeed my natural voice. A strain on the ears, is it not? I had a terrible fever as a child and my throat was pure agony for weeks. The doctor believes the illness damaged my vocal cords. It has been very frustrating when meeting new people, as few can endure my voice for long. I do not have any suitors as a result. Or many friends." She smiled at Irene. "But there are a handful who have been most kind."

Irene sat, mute with shock. And a fair degree of shame. She had never been kind to Olivia. Irene had let her tag along for company. She had used her, as she was doing today. And never, in all that time, had she asked herself *why* Olivia maintained an awful quality to her voice if she could change it. Irene had just thought her too simple-minded to know better.

"I never knew that about your illness," Irene said, mouth agape.

"Well, we weren't friends then yet." Olivia shrugged. "And, to your credit, you never mentioned it once when we were."

Mrs. D'Arby bathed Irene in the warmth of a sudden smile. "That is most commendable, my dear. Your mother must be so proud to have a daughter with such rare qualities."

Irene said nothing. Possibly this only served to make her appear modest, when really, she was too embarrassed to speak. She did not deserve Olivia. Some might say she had done the poor thing a kindness by keeping her as a friend, but Irene now knew it was quite the opposite. *Olivia* was the true friend.

"Shall we order?" Olivia inquired. "They do excellent meringues here. Have you tried them? If you choose something else, you shall have one of mine. They are like sugared air." She looked up dreamily, as if she could picture the meringues before her, the taste already upon her tongue.

"I am something of a traditionalist," said Mrs. D'Arby. "I will be having a scone with jam and cream."

"That is my favorite, too," said Irene.

Mrs. D'Arby looked pleased. "Is it? How interesting."

"Perhaps your tastes run in the family," said Olivia. "You are related, after all."

"Hmm, yes," replied the older woman.

"I can certainly see the resemblance," Olivia continued. "Are you related on her mother's or her father's side?"

"Her mother's," answered Mrs. D'Arby at the exact moment that Irene said, "My father's."

The two women stared at each other.

"Well, which is it?" Olivia asked.

"I defer to my cousin on this," said Irene hurriedly. "I just assumed it was my father's side because Mrs. D'Arby looks nothing like my mother. I'll admit I am not one for paying attention to the details of the family line."

"Well, Mrs. D'Arby has certainly got your fine features, Irene," Olivia continued. "The resemblance is quite uncanny."

Irene had not been much focused on her older guest's looks, other than to note with great relief that she had dressed perfectly for the part she must play. But now that Olivia had pointed it out, Irene could see it too: the slightly long nose that was not too long; the very dark eyes; the elongated neck and narrow face. In short, she was, in many ways, an older version of Irene.

Mrs. D'Arby, however, must have lost interest in the topic, for she had her long, slender arm in the air and was attempting to catch the attention of a server. She made no eye contact with Irene or her friend, intent on locking on to the gaze of a waiter instead.

Soon a very neat and well-groomed—albeit a little short— fellow hurried over.

"Good day, ladies. How may I help you? Would you like to know our specials?"

"We will have two orders of scones, a plate of meringues, and a pot of Congou tea," Mrs. D'Arby said smartly. "Will you be wanting milk or sugar?" she asked the others. They shook their heads.

"I will have that for you shortly, ma'am," the waiter said with a small bow before walking away with trim steps toward the kitchen.

"When last have you seen my friend, Mrs. D'Arby?" asked Olivia. "I gather you have been away for some time."

The abbess looked at Irene with an empty sort of gaze, as if her eyes, despite being focused on Irene, were seeing something else, perhaps a distant memory. Her mouth softened and she said, "I believe it was when you were still a baby. Such a tiny thing you were. A fragile bundle in your mother's arms. You had your father's mouth, but the rest were… your mother's."

"So, in a sense," said Olivia, "you are really meeting for the first time now."

Mrs. D'Arby nodded. "That is true."

Something in the way the woman had spoken of her told Irene that this was not some fabrication to satisfy Olivia's curiosity. "I am amazed at your description of me," Irene pondered aloud. "Everyone considers Amelia to be the echo of my mother. I just assumed my looks must have come to me through a more roundabout route—an aunt twice removed or something like that. And yet you say I looked just like her as a baby. Have I changed that much?"

There was a long pause. "No," Mrs. D'Arby answered eventually. "I would say it is your mother who has changed."

"That is odd," Olivia said. "I have known the family for some years and Mrs. Sangford has been quite consistent in her appearance."

"The change must have occurred many years ago then," answered Mrs. D'Arby. "Be that as it may, I am happy to see my cousin looking so well. Especially given the recent injury. And yet here you are, Irene, taking tea as if nothing had happened." She tilted to the side to get a better look at Irene's unusual seat. "What a marvel this chair is! I doubt such an outing would have been possible without it."

"It was a gift from Mr. Nathaniel Macrae," Olivia piped up, evidently delighted that no one was speaking over her as they so often did. "He has been *most* attentive to her needs." A knowing grin accompanied the comment.

"Has he indeed? I am surprised your father tolerates your acquaintance with him, my dear. Mr. Macrae has been known to frequent…" Mrs. D'Arby stopped suddenly, her face frozen as if caught out in a misstep.

"Oh, we know all about Mr. Macrae's reputation," said Olivia, sharing a look with Irene. Or trying to. Irene fought to keep a neutral expression. Madame Dubois had almost given away her intimate knowledge of the gentleman. And Olivia, it seemed, had picked up on the clue, for she added, "I am amazed his reputation has reached Belgium."

"Hardly," Mrs. D'Arby answered, waving a hand dismissively. "But Mrs. Sangford writes to me and has spoken of Mr. Macrae's kindness, as well as his… shall we say… *other* qualities."

Irene breathed out. She had to hand it to Madame Dubois. She was a smooth liar. But it did make her wonder if she would ever get the truth she wanted from the woman if she was so adept at creating *untruths* at a moment's notice.

"My father appreciates the services Mr. Macrae has rendered our family," Irene said. "He does not have to approve of the man's lifestyle to be grateful for his brave and generous actions."

Mrs. D'Arby pursed her lips. "It seems to me Mr. Macrae is no less a rogue than so many of the titled lords to whom your father would offer your hand in marriage."

"Isn't that the truth!" Olivia said with feeling.

Irene rolled her eyes inwardly. Olivia was always game for a good bit of gossip.

A tray floated through the space between them and the waiter, having approached in impressive silence, began to unpack the tea pot and cups with saucers, causing Olivia to turn expectantly and discover a second waiter with a tiered display of scones and meringues in one hand and another tray with thick strawberry jam, cream, and a small pile of plates in the other. Needless to say, all gossip was immediately forgotten. It was only an excellent upbringing that would have kept Irene's treat-loving friend from grabbing the gooey sweetness from the waiter and shoving it between her otherwise-delicate lips.

Irene stifled a smile. Olivia's fondness for all things baked and sugary had always been a cause of condescension in Irene's mind. But today, she saw an innocent enthusiasm. Olivia had so few prospects. Irene understood that now. Despite her doll-like features and pretty golden ringlets, Olivia would be unlikely to find a mate who could bear her speech. Unless she married some wizened old man who was at least partially deaf. Why should something as simple as a tartlet or meringue not bring her joy?

Olivia held herself back. Then, as soon as it was polite to do so, she placed a single meringue upon her plate, smiled at the other ladies at the table, and lifted the light confection to her mouth. Her eyes closed as she let it melt upon her tongue. Her teeth procured a bite, crumbs tumbling to her plate, which Irene knew her friend would look at sadly after the bulk of the treat was consumed.

When Olivia's eyes opened once more, she blushed at the way Irene was studying her. "Are you not going to have your scone? It is best while still warm from the oven."

Irene's gaze dropped to her empty plate.

"Shall I pour tea for you?" asked Mrs. D'Arby, who must have noticed that the cups remained empty also.

Irene nodded, pushing her cup and saucer across the table-cloth toward the older woman.

"Have you known many rogues in Belgium?" asked Olivia, returning to the interrupted topic.

"No," answered the abbess, her eyes upon each of the three cups as she poured. "But I have known a good many here in Munro."

Olivia's eyes lit up, her meringue temporarily forgotten.

"Anyone we might know?"

"That is very likely," said Mrs. D'Arby, returning the pot to its stand.

"Anyone with a story worthy of extortion?" Irene asked suddenly. She wasn't entirely sure what had possessed her to fling the question out like that. Especially with Olivia still at the table. Mostly it was the hope of catching Madame Dubois off-guard.

Instead, the woman calmly lifted her own cup to her lips and sipped discreetly at the richly flavored liquid.

It was Olivia who pressed the matter. "Do you know, Irene, I think your cousin has a really good tale to tell. The best ones always have to be drawn out for maximum effect. I believe Mrs. D'Arby has a story as delicious as… well, as this meringue here." She promptly took another bite as if to test the theory.

"I would be a poor keeper of secrets if I shared such sordid details with refined ladies," Mrs. D'Arby said grimly.

"And yet here you are," came Irene's sharp response. "No one forced you to come."

"Didn't they?" the abbess replied, her tone suggesting a measure of extortion had already occurred.

Irene glared at her. "Why don't you just come out with it? Or shall I bring the matter to my mother's attention?"

"Your mother!" The abbess scoffed. "She would be far less shocked than you think."

Olivia looked from one lady to the other, her forehead creasing at their strange talk. It was too late to maneuver Olivia from the table as Irene had previously planned. Besides, she had finally gotten the abbess to take the bait. Olivia would have to bear witness to whatever was revealed.

"Are you saying my mother knows?" Irene asked, taken aback.

Madame Dubois leaned back and gathered herself. "This is neither the time nor the place." She indicated to Olivia with a tilt of her head.

"Madame," said Irene, carelessly letting the title slip, "there will never be an appropriate time for such an expensive truth. Unless you are afraid the well will run dry. I suggest that Miss Bathurst can be trusted to keep my confidence."

It was a strange realization. Olivia could be trusted. She had misjudged her all these years. She had always known Olivia to be a simple creature, easily manipulated. It had never occurred to her that Olivia had been so grateful for her friendship that she had merely acted according to the example that Irene had set. If Irene was mean and sarcastic, so was Olivia. If Irene made snide, gossipy remarks, Olivia echoed them. But if Irene demanded trust and secrecy, Olivia would gladly give these, too. And these qualities might very well suit her nature all the better.

Olivia, whose frown had been setting deeper and deeper into her brow, immediately threw it off and sat up a little straighter. "You can count on me, Irene. I enjoy some tattle as much as the next person, but I would never want to see you hurt. If you need me to keep a secret for you, I will do so, and gladly."

Irene took a moment to digest this declaration. She had always looked down on Olivia with her silly voice, her embarrassing keenness for cakes, and her willingness to do what she was told if Irene was doing the telling. But even at her most condescending, Irene had known Olivia to be a loyal friend. She had simply never appreciated it before. Whenever it had suited her, she had manipulated and selfishly used her friend to further her own interests. Yet she had never recognized what a good friend Olivia actually was.

Well, she saw it now.

"Yes, I think we may speak safely at this table," she declared. "And speak you shall. If you were so nonchalant about my mother's reaction, you would have let me take the secret to her and not been persuaded to meet me."

Madame Dubois gazed intently at Irene. "I have come to meet you for my own selfish reasons. I do not care what the Sangfords think of me. Nor have I been in need of their money for a very long time. It has all been for *you*."

Irene's thoughts ground to a halt. She shook herself mentally. This was not what she had expected. A secret, yes. One shocking enough to warrant a fee to stay hidden, certainly. But what on earth could it have to do with *her*?

"This is your last chance to leave things as they are," warned the abbess. And yet there was no threat to her tone. Instead, sadness lay shallow in her eyes.

A measure of doubt crept in. If her mother knew her father had been paying the monthly ransom for this woman's silence— even knew *why*—and they had felt it better to keep it to themselves, it might be best to leave well enough alone. And yet... her father's behavior was becoming increasingly erratic. Something was up. And this was the only secret she knew he was harboring. Irene had no idea where else to start unraveling the mystery within their home. She didn't like that there was one in the first place.

It was time for the truth to out.

CHAPTER TWELVE

"I WANT TO know," Irene said aloud.

"All right, then," said the abbess. No fear touched her voice. She sat calmly with hands folded upon the tablecloth. A soft smile crept from the corners of her mouth and settled in her eyes, which looked warmly upon Irene. All of these small gestures of reassurance were far more disconcerting than if Madame Dubois had simply blurted out some fiendish facts. Irene had prepared herself for such a confrontation. But kindness and compassion? These undid her composure.

"Four and twenty years ago," began Madame Dubois, "a very sheltered daughter of a marquess met a gentleman of good standing and a little money at a private ball at their home. She was a studious sort of young woman, her nose more oft in a book than her hair was in ribbons. Perhaps she was a little too pale from all the hours she spent within the library. Possibly she was not as womanly of shape as men might want. As it may be, she was getting on in years, her coming out many seasons behind her, and no suitor won. Nor did her parents make great work of it, for she must marry well—meaning, of course, a title and money—or not at all."

Irene fought the urge to fidget in her chair. The story was sounding painfully familiar.

"The scarcity of such men," continued the abbess, "further

diminished her chances of marriage, and the idea of happiness within such an arrangement certainly played no role at all.

"Until the ball," said Olivia breathlessly, hanging on every word.

Madame Dubois's demeanor shifted. She spread the fingers of her hand that rested upon the tablecloth, then drew them back protectively and tucked them into her lap.

"In the young lady's defense," she said abruptly, "I would say that she was caught off guard by his attention, having never been offered anything of the like before. She did not question his motives. Why should she? No one had lied to her before. Why should she suspect this lovely creature who was giving her the sort of attention every woman yearns for? No, indeed, she drank it in. Became intoxicated with love, and then desire.

"He visited their home frequently after that night until her father, suspicious of his intentions and absolutely set against their match, forbade his return.

"But it was too late. The newly acquired emotions became a passion that burrowed into the core of her being and would not be rooted out. They began to meet in secret. Not long after, she gave herself to him, willingly and gladly. And the happiness that had eluded her all her life now bloomed within her."

The voice of Madame Dubois grew soft, as if to balance the hard truth that must follow.

"Also within her, bloomed the seed of life."

"She was with child!" Olivia gasped, unable to contain herself any longer. "Her father must have been furious! Were they forced to wed?"

The abbess lowered her eyes, wincing as if in pain. "No. It was quite the opposite. Her father denounced them both." A pause. A deep breath. "He accused his daughter of being little better than a whore."

Irene felt sick to her core. It was all too clear now. This young man, terrible as the thought was, had been her very own father before he had wed her mother. Why else would he need to pay for Madame Dubois's silence? His youthful dalliance would have undone all his efforts for a good match, both for himself and for his legitimate children to follow. But where was the babe? Had the abbess raised the child? There were more questions than ever before!

"And her lover?" Olivia wanted to know, her neck straining forward as though to draw the answer from the narrator by sheer willpower. "Tell me he made an honest woman of her!"

"Ah, Miss Bathurst." The woman gave a rueful smile. "You are full of innocent hope, as was the daughter of the marquess. But it now became clear that her lover had *meant* to produce fruit in her womb to force her father's hand, so recklessly and selfishly had he sought a superior match with her. He had never dared to think a father could abandon his daughter if her actions displeased him. The foolish man had underestimated the marquess's cold insistence on a match of proper status and wealth. When his lordship's daughter made this impossible, she was discarded with the clothes on her back and a baby in her belly."

Irene shuddered. Where was the child now? Irene's mother was not the daughter of a marquess, so the woman and child had been abandoned. It painted a very cruel picture of her father, which did not match her own experience of him. Yes, he was cold and ambitious, but to be so utterly ruthless? It was bad enough to think of him manipulating a woman into marriage. But the suggestion that he could doom his own child to ignominy sent a burning indignation through her veins.

"My father would never do such a thing!" Irene said, a little too loudly. Nearby customers threw disapproving looks her way before resuming their own, less vociferous conversations. Her cheeks grew warm and yet she repeated insistently, "My father would never abandon his responsibilities."

"It turns out you are right," Madame Dubois replied. "To a point. Unlike the marquess, the young gentleman did not leave his lover to her own fate. Not entirely. But he did not marry her. For he had ambition, and she could no longer satisfy it."

"Hold on a minute." Olivia was shaking her head. "What does this have to do with Mr. Sangford?"

The abbess raised an eyebrow at Irene. "How much do you want her to know?"

"Everything," Irene answered through gritted teeth. "I cannot bear this news alone."

"Very well. As it happens, Miss Bathurst, the gentleman lover of this story is none other than Mr. Albert Sangford."

The wheels behind Olivia's eyes turned rather slowly until, at last, her mouth formed a large, undignified oval, which her hand flew up to cover. She turned wide-eyed to Irene and said in a hushed voice, "Then you have a sibling somewhere whom your father has not told you about. What a shock! I wonder if you've ever met them without realizing...'"

Madame Dubois interrupted. "I'm afraid you've drawn the wrong conclusion, Miss Bathurst. The child in question who was born out of wedlock is your own friend, Miss Irene Sangford."

The words hit Irene like a mallet to the chest. "What?" Panic clenched at her heart. "It was me?" Years of false truths upon which she had built her entire life began to wobble dangerously. "But my mother..." Another tremor. "She is not the daughter of a marquess." Irene raised her eyes hopefully to the abbess. "Is she?"

Madame Dubois reached a hand across the table, but Irene did not take it. The woman withdrew it with a sigh. "No, my dear. Your parents never married. Your father paid your mother ten pounds a month to take care of herself and to keep his secret—*their* secret—confined to their knowledge alone."

She waited for Irene to understand. It did not take long, but to Irene, the shift felt slow and monumental, akin to a mountainside when an avalanche robbed it of its snowy skin.

Irene's head lifted as if through the treacle of a terrible dream. Her eyes met her mother's. Her breath hitched. Her mother. It was so obvious now. The disdain she had always received from her supposed mother... Should she call her Mrs. Sangford now? She could certainly never think of her as family again.

All those years and the woman had known Irene was not her daughter. She must have hated Irene, having to raise another woman's child—daughter of her husband's lover—as her own. Small wonder she treated her like a stepchild. That was exactly what Irene was.

But if the world believed Irene was her daughter, she must have married Albert Sangford almost immediately. How on earth had her father persuaded her to do that?

"I don't understand. Why am I living with my father? Why did my mo… I mean Mrs. Sangford agree to such an arrangement?" Irene asked. Madame Dubois opened her mouth to answer, but Irene quickly added, "And why did you give me up?"

"Ah, my dear," her mother answered, "you know the answer to that last question. What could I offer you? With your father, there was the chance for you to have a stable life and a good match. I could not raise you among the women who took me in. Even though I did not share in their lifestyle—since the ten pounds covered my rent and expenses—it was not the sort of place to introduce a child to the world. Nor have I done so."

"You would have loved me."

"Your father has loved you. In his way."

"It is not the same."

"No," said the abbess sadly, "I suppose it is not."

"Do *you* love me at all?" Irene's voice trembled as she spoke. She felt small, worthless, unwanted.

Madame Dubois took some time to answer. A tear slipped down her elegant cheek. Then another. She bit her lip and nodded, seemingly unable to speak. "Oh, yes," she managed, her voice barely a whisper.

The weight of her words, few as they were, sat upon Irene with some confusion. A mother who loved her. It should have been a gift. Even after all these years. But the knowledge was tainted with a sense of betrayal. Where had that love been when she had needed it? Ah yes, it had been sold for a ten-pound-a-month muzzle. A brick of resentment hardened in her heart.

Olivia, who had wisely kept from saying anything during the momentous revelation, now reached a hand across and folded it around Irene's where it lay, paralyzed, in her lap.

"Your secret is safe with me," Olivia said very softly. "You are a fine woman, Irene. Your origins do not change that."

"I am so grateful you have a good friend," said Madame Dubois, her voice growing stronger as she briskly wiped the tears from her face. "I regret that I have been unable to play any role at all. But you must know, Irene, that I have followed your life closely. I cannot expect you to accept me as your mother, but I hope you will count me among your loyal friends. Even if we can never be seen together in public after today. For your sake, that is."

"'F-Friends'?" Irene spluttered. "After you took money for your secret for decades, even when you had needed payment no longer, having established yourself in business? And you know I am being kind to describe it as such."

"The money! You think I cared for that?!" The abbess hissed, her anger likely only contained so that none about them might notice. "I had my heart broken. My family abandoned me. I was punished for knowing love briefly and then never again. And the man who seduced me took everything. Everything! Do you understand? I could not even have the comfort of knowing my own child. And yet everything I did, I did for you. Giving you up. Taking the money. I haven't spent a penny in twenty years. It has all been set aside for you."

Irene froze. "What do you mean?"

"Secrets have a way of worming their way to the surface. I knew that there was always going to be the chance that the conditions of your birth would be made known. I have saved up nearly three thousand pounds in investments and interest. If you should ever have need of it, it will grant you your freedom. You don't need to rely on your father's protection, or the whim of a husband. You can make your own way, and comfortably so."

"What sort of freedom would the daughter of a brothel madam have in society?" Irene asked bitterly.

Olivia gasped but did not withdraw her hand.

"I suspect it would be the same sort of freedom I enjoy now," said her mother with a shrug. "The freedom to come and go as I please. To choose whose company I keep. Indeed, I would say I have met at *least* as many lords and other gentlemen as you have. Perhaps I do not attend balls or sit around the dinner table with family who have lied to me all my life. But I am content enough. One might even say that you would find a happier match if you did not have to abide by your father's strict standards."

"Oh, yes." Irene sneered. "I would definitely find a quality sort of man when my heritage is known."

Her mother sighed. "I understand. This is a shock. Does it help to remind you I did not wish for you to know? That I would have protected you as long as possible?"

"No."

"Irene," said Olivia carefully, "your mother carries far less blame than the men who left her out in the cold. Even if your father had married her, she would have been little more than a prize to him. And your grandfather... Well, his cruelty was simply abominable. He could have sent the child... you... to a good home with a decent couple who were unable to have children. You might have grown up without shame and in the bosom of a loving family. And your mother could have married another and held her head high among society. You are not the only one who has lost much. In fact, you have—as far as the rest of the world is concerned—lost nothing at all."

"I suppose," Irene replied, her lips twisting as she spoke. "I should be grateful to finally understand why the only mother I have ever known has so clearly despised me. Or that she agreed to raise me at all. Quite frankly, I do not understand that at all."

"I wish I could help you," said Madame Dubois, "but I have not been made privy to those details. I only knew you were safe—at least physically so—and had a promising future. You will have to ask your father to furnish the rest of the story."

Irene pressed her lips together. "Then that is what I shall do."

"Is that wise?" asked Olivia. "Mrs. Sangford barely suffers your presence now as it is. If she knows the sham is over, what reason will she have to show you any courtesy at all?"

A nasty sort of smile formed in answer. "Oh, I think she might be motivated to be *much* friendlier, in fact," suggested Irene. "That is, if she does not want the world to know what they have been up to. Imagine the shame for poor, dear Amelia if it is discovered that her half-sister is illegitimate and that her parents have lied to the entire *ton*."

"But you cannot threaten her with the truth unless you are willing to reveal your own secret to the world," protested Olivia.

"Do you know, Olivia?" said Irene, withdrawing her hand from her friend's. "I feel oddly relieved. I never had a chance to be loved as I should be. Father let his wife and younger daughter enjoy any and every opportunity to shut me out. It made me bitter and taught me nothing of kindness or compassion. I have pushed people away, been arrogant and condescending. After all, what did it matter? I was never going to be cherished, anyway.

"But now I see that little Irene was *not* unworthy. Oh, I certainly tore down my own reputation later. I wonder, though, if I would have been as careless with it if I had been shown a better example. Perhaps it is not too late to find out."

Olivia's eyes were wide, and she hugged herself as if the risk were hers. "What are you going to do?" she asked.

"I'm going to find out the whole truth. Every last bit of it. And I am going to hold my father accountable. And that wife of his. And then I will start living my life rather differently, I think. For one, I will no longer seek some man of title just to please them."

Her friend, apparently quite taken with the entire plan and far from shocked, clapped her hands in delight, her eyes shining. "You could seek a closer acquaintance with Mr. Macrae! I think he would like that. I have seen how he looks at you."

"Mr. Macrae might be a closer ally than you realize," her

mother said suddenly.

"What do you mean?" asked Irene.

"He knows."

"He knows? What does he know?"

"Everything. About your father's payments. Our connection. The conditions of your birth."

Irene did not think anything could shock her more than the news she had already learned at this table. Here, among scones and Congou tea, her understanding of who she was had shifted and stumbled. But it had been salvaged somewhat by the knowledge that only a very small circle shared this new understanding, all of whom—barring Olivia—stood to lose much if anyone learned the truth. Even her mother, whose reputation was already ruined, seemed eager to protect Irene's, and would be gutted if she were hurt.

Mr. Macrae, however, was a wild card. Irene did not like to think of him as a treacherous sort. After all, he had gone out of his way to help her in the park, with the newspaper, and then with the wheeled contrivance. He had no reason to betray her. And yet the mere fact that he'd known her terrible secret... Even before she had!

"How did he find out?" She wanted to know.

"He came to me with knowledge of the payments, just as you did. Though, in his case, he marched straight into my office and demanded to know why I was extorting your father, or words to that effect. Mr. Macrae was afraid that such a secret could be used against him... your father, I mean. He did not want to see you hurt in the process. Mr. Macrae definitely had your interests at heart."

Oh, good, Irene thought limply. The one man whom she so deeply admired, who made her heart pound against her breast, knew she was little more than a bastard. He understood what sort of parents had raised her. A mother who despised her very existence. And a father whose ruthless ambition saw no difficulty in seducing a woman and then robbing her of her only child. Was that all Irene had been to Albert Sangford? A tool to marry into the aristocracy?

And Nathaniel Macrae knew it all. Oh, the shame of it! He probably pitied her. She did not *want* his pity, nor his protection. Not if it meant he gave them only as a consolation instead of true friendship.

"Pardon my asking," said Olivia, "but how would Mr. Macrae know about the payments if neither you nor Mr. Sangford spoke of it? There must be a third source."

"It was certainly a surprise to me when he mentioned it," answered Madame Dubois. "How did *you* discover it?" she asked Irene.

"It was recorded in my father's ledger," Irene answered absently, for her thoughts were racing now. The thread… Someone had been at that ledger before her. Her father had been convinced of it. It had rattled his confidence. And he had been jittery ever since. Could it have been Mr. Macrae? But how would he have gained entry to the room? Not only that, from what she had gathered, the ledger was typically locked away. How would he have accessed it? Could he have bribed the maid? And why would he do that?

"I see," said Madame Dubois. "Well, he is certainly resourceful."

"You think he really could do such a thing?" Irene felt sick at the thought. If so, Mr. Macrae was not the man she thought he was.

"I would say," her mother answered cautiously, "that these are matters for discussion between you and the gentleman."

"What sort of *gentleman* snoops in the affairs of others?" Irene said more to herself than in reply to her mother's advice. The fact that her mother had, up till an hour ago, been simply a name associated with scandal and intrigue, did little to comfort Irene. Taking advice from her was even more surreal.

"I think," said Irene, pushing the plate and its untouched scone from her, "I would like to go home. There is too much I don't know. And I need time to make sense of what I have learned. I have much to think on. And, most likely, some very unpleasant conversations to have." She beckoned across the spacious room to Cedric, the footman who had been standing in readiness at the entrance to the tea room before turning her attention to Miss Bathurst. "Olivia, please forgive me for cutting our time short."

"Of course. Er… do you think I might finish my meringues before we go?"

"If you are willing to eat them in haste, for the footman already approaches."

Olivia promptly and unapologetically began to consume the rest of her sweet confections one after the other, barely able to truly savor them and yet clearly preferring that to abandoning the pleasure of them entirely.

"Whatever happens," said Madame Dubois, her entire body leaning forward to emphasize her words, "you have my support. I have enough money for you to make your own way if you choose to. And my door, regardless of the business it is attached to, is always open to you."

Cedric appeared at Irene's elbow before she could answer. "You wanted me, Miss Sangford?"

"We are leaving. You may direct my chair to the carriage I assume Barton has waiting not too far from here."

Cedric swallowed his obvious surprise at their premature departure and took hold of the handles at the back of the wheeled chair, pulling Irene away from the table to turn her about.

Olivia, still licking the last of the sugar from her lips, grabbed a napkin to dust her fingers clean before rising hastily to follow Irene.

Madame Dubois, about to be rather abruptly deserted, stood up and called urgently, "Miss Sangford!"

Cedric paused for Irene to answer. She turned in her chair. "Yes?"

"Please do not be a stranger. Even the occasional letter will do. And if you ever need anything. Anything at all…" Her expression was so keen that Irene could not help but feel sorry for her.

"Thank you." What more could she say? She was not ready to make any sort of promise. "It has been a challenging day. You will understand if I need time."

"Yes." The abbess's face fell. She took a quick breath, squared her shoulders, and added, "Of course. I understand perfectly." She forced a small smile. "I wish you well."

Irene sat back against the deep cushioning of the chair. "We can go now," she instructed Cedric. "Come on, Olivia."

She did not look back again. The agony in her mother's face was unbearable. Irene was barely holding on to her own dignity, such as it was. For who was she now? Even if she said nothing to her father, she was changed within.

Olivia tried to make conversation on the way home. Irene could only think that the poor thing had never before had so much opportunity to talk without interruption. What she actually said remained unheard, for Irene let the words flow over her without taking in their meaning. There was probably an attempt at distraction. And a good dose of commiseration and reassurance. Irene remained quiet. After a while, Olivia, too, fell silent, until the carriage pulled up at her front door. She stepped down, guided by Cedric's strong hand, then looked up at her friend.

"I hate to leave you like this. Shall I call on you tomorrow and see how matters are progressing?"

Irene shook her head. "I will let you know when I am ready to receive a guest." To the groom, she called, "Home, please, Barton."

The carriage jerked forward. The movement was as sudden and uncomfortable as every bit of information that Irene had collected this day. She felt raw and vulnerable. And yet, for the first time, she had answers. And choices.

It wasn't very far to the Sangford home. The horses clopped along the cobbled street, their rhythm strangely soothing. Irene allowed herself to release a small measure of tension, breathing out slowly as she prepared herself to enter a house where she no longer felt she belonged.

At the corner of their fenced property, Barton took a wide turn before heading into the mews, partly—Irene noticed now—to avoid a man who stood, cap pulled low over his eyes, refusing to move. As they drew past him, he pushed his cap back and looked up directly into Irene's face, his eyes boring into hers.

A terrifying chill set into her bones. She *knew* that mouth, that nose, that scarred eyebrow. But most of all, she would never forget those eyes. They looked at her now with the same intensity as they had that day in Munro Park. The day when he had burst forth from behind the holm oak, knife in hand, and caused her horse to rear up and throw her.

Now, as if they, too, remembered him, the horses shied away from the man, their hooves clattering on the cobbles as they stamped restlessly. The carriage stalled and Barton argued with the animals to move on.

Seizing the opportunity, the stranger stepped up the window of the carriage and leaned in. A slow, satisfied smile grew from his unshaved jaw. "So you *know* me, then, Miss Sangford." The softness of his voice only made it feel more threatening. "I thought you might. Didn't put much stock in those lies about you losing your memory. Guess that means I'll be seeing you again. Soon enough."

The horses settled under Barton's coaxing, and the carriage proceeded smoothly farther down the mews, the man and his disturbing leer falling out of sight. But Irene could still see it before her, clear as day.

Every limb on her body sat frozen with fear while her heart beat wildly, its cadence dangerously fast.

Cedric had gone to fetch another to help him get the wheeled chair down from the roof of the carriage. He readied it for Irene, then stepped up into the carriage to lift her out.

"Ready, miss?"

Irene forced herself to release her arms from their torpor. She threw them around Cedric's neck, gripping on to him like a life-raft.

"Are you all right, Miss Sangford?"

"I think I need to lie down. It's all been too much."

"I shall take you directly upstairs," said the lad, bypassing the chair and carrying her straight into the house.

"Miss Sangford, you're home early," said Hutchins as another footman opened the door. "Everything in order? You look rather pale."

Irene could not be sure he worried for her or himself, for the meeting with a woman of ill repute had been made possible by him.

"Miss Sangford is tired," Cedric explained. "I am taking her upstairs. Send for Miss Finnegan, will you?"

Once transported to the sanctuary of her room, Irene at last began to breathe a little easier. But was she truly safe? In this house where people had lied to her all her life? And now that the assailant from Munro Park had actually threatened her?

Every fiber of her being called silently for Mr. Macrae to rescue her and comfort her. Yet she was no longer certain she could trust him. Without him, she felt so terribly alone.

Her future, her very safety, were all undecided. And she could not rely on the loyalty or strength of the one man on whom she wanted to depend.

The emotion of the day began to take its toll. A tremor rose within her, working its way up to the surface until she was shaking violently. The maid came in, gasped at the sight of her lady in such a state, and called at once for Mrs. Sangford.

Between them, they undressed her and tucked her into bed, her leg-in-cast carefully shifted so that she may lie comfortably. Then the stranger who was her mother sent for the doctor. But by the time he'd arrived, Irene was already asleep, exhausted by the day's trials, her dreams racked with fear and isolation, the hope of waking and escaping them no hope at all.

CHAPTER THIRTEEN

The following day, Saturday, March 29th, 1817

LORD HOWELL PACED the length of his study, his long legs making short work of it. He spun on his heel and threw out an exasperated hand.

"How did we not know about this? More than a hundred men arrested, Bill O'Neal among them, and not a word from any of our informants. Even Simmons was caught unawares. Not a breath of this conspiracy was in the air for them to get a whiff of it. How is that possible?"

"I would suggest, your lordship," Nathaniel said grimly, "that is because there *was* no conspiracy."

"What are you talking about? Men were taken off to London in irons by the dozens! That would not happen unless they had proof of a planned uprising."

"And where is this proof?" asked Nathaniel. "How is it that neither you nor I nor our vast network of informants had the faintest inkling that such an uprising was about to take place?"

"What are you saying? That it is all a lie?" The viscount scoffed. "Why would anyone make this up?"

"Think about it, your lordship. The march earlier this month was broken up. Bill O'Neal escaped with his life and disappeared. All seemed well for the time being. But the mill owners had no guarantees. At any given moment, there may have been further disruptions. O'Neal could not be found to make an example of him. He might have continued to plot with his comrades. What was there to discourage the workers from further protest? Clearly, they were still meeting. They had not given up their cause. The situation was unstable. But that could be remedied. All it would take was for one trusted voice to cry foul to the authorities, and suddenly, the meeting the workers were having was a planned conspiracy. And of such a scale that immediate arrest was warranted."

"You underestimate the severity of the situation, I think, Macrae," said the viscount gruffly. "There was to be an attack on local officials to liberate those protestors already imprisoned. They were going to burn down the mills." He threw out an arm to show the extent of the issue. "As many as fifty thousand workers were set to take part. The government has had to put emergency measures into effect."

Nathaniel crossed his arms. "All very convenient, I would say."

Lord Howell pulled up short. "You really think the conspiracy is *against* the protestors rather than of their own making?"

"It serves the purpose of the mill owners very well, don't you think? Thus far, the workers have shown no violent tendencies at all. Not during the march that was disrupted two weeks ago, nor since. They carried no weapons then, only blankets to sleep by the roadside as they headed to London to deliver their concerns to the Regent in writing."

Nathaniel released a hand to gesture with. "The mill owners, on the other hand—or someone sharing their interests—hired an assassin to kill O'Neal. They have not shied from violence. It is far more likely that *they* would create a scenario to bring the situation under their control, offering 'proof' of an imagined situation so brutal and unsettling that action had to be taken at once to prevent it. They are strongly motivated to do this because the longer any unrest continues, the more money they lose."

Lord Howell tapped his hand against his thigh. "You've made your point, Macrae. I must unhappily agree with you. But it grieves me that justice could so easily be skewed."

"It is only a theory. But every other explanation rings false to me. I only wish I knew who had the ear of the magistrates. Whoever they are, they acted quickly enough for us to have no time to discover either their identities or their intent."

Lord Howell tapped a grim tattoo with his finger against his leg. "They would be men of power, no doubt, if they expected the magistrates to take them seriously without any solid proof. I'd hate to think any of the officials themselves were involved."

"What about Cranbourn? His title would lend him credibility."

"*Hmph*," grumbled the viscount. "I wouldn't trust him within a ten-foot radius of my purse. Proper scoundrel, him. Just goes to show that money and a barony can't buy integrity. Simmons should have a thorough report on him any day now."

"I think," said Nathaniel, after a short pause to consider their options, "it's time I paid a visit to Shelby's, find out what sort of talk the gentlemen are involved in at this club. A few drinks should loosen some lips. Though I'll likely have better luck with the servants. People of that sort often forget who's listening because they hardly know the servants are in the room. I sometimes think they look at the gin in their hands and wonder how it got there."

Lord Howell snorted. "Too true. That's why I prefer to visit with friends at my home, where I can handpick my guests." He cast a thoughtful glance at Nathaniel. "Speaking of arrogant society, how goes your investigation into Albert Sangford?"

Nathaniel carefully sifted through the information he had acquired on the man. Much of it had nothing to do with the case at hand and did not warrant sharing. He hadn't yet decided what to do with all he had learned. Nothing for now, at least. Not when innocent parties could be hurt.

"Sangford is certainly not a man to be trusted," he said, picking out a relevant detail. "He is as ruthless as he is secretive. Whether that makes him guilty of conspiracy, I cannot say. Not yet, anyway. But I am making progress. An evening at Shelby's should fill in more of the picture."

Lord Howell nodded slowly, his mouth drawn askew. "It seems the apple didn't fall far from the tree, then. Miss Sangford takes after her father in every way, if your description of him is any indication."

Nathaniel weighed up the merit of staying silent. He just couldn't. Not if the viscount was going to slander her.

"I think you'll find, your lordship, that Miss Sangford is much changed. Whatever your past experience of her, she is not that person anymore. Her father, by contrast, is not afraid to take what he wants. Whether that involves him in the attempt on the life of Bill O'Neal, I hope to determine very soon."

Lord Howell rested his gaze upon Nathaniel. The viscount was a thoughtful man. A rarity among his peers. He was also willing to listen and learn: an uncommon quality among men of *any* standing. If he was quiet, it was because he was taking seriously what had been said.

"I understand you to be a man of intelligence, Macrae."

"Thank you, your lordship."

"I would not like to call that into question."

"But you are considering it?"

"I am merely pondering how it is that you have reached this conclusion about Miss Sangford."

"Through the usual means, sir. Investigation and observation."

"And you are not being led at all by, say, more *worldly* influences?"

"By that do you mean, do I find her attractive, and has a carnal interest swayed my judgment?"

The viscount cleared his throat. "Yes, well, you've always been one to speak plainly. And that *is* what I meant, though I do try to maintain a modicum of genteel speech."

"As you say, sir, I speak bluntly. And I can say, without beating about the bush, that my impression of Miss Sangford has been guided by her character and nothing else. I would happily embrace friendship with her if that would not be a conflict of interests."

"And this admiration in no way affects your clarity of thought?"

Nathaniel drew his lips into a tight, thin line. "If her father must be arrested, I will deliver evidence against him in court. That doesn't mean I have to enjoy doing it."

Lord Howell straightened to his full, impressive height. "Mr. Macrae, if I thought you were the sort of man who derived pleasure from the suffering of others, even if they deserved it from a legal perspective, I would have no dealings with you."

"That is good to know."

"I shall confine further opinion on Miss Sangford to my own thoughts as you have experienced a version of her that I have not. We shall agree to disagree until one of us is proven wrong. If she is truly changed, it would be unexpected, but I have never minded a pleasant surprise."

"Indeed, sir."

"I suppose that is all for now. We shall meet again as soon as either of us has further facts to add to the case."

"Very well. I shall see myself out. Good day to you, Lord Howell."

"Good day to you, sir."

Before Nathaniel had even turned to leave, the viscount had moved toward his desk. No doubt a number of other issues waited for his lordship's attention. Nathaniel was no longer one of them.

He ran his fingers through his hair as a form of self-soothing. This investigation was taking a turn he had not expected. Certainly, he was discovering plenty of astonishing facts, but none of them were bringing him any closer to solving the case.

Nathaniel's tread as he left Munro House was heavy. As much as he despised Sangford for all he had done as a young man, he would rather prove his innocence now if that would spare his eldest daughter further disgrace. It was just as well she knew nothing. She did not deserve the shame of illegitimacy any more than she did being treated as the unwanted stepdaughter she was.

These facts were fortunately not pertinent to the case, and she might be spared any humiliation in the use of them. Unless… Unless Sangford's secret was being used to control him. He might not be the mastermind, but someone even more ruthless than he could have been pulling the strings, with Sangford merely a puppet, carrying out the more disagreeable tasks and perhaps being offered up as the scapegoat in the event of their plans coming to light.

It was vital that Nathaniel discovered the truth. Better him than another. No one else would consider Miss Sangford in their handling of the matter. And she *must* be considered. She was a real person, with thoughts and feelings and…

Nathaniel stopped himself. Why did his mind linger on her slender neck? The way it curved as she gazed up at him, elegant and seductive without even trying. The way it rested, trusting and calm, on his shoulder when he lifted and carried her. The smooth, ivory skin. His mouth would slip so easily onto its silky surface…

No, no! He must not think of her in that way! He had no chance with her. If all turned out well with her father, she would not give Nathaniel a second glance, except to enjoy his looks as so many women did. He would be nothing more than a fine friend. And even friendship might fade when her need of him was done.

But worse, so much worse, would be if Albert Sangford was up to his eyeballs in trouble and Nathaniel then ferreted out the evidence for it. She would never forgive him. Her name would be ruined along with her father's. It wouldn't matter that the blame was Sangford's. His daughter would suffer. And her suffering would be equated with Nathaniel meddling in their affairs.

Confound it! He must rein in these feelings that threatened to shake his good judgment from him. If only they would cease creeping up on him whenever he let his guard down!

Tonight, he would spend time among the supposed gentlemen at Shelby's. It did not really matter if any of the men they were currently watching were actually there. He could learn much from the talk of others. He might even glean information to help with a future case. No knowledge was ever wasted. It tied the social network together like a sprawling web. One carefully placed finger strumming a single cord would send ripples across the entire interwoven structure.

Tonight he hoped to add a few strands.

CHAPTER FOURTEEN

WARM LIGHT BATHED the steps leading up to the gentle-men's club, creating pools of visibility around the feet of those ascending with great dignity and departing sometimes with less of it. For some, poor judgment in the excesses of drink, or a devastatingly large wager lost, meant that top hats could not hide a face that was red with liquor or humiliation, and legs no longer supported all that was needed to maintain self-respect. Such men were easy to interrogate without them even knowing it.

Before Nathaniel had even entered the building, he had spotted his first promising mark.

The short, blunt shape of Harry Bligh had taken a single step, then paused uncertainly. He felt his pocket, appeared unsatisfied with what he had discovered, and lifted his hat to rub his hands over his very short hair in a manner universally suggestive that a solution to a problem was not forthcoming.

"Bligh!" Nathaniel greeted him with the enthusiasm of an old friend, which he certainly was not. It was therefore no surprise the man's brow furrowed and he shoved his hat back down, hard, onto his head. Nathaniel leaned over, held up a hand to the side of his mouth, and said in a conspiratorial fashion, "I've got a full purse and no one with whom to spend it. What say you and I make our fortune at the tables? You any good at playing brag? I can never read my chances well, and you look like a man who knows his business. What do you say? I'll split my profits with you if we have any luck."

The change in Bligh's expression was nothing short of miraculous. His beady, black eyes gleamed at the possible shift in fortune. He licked his dry lips and nodded. "Ay, I reckon I could be persuaded to keep company with ye."

The accent threw Nathaniel for a second. Then he remembered: Bligh was only a gentleman by new-world money and old-world in-laws. His eldest daughter had bought her way into a noble family with an exceedingly handsome dowry. And Mr. Bligh now frequented the haunts of gentlemen where he was not so much accepted as tolerated. In truth, his pocketbook was more welcome than he, and if he had emptied it unintentionally tonight, he would have no further excuse to hang about all the men of good breeding, whether *they* had coin to spend or not.

Now, however, accompanied by a man as frowned upon as Nathaniel, but with the promise of cash to throw about, Bligh marched smartly back up the steps and into the bright space that constituted the entrance to Shelby's.

Several frowns met Bligh's return, but neither paid the implied disapproval any mind. They gave up their coats and gloves and hats to the footman, who offered them stubs with which to collect the items again upon their departure. Settling at one of the tables where a game of brag could be started, Nathaniel beckoned to a waiter and ordered an excellent brandy for each of them. The amber liquid made Bligh that much friendlier toward him, and it wasn't long before conversation flowed smoothly as the card game progressed.

"Come, Bligh, what is your guess? Do I stay or do I fold?"

The fellow peered closer at the three cards in Nathaniel's hand. "Ay, that's a fine hand you've got there, Macrae. You should not only stay in the game, but raise the stakes."

"You think so? I have nothing to match that card." Nathaniel pointed at the card to the right of the others.

"That card won't be needing a match," answered Bligh in a

voice that was both low and yet intended to be heard.

Nathaniel shrugged. "If you say so. I will trust your counsel." He promptly said, "I brag," and raised the wager.

A grumbling ensued about the table. The gentleman whose hand was to follow Nathaniel's threw his cards down dramatically. "Pass," he said morosely.

The rest of the players followed suit until only one other remained. This gentleman sat back and tapped his cards on the table. "I think you are bluffing, sir. You don't have the wild card any more than I do. And since I already have a pair of jacks, I believe it is unlikely you have the knave of clubs. Therefore, I will see you." And he spread his cards face up for all to see. Two jacks and an eight.

Nathaniel kept his face free of emotion. "You are right. I do not have the knave of clubs. I had a king I hoped to pair for a higher score. But," he said, laying his hand, face up, upon the table, "I believe two queens still win the round. One tends to underestimate the value of women."

"Well played, Mr. Macrae," said a voice ominously behind him.

Nathaniel twisted around to see the mealy face of Phineas Pratt. *Well, well, the suspects are gathering.* "I have Mr. Bligh to thank," he answered pleasantly. "He has been offering me sound advice on when to play and when to fold. I am too easily distracted to read the faces of the other players. Without him, I would have had to rely solely on Lady Luck."

"Did you not just say one too easily underestimate's a woman's worth?" It was a simple question, lighthearted, even. But Mr. Pratt managed to insinuate a threat, as he always did. As if Nathaniel had been caught in a lie. A lie with consequences.

"You have me there." Nathaniel smiled good-naturedly. "It was remiss of me to forget the powers of Lady Luck. She has made many a man's fortune."

"I prefer to rely on planning," said Pratt.

Oh, yes? Nathaniel was dying to ask. *And what sort of planning have you been up to?*

"Would you care to join us, Mr. Pratt?" He indicated an empty seat at the table. "We are about to play the last stakes. Let us say I ask Bligh not to help me, and we pit Lady Luck against your planning. That is, if the good lady will have me." Nathaniel flashed one of his broad, disarming smiles.

"Planning doesn't come into this game," said Pratt. "Too much is left to chance. Those are not the sort of odds I like to wager with."

"Ah, well, then I am happy to continue using the excellent assistance of Mr. Bligh here. If you will excuse us."

Mr. Pratt continued to hover. He said nothing further, but Harry Bligh grew increasingly restless at Nathaniel's side.

"Er… If you'll pardon me, Mr. Macrae," Bligh said after a minute or two. "I have a meeting I forgot about. Thank ye for the drink. But I must be on my way. Enjoy the rest of yer evening."

"If you're sure…" Nathaniel began, but Bligh was already plodding heavily in the direction of the coffee room.

"Good night to you, Mr. Macrae," said Phineas Pratt and turned to leave, but not before glancing at the card table and adding, "Don't take too many risks."

It should have been a simple, parting statement. But Pratt's manner of speech left Nathaniel with a prickling sensation at the base of his neck. The man really had an uncanny way of suggesting a threat where one would not normally presume there to be any. Then again, there *was* the possibility that Pratt knew something.

A surge of self-doubt unsettled Nathaniel. He had been careful, had he not? He had not investigated anyone directly other than Albert Sangford. And Madame Dubois was, despite her profession, a woman of discretion. The only person who could place Nathaniel anywhere near this case was the would-be assassin. If either that rogue or Mr. Sangford suspected him of more than a passing involvement, Pratt would be on alert. But which one would have guessed that he was part of an investigation?

He inhaled deeply and let it out slowly. He was letting Pratt's disquieting tones get to him when, in all likelihood, the fellow's words had been innocent. For the next few minutes, Nathaniel focused his attention on the game of cards. But not enough. He lost, though not badly, having folded when the stakes had begun to climb.

The cards were dealt for a new game. Nathaniel stood and collected his earlier winnings, pocketing half and keeping the rest in his closed hand. He had not come here to gamble. His mission was still incomplete.

His long legs covered the distance to the coffee room in record time. Upon reaching the doorway, he slowed, his eyes searching the room for particular familiar faces. There, in a far back corner, sat Bligh and Pratt.

Nathaniel was about to approach when a movement near the two men made him pause. Elias Upton, Baron Cranbourn, was almost upon them. Both men looked up without surprise, as if he were expected. With barely a greeting, Cranbourn slid into an empty seat and joined them.

Stepping back from the doorway, Nathaniel withdrew several paces into the hallway, then crossed to its opposite end, from where he could observe the staircase to the ground floor. If Mr. Sangford was coming to this meeting, Nathaniel wanted to remain unnoticed until he was ready to show himself.

He waited a good ten minutes, but there was no sign of Sangford. Unless he had entered through the dining room, Nathaniel should have spotted him. Why was he not joining them? What sort of meeting excluded Albert Sangford? Had they turned against him? Or did it happen to be a discussion that did not concern him?

Nathaniel could wait no longer. If he was going to learn anything, he needed to be in that room.

As nonchalantly as possible, he sauntered into the coffee room, making his way past several small groups of visiting members until he reached a small table with only two seats near the back. One table separated him from the trio he wanted to observe. He sat down with his back to them, taking the coins now made warm by his fist and dropping them softly upon the tabletop so that they barely clinked at all. Calling a waiter over, he requested a copy of the day's newspaper, a sandwich, and a glass of wine. For anything more sustaining, he would need to shift to the dining room, and that would undo the point of being here.

The newspaper and wine arrived almost immediately. Nathaniel unfolded the pages and took a sip from his glass. For all the world, he was a typical gentleman enjoying a light meal, a quiet read and an undisturbed evening at the club away from the fuss of the more mundane aspects of life.

He heard his name mentioned. It was neither a gruff nor vaguely threatening voice, ergo it must have been Cranbourn who spoke. Nathaniel kept a cool guise sipping his drink and turning the page of his newspaper. He did not look up or turn around. They did not exist, or so he would have it appear.

His sandwich arrived and Nathaniel lay into it with vigor, peering over his plate at the article in front of him. It was not long before the trio behind him relaxed enough to speak more freely.

"We should make an example of him," said Cranbourn.

Nathaniel's ears pricked up at these ominous words. They couldn't have been talking about Bill O'Neal. The man was in custody as a guest of His Majesty's prison service. Strangely enough, he was probably safer there, his supposedly treasonous crime not yet proven, than he was in Munro, where an assassin sought to silence him permanently.

Is it possible they meant Albert Sangford? Had they turned on him? Did he want to be released of his pact with them?

"He won't back down unless we make him," said Pratt.

"He is a gentleman," Bligh pointed out. "Not some nobody like O'Neal. People will pay attention if a man of society dies suddenly."

Nathaniel froze. Ice trickled down his spine. It was as good as a confession. Murder. Conspiracy. O'Neal mentioned by name. He *knew* the mill owners had to have been involved.

"Who said anything about dying?" Cranbourn spoke without emotion, as if the topic of discussion were akin to placing an order for yarn. "Just a little *discouragement*."

"He's stubborn," grumbled Bligh. "And as long as Miss Sangford is in the mix, I don't know if he can be made to listen."

"She's already been given a good fright," Cranbourn said in what could only be described as a tone of self-satisfaction. "When she shares that little tidbit of news, I think it might give him pause."

"Or embolden him. He is loyal to her."

Nathaniel's heart was thudding so loudly that he did not hear what the men said next. What was this fright they talked of? What had they done to Miss Sangford? It had been two weeks since he had last seen her, but one of his informants would surely have let him know if she was in danger. Or had she told her father, and he had assured her he would handle it himself? Nathaniel was not accustomed to being left out of the know. He did not like the feel of it at all.

"So, we are agreed? My man will see to it." Cranbourn said.

"When?" asked Bligh. "The longer we wait, the more he puts us at risk."

"It should be tonight."

Pratt's words carried a disturbing element of finality, which was only further emphasized when Cranbourn added. "So be it."

Nathaniel stood so abruptly, he surprised even himself. He had to get to the Sangford house immediately. Warn Mr. Sangford. Even if it meant pounding on their door at this late hour. He wouldn't have much of a head start. Who knew how easily Cranbourn could get instructions to his underling?

The next thing he knew, Bligh was at his elbow.

"Mr. Macrae," the stocky figure said. "Did the rest of yer game go well without my help?"

Nathaniel watched as Cranbourn strode from the room.

"Yes. Er, actually, no. But it is no matter. It is only money, after all." He tried to assume a casualness about him, but time was of the essence and his communication with Bligh no longer served a helpful purpose.

"Speaking of money…" Bligh let the words hang in the air.

Nathaniel blinked without comprehension.

Bligh's gaze fell to the table Nathaniel had just vacated.

"Ah," Nathaniel replied, understanding dawning. "That." The coins lay abandoned where he had left them in a little heap. "Those are, in fact, yours. I had kept them aside to give to you when your meeting was done. Please, take them."

"Perhaps I can buy ye dinner with these generous winnings," Bligh suggested. "To make up for the rude way I abandoned ye earlier. What do ye say to that, Mr. Macrae?"

"I say that I have an appointment to keep. Another time, maybe."

"Not even a quick brandy? That was a particularly good vintage we had before. Very smooth. Can I not return the kindness?"

"Sadly, no. If you'll excuse me."

Nathaniel almost *ran* from the room. He drummed down the stairs and drew his ticket stub from his pocket as he crossed the foyer. His foot tapped impatiently until the staff brought him his coat, hat, and gloves. He did not stop to put them on, but rather flew out the door to hail a hackney.

One drew up as if in anticipation of his needs. He had just put his foot upon the step, his coat slung over one arm, his gloves tucked into his hat in the same hand, when a sharp pain pierced his skull.

An explosion of agony spread through his brain. He grew unsteady, his mind confused. Nathaniel fell back into the road, a darkness greater than the moonlit night reaching to claim him.

Just as Nathaniel was about to lose consciousness, a figure bent over him. A familiar face grinned down into his. Memories flashed into the approaching oblivion. Munro Park. A knife.

"Hullo, Mr. Macrae," said the voice as Nathaniel's mind grew blank. "My employer sends his greetings. Best to mind your own business from now on. Or Miss Sangford will suffer a similar fate."

Footfalls receded from Nathaniel's limp body. A wave of nausea rolled over him. Then all his senses left him.

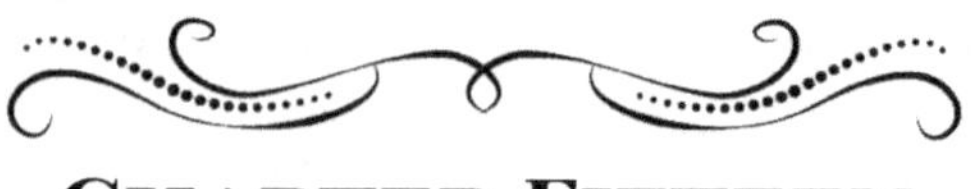

CHAPTER FIFTEEN

Wednesday, April 2nd, 1817

IRENE HAD NOT left the house since the day her whole life had been turned on its head. She had thought to confront her father and "mother," find out the rest of the story, but she could not bear to talk about it. It was bad enough rolling through the house in Mr. Macrae's wheeled chair, wondering what *he* must think of her.

She should not have been surprised that he avoided her now. He had done the neighborly thing, helping a young woman in distress. But what more must he do in her company? How could he look at her, knowing all he did about her? He could only see a pretense at legitimacy. A babe cast off by her mother, purchased by her father to be used as he had used her mother: to further his mission for what he most desired, a connection to a title.

What disgust Mr. Macrae must feel for their entire family! A feeling she shared all too well.

For the time being, Irene had no desire to know more about her past. At least her "mother's" and sister's jibes did not affect her anymore. Mrs. Sangford had chosen an ignoble route while raising her husband's daughter. She could have been kind, taken pity on an innocent child. Instead, she had done the bare minimum. Irene no longer sought her affection or approval. It was actually a relief. No more confusion about why Amelia was preferred. No more hope that things might change. Irene was now free to reject them in turn, without guilt.

Her father, however, was a completely different matter. They had never been particularly close, but he had not been unkind to her. He was even known to have shown her the odd bit of sentiment. But always the *grand purpose* came first: find a husband with title and wealth. Knowing what she did about his treatment of her mother, Irene could see that this goal had always been at the forefront of his mind. It superseded all else. He would sacrifice anything to achieve it. Any tenderness lay deep in the shadow of his ambitions.

For this reason, and because, as a woman, she could not ignore his betrayal of her mother, Irene could not talk to him. Even simple conversation at the dinner table had ground to a halt. Mrs. Sangford had noted, with the usual condescension, that meals were strangely quiet without Irene's sarcastic interjections. But Irene could not be provoked. Her silence was more disturbing to the family than her sharp tongue, and the rest of their small family often subsided into uninterrupted chewing when they could neither goad nor entice her to talk.

However, she had to talk to *somebody*. The appearance of the Munro Park villain with his casual threat, right on the doorstep of her home, could not be ignored. And until Irene decided whom she could trust, she dared not leave the house, not even to sit in the garden. Her inability to move freely, to run if she must, further terrified her, making her a prisoner in her father's house.

Olivia had popped in once or twice, but Irene was terrible company. She did not want to worry her friend and did not speak of her fears. But the existence of such fears spoiled the mood of the visits. When Olivia could not get to the bottom of what troubled Irene, she withdrew, no doubt feeling helpless and rejected, which only added to Irene's frustration.

Her natural urge was to reach out to Mr. Macrae. He was the only man who had taken her seriously and to whom she had felt she could turn. But both these assumptions were now up for debate. Would he have anything to do with her anymore, knowing what he did? More importantly, how had he acquired that information? *Had* he sneaked into her father's office? And why would he have done that at all? It just didn't make sense!

A confrontation with him would be just as painful as the one with her father, if not more so. She actually cared what Mr. Macrae thought of her. If he refused to meet with her or looked at her with pity—or worse, derision—she could not bear it. Better not to reach out to him at all and keep the happy memory of his last visit safe and unsullied in her heart.

When the confinement of the house began to suffocate her, trapped as she was with the people she trusted the least, Irene could stand it no longer. There was one person who might help, even if it was for a price.

"Hutchins," Irene said in a low voice when she cornered him in the hallway, having exhausted herself traversing the downstairs rooms in search of him. "I have a letter for you to deliver."

The butler's face fell. "Please, Miss Sangford. I can't. The master is already suspicious of everyone ever since the day he accused the staff of snooping in his study. Every time I arrange for one of these letters to make their way to *her*, I am risking my position here."

"But you're going to do it, anyway, Hutchins." Her voice was firm, but with an edge of pleading.

They stared at each other for the briefest of time before he held out his hand. "Lord have mercy on me. I don't know why I cannot say 'no' to you, Miss Sangford."

"I do appreciate it, Hutchins," Irene said softly, passing him the letter for Madame Dubois. "More than you can imagine. I have no allies in this house. You are as close to one as I can hope for at present."

The good-natured face of the family butler puckered. "Why would you say that, miss? Is something wrong? You haven't been yourself since the day you went to tea. I knew you shouldn't have been talking to this woman." He waggled the letter in his hand.

"She is not the cause of my misery, Hutchins. Merely the

means by which I discovered it. Let's leave it at that, shall we?"

"Would it not be better to speak to Mr. Sangford about what-ever worries you?"

"No."

"What about Mr. Macrae? He seems a good sort. Better than *her*, at least." He indicated the letter.

Irene noticed he did not suggest she confide in Mrs. Sangford or Amelia. It occurred to her that the servants were a lot more observant than she had previously considered.

"I'm surprised at you, Hutchins," she answered. "It is no more appropriate for me to write to an unrelated man of *any* sort than to write to a woman like *that*."

The butler had the good grace to blush at her comment. "No, I suppose not. Silly of me to suggest it." He hesitated. "I… That is, we…" Irene assumed he meant the staff as a whole. "That is to say, we care what happens to you."

The statement was simple and sincere and caught Irene completely off guard. No one in her whole life had declared such straightforward concern for her. His words pierced her heart. Her breath caught and released in a gasp.

Irene fought back the tears that stung at her eyes, swallowing down the lump that was forming in her throat. She remained quiet until she could speak without her voice trembling. "That is very kind," she said almost breathlessly. She was all too aware that her skin must have been quite pink with the effort of controlling her emotions.

No doubt Hutchins knew what her sudden rosy hue implied. "I'll just see to this letter, shall I?" His voice was gentle, like a father's should have been if he'd truly loved his child. "And then I will arrange for some tea in the library. No one but you seems to spend time there. You can have the space all to yourself. I've never had a problem a good cup of tea didn't soothe." He tapped the side of his nose and lowered his voice to a whisper. "I might even put a drop of brandy in it."

Some of the weight she had been carrying on her shoulders

slid free with Hutchins's show of camaraderie. She managed a smile. "I'll wait for you in the library, then."

"Yes, miss." The butler resumed a degree of formality as one of the maids squeezed past Irene's wheeled chair on her way to clean the next room. "Shall I push the chair into the library for you?"

"No, Hutchins. I can manage. You have more important work to do." With that, Irene maneuvered one wheel to turn her domestic vehicle around and head to the agreed-upon room.

A short while later, Hutchins returned with a tray of suspiciously strong tea and a plate of biscuits. "The... er... 'package' has been handed to a passing hackney driver. He was happy to take payment for it as if for a customer. I told him to wait for a reply and bring it to the back door, addressed to me."

"That is very good of you." Irene meant every word. Hutchins had done more than had been asked of him. He must have sensed the urgency of the matter. Or, at least, he knew that a quick reply would take the edge off Irene's agitation.

Irene sipped her tea, which left a glow in her belly and definitely softened the corners of her mood. She browsed the shelves of books that she could reach. Eying more interesting volumes higher up, she was tempted to lift herself onto her good leg. The discomfort of the broken limb had faded significantly. But she heeded the surgeon's warning. Three and a half weeks was nowhere near the two months she had been told to wait before putting any stress on that leg.

The tea and its special contents had the hoped-for calming effect. A few chapters of a favorite book later, Irene was nodding to stay awake.

Footfalls and a soft click of the door closing snapped her back into full alertness.

"It has come, Miss Sangford." Hutchins held out a letter written in a hand Irene had grown to recognize.

"That was very quick!" She turned it over to pull at the seal and unfold the page to release the message. Her eyes flew from line to line, widening as she read. "What?! No!"

Hutchins stepped closer, then halted, no doubt conflicted between showing care and maintaining proper distance.

Irene forced herself to start again, taking in every word.

"Dearest Irene," the letter began. These two simple words had immediately disturbed her equilibrium. They claimed a familiarity that, though deserved by blood, had not yet been truly earned by relationship. Even so, Irene warmed at the sentiment. Here was someone who had considered her needs above their own, giving up the precious bond of mother to child for her daughter's sake, despite the outcome not having been all she had hoped for.

"I am grateful you consider me worthy to hear your concerns. I understand that the situation in which you find yourself at home is unenviable. I regret that it has come to this. As promised, I will do everything in my power to assist you.

"It may interest you to know that I have several men in my employ in addition to my ladies. They ensure that the visitors to my establishment remain sensible. I have dispatched one of them at once to watch your home. I am pleased to say these men are a special breed: inconspicuous, incorruptible, and brutal. You will not be aware of his presence, but he will be there nonetheless. If the assailant from Munro Park even approaches your home, he will be spotted and dealt with. Thoroughly. I will rotate my men on a two-hour basis to keep their senses acute and their attention sharp. Do not worry yourself further on this matter. You are quite safe."

If the letter had only ended there, Irene would have breathed a deep sigh of relief. But it did not.

"I assume you have chosen to rely on me because Mr. Macrae cannot assist you. There is no doubt in my mind that the man who has threatened you is the very one who has done the poor gentleman such harm. It must have been a terrible blow to lay him out like that. I understand he is conscious but has had a fever which has only just broken in the last day or two. The swelling of the head wound would have come down significantly by now. I am sure it is only a matter of time before the charming rascal is ready to call on you again. I doubt much could keep him from you. Until then, I am grateful to be at your service."

All that remained of the letter was the usual polite greeting. Irene cared nothing for it. Her mind was reeling with the shock of what had happened to Mr. Macrae. Why had no one told her about it? Then again, who would think she'd want to know? Her stepmother and sister, if they had been told, would likely have mentioned it just to see her reaction. In the absence of them toying with her in this way, Irene assumed they must not have known, either.

Why was Madame Dubois so certain it was the man from Munro Park who had attacked him? And why *had* he assaulted him? Irene hated being unable to ask these questions to those who could answer her. It was vexing to have so little control over her life. Why should she not hasten to the home of the Macraes and see for herself that all was well? Why could she not soothe his brow with a cool cloth, like a sister?

Then again, did she want to be anything like a sister? If her circumstances had been different, she might have been brave enough to hint at her feelings to him. Yet the *ton* viewed him as beneath her. What a joke! How ironic that his reputation kept her family from considering him as a suitor when it was *her* reputation that was truly in a shambles! If the black marks against him had been as well-kept a secret as hers, perhaps there would have been a chance…

Irene's heart ached at the thought. What she wouldn't give for a chance with Mr. Macrae. To run her fingers though his thick, dark-blonde hair. To cup his sculpted jaw in her palms and press a tender kiss upon his perfectly curved mouth. To have him wrap his strong arms about her, drawing her closer, close enough to hear his heartbeat with her ear upon his breast.

But there was always the question of the infernal title.

Revulsion at the very idea of a noble rank swelled up within her like bilge water. Her father's craving for that connection had cost her mother everything. Irene wanted nothing to do with it. If she had not had to confine her choices to men of nobility…

Ha! She scoffed at the very word. Nobility, indeed!

Mr. Macrae was the noblest of them all.

Irene wished she were braver. Then she would cast off her false identity, throw all her father's tiresome expectations to the wind, and embrace a life with Nathaniel Macrae.

But even then he would not have her, would he? And who could blame him? A rakish gentleman was still far superior to a woman of illegitimate birth. It shouldn't have been thus, but it was. And there was absolutely nothing she could do about it.

Irene balled her fists tightly. Either she lived a lie and married no one, for she was reaching the end of a long line of possible suitors with the sought-after title, and her youth was fading while new debutantes came out each season. Or she revealed the truth about her origins, and married… whom? An equally disgraced fellow she should consider herself grateful to have caught the eye of? Either way, her prospects were grim.

In the middle of her swirling hopelessness, Irene remembered a small ray of comfort. Olivia Bathurst had not denounced her. Five days had gone by and not a single rumor was doing the rounds. Olivia had kept her secret.

If Irene were to send for her, she knew Olivia would come. It was Irene's own choice that kept Olivia from helping more. If Irene wanted, she could confide in Olivia. She had proven herself a true friend.

The beam of hope widened. Was it possible… Was there any chance that Mr. Macrae would do as Olivia had done? He was such an honorable man, despite his gaudy reputation. She would value his friendship above any other, if she could have it.

She must speak with him. Have it out with him. No more secrets between them. If he was going to reject her, he must remember the guilt truly lay with her father and not herself. If Mr. Macrae could hang about with rough sailors and ladies of ill repute, to mention but a few of his questionable acquaintances, why should he look down on her because of a birth she'd had no say in?

Irene had not suddenly changed since their first meeting. If he could show her kindness before, why could he not do so now?

Yes, she liked this thinking. She felt stronger already.

And if they were going to be friends, she must show herself a good friend, too. She would write to his mother. That would be acceptable. Irene could visit him with Olivia if his mother extended the invitation. She would write to the lady at once. At least such a letter would require no subterfuge on her behalf from Hutchins, who had already done more for her than her own family.

The butler! Ah, the poor dear had been waiting patiently all this time for some sign from Irene that all was well. He had maintained his distance, but a furrow had been etched into his brow as he worried for her.

"Hutchins," she said at last.

He exhaled as if he had been holding his breath for some time. "Yes, Miss Sangford. How can I help?"

"I will need paper and pen on that table over there. It should be low enough for me to write on."

She saw the frown return.

"Oh, no, I am not writing to *her*. I am preparing a letter to Mrs. Macrae. It would appear that her son has been injured. I would like to send my good wishes for his full recovery."

"Injured, miss? I hope it's not serious."

"I'm afraid the harm done was significant. But it seems he is starting to recover. I would feel a lot better if I could confirm that."

"Of course, miss." Hutchins cheered up significantly now that he had something to do that fell within his usual realm of duties. "I will send a footman to deliver the letter as soon as you have finished writing it. I think we should all be much happier knowing Mr. Macrae is out of the woods. He is a good sort, if I may make so bold as to say."

"You certainly may, Hutchins. Now, if you would be so kind…"

"Ah, yes, I will bring pen and paper at once." He turned smartly and was out of the door as quickly as his dignified posture would allow.

It was a small step. But Irene had grabbed the first fistful of control over her life. She felt almost giddy with the freedom of it. If she had her way, Nathaniel Macrae would not get rid of her so easily. And if he would let her, she would be honored to fuss over him a little as he had done for her. Even it was just to read to him while he rested or pour him a fresh cup of tea.

And woe betide the vermin who had done this to him! She almost hoped the wretch would turn up at her home so that Madame Dubois's man could set upon him and dole out his just desserts. That would be very satisfying indeed!

Irene allowed herself a moment of reflection. It was odd who her most loyal supporters had turned out to be. Olivia Bathurst, who had never drawn attention to herself except involuntarily through her speech, now quietly offered true, solid friendship. Then there was Madame Dubois, her mother, though the idea of it still sat strangely in Irene's mind. And the servants in their home, who went about their business and owed her nothing other than what their duties demanded yet looked out for her in small, unexpected ways. Best of all, Mr. Macrae, a scoundrel and a rake, and the most wonderful man she had ever met.

When she thought about it like this, Irene felt curiously blessed. Much of the humiliation and sorrow she had endured these past days retreated a little distance from her.

All she needed was an invitation from Mrs. Macrae and her heart would grow lighter still.

As if on cue, Hutchins returned with the tray and began to set out the paper, ink, and quill for Irene who now wheeled herself over to the small table.

"Wait here, if you don't mind, Hutchins. I won't be long."

The butler assumed his stiff position and cast his gaze across the room.

Irene made herself comfortable, dipped the quill in ink, and began at once to write, each word purposefully reaching for a future she was choosing for herself.

CHAPTER SIXTEEN

Thursday, April 3rd, 1817

THE POUNDING IN Nathaniel's head had finally begun to die down. His mother, not one to have doctors prescribe laudanum when so many good English subjects were succumbing to its addictive effects, had preferred the virtues of various herbs as tinctures for pain, as well as pastes for swelling. These had worked remarkably well, although Nathaniel was uncomfortably aware that his bandaged head smelled rather strongly of turmeric and vinegar. Still, it was better than the alternative he had started with, which included a massive lump and disabling pain.

Several days had been lost to him. Several more stretched equally fruitlessly ahead, for his mother had no intention of letting him out of her sight until he was strong enough to her satisfaction.

It was terrible timing, for he had proof at last that Cranbourn, Pratt, and Bligh—if not Sangford too—were behind the attack on Bill O'Neal. How they knew he had been investigating them, he could not fathom, and his head had hurt too much to work it out. But this morning he had managed to dictate a letter for Lord Howell to his ever-patient mother, updating the viscount on all that Nathaniel had discovered, and how Cranbourn's man had been behind the attack on his own poor, bruised skull.

He was just starting to sit up gingerly when his mother came into his room and announced, quite amicably, that Misses Irene

Sangford and Olivia Bathurst would be calling on him in an hour, and that his valet was on his way to give Nathaniel a wash and shave.

"How is it, Mother dearest," he wanted to know, "that I am not well enough to work, yet I am able to receive the company of ladies?"

"Miss Sangford is worried about you," his mother remarked while fluffing his pillow behind him. "She will not be assured you are safe and well until she has seen it with her own two eyes. Miss Bathurst, I believe, is the obligatory chaperone."

"Surely you don't intend for them to come into my chambers? These are ladies, Mother, not the sort of riffraff I do business with."

"Do calm yourself, Nathaniel. I am not quite so desperate for a daughter-in-law that I would sully these ladies' reputations just to force one of them into marriage. Though, from what you have said, I understand they are both lovely to look at and enjoy your company. I should be so lucky that you might fall for either of them."

Nathaniel sighed. "Neither of their families would want anything to do with me as a son-in-law."

His mother shrugged. "And yet Mr. Sangford has invited us all to dinner ten days from now. Apparently, he wishes to thank us for raising such a kind gentleman who has his daughter's best interests at heart.

"This is the first I hear of it," said Nathaniel, genuinely surprised.

"Well, you *were* unconscious when the letter came, so there is that."

Nathaniel watched his mother tuck a coal-black lock of hair behind her ear, a telltale sign that she was secretly delighted but was making a concerted effort not to show it. Her face showed no further clue as to her thoughts, but he could guess well enough what they were.

"Mr. Sangford seeks a title for his daughters," he said flatly.

"That is a pity. Not much use for a title these days. Money is a better currency, and I am pleased to say we have more than enough of it for a good match."

Nathaniel softened toward her. It was not her fault he had chosen a path that ruined his reputation. "You know how things stand, Mother dear. Not a lot of women or their families would consider me a catch."

Mrs. Macrae sat herself down in the chair next to his bed and smoothed her skirts. "There's a pretty maid, new in the kitchen," she said to her own knees, for she certainly could not look her son in the eye. "Lovely, wide, child-bearing hips. Could you be persuaded to…"

"*Mother!*"

"Oh." Mrs. Macrae's enthusiasm fizzled out. "I suppose not." A new thought must have occurred to her, for she perked right up again. "Anyway, we're going to get you settled in the conservatory. Lovely and warm there, with a marvelous view. Time for you to have a change of scenery. It will do you good."

"And make it possible for me to receive guests," he added dryly.

"Why, yes, as it happens. That will do you good, too."

"Don't get your hopes up. This visit will amount to nothing."

His mother wisely decided to say nothing further, but she did tuck another errant lock of hair behind her ear.

Things happened rather quickly after that. Or to Nathaniel's bleary head, they felt as if they did. All he knew was that, an hour later, he was clean, shaven, and helped down to the settee in the conservatory, a blanket over his knees, and two young women of the *ton* coming forward to ascertain his well-being.

Miss Bathurst wheeled Miss Sangford toward him, but when she stopped short at the nearest seat, Miss Sangford grabbed the handles and moved herself closer, so that she came right up to Nathaniel and looked him appraisingly up and down.

"I am relieved to find you more recovered than I had been led to expect," she said, pushing her chair back to a more appropriate distance. "You gave us quite the fright, Mr. Macrae." She blinked slowly. "And it saddened me that our friendship was not well enough established for the news of your injury to have reached me sooner."

Nathaniel knew, without looking, that his mother would have both hands tucked around her ears.

"How *did* you find out?" Mrs. Macrae asked their guest.

"Through a mutual acquaintance," Miss Sangford answered. "A lady by the name of Dubois."

Nathaniel started. His face had definitely betrayed him, for the shock was too sudden to hide.

"I do not know this name," his mother mused, "but Nathaniel has such a broad range of... *friends* that I am unlikely to know them all."

"Your son has shown me such kindness," Miss Sangford continued. "Not the least of which has been this life-altering wheeled chair, without which I would have been housebound for a full two months." Miss Sangford kept her sights focused on Nathaniel's mother, but he could not help feeling the words were for him. "I do miss his visits, though. I understand he has been fulfilling the duties of a good son, a noble reason to explain his scarcity."

Mrs. Macrae cocked her head toward Nathaniel. "Such a good lad, my son. Of course, if I had known he was neglecting his duties of friendship, I might have been less demanding with my own."

Nathaniel felt the implied glare to his very core.

"Well, then, since Nathaniel has been remiss with his visits," his mother continued, "I would love for both you young ladies to stay a while instead of the usual brief courtesy call. My son could use the distraction, and it seems, Miss Sangford, that you would be equally pleased to have an outing from home."

"Mother, I am sure the—" Nathaniel began urgently, afraid of what a longer visit might unearth. Both his mother and Miss Sangford, it appeared, had plans for him.

"We would be delighted, Mrs. Macrae," Miss Sangford said smoothly, settling back into the wicker chair. "Wouldn't we, Olivia?"

"Absolutely," Miss Bathurst said very softly. "If it is not too much trouble."

"I'm afraid you'll have to speak up, dear," said Nathaniel's mother. "These old ears need all the help they can get."

Miss Bathurst looked at her friend, took a breath, and repeated herself more audibly, her distinctive sound no doubt something Mrs. Macrae was wholly unprepared for.

"Oh," said their hostess. "Oh, I see. Yes. Ah. No trouble at all." She turned to Nathaniel and widened her eyes at him. He pretended not to notice. If his mother was going to plot with Miss Sangford against him, he would not acknowledge her shock at Miss Bathurst's voice. She would simply have to grin and bear it for the lovely long visit she had just made possible.

Miss Sangford's creamy brow furrowed. "It is odd that someone should attack you so violently, Mr. Macrae, and yet not even bother to steal your purse. Madame Dubois seems to think we have a common enemy. Do you have any idea why the fellow should assault you so viciously when he has made no such attempt on my person? Not that I am ungrateful, you understand. Still, it does seem very strange."

"How did you know it wasn't a robbery?" Nathaniel wanted to know.

"Er…" His mother had turned a particular shade of pink. "It is possible that I shared some of my concerns when I wrote back to Miss Sangford. It is not often a young lady shows such kind interest in our family. I may have gotten a little carried away."

This, thought Nathaniel, *is exactly why I don't get involved with young ladies in the first place.*

"Now that you mention it, Miss Sangford," his mother continued, "I remember reading about your ghastly incident in Munro Park. Too terrible. Though I also seem to recall you remember very little of it. That would make my Nathaniel the only witness to the crime." She pursed her lips and tapped her fingertips against the opposite forearm. "This Madame Dubois, she must have interesting connections to know so much. I am surprised, since people tend not to confide in the French. Not after all those years of war, you know. What did she say, exactly? Was it simply a warning, then, or a failed attempt on my son's life?"

The conversation, in Nathaniel's opinion, was getting wildly out of control. Miss Sangford and his mother were tripping along merrily into waters that were potentially dangerous and best kept in the seclusion of his own mind.

"Shall we ring for tea, Mother?" he said, aware that a desperate edge had slipped into his voice. This would not do. It would not do at all. He must get the situation in hand. Steer it in a different direction.

But the ladies did not share his approach.

"Ah. Tea. Yes," said his mother. She rose, tugged gently on the bell pull, then sat down again briskly and resumed her interrogation.

"You were saying, Miss Sangford?"

The young lady shrugged. "I am not privy to all of Madame Dubois's knowledge. But I do know that my person is safe thanks to her interference. She really is a surprisingly influential woman." Miss Sangford lowered her lashes, only to lift her gaze at Nathaniel. "But then *you* know this, Mr. Macrae. I understand she has shared some very deep insights with us both. Wisdom that was worth at least ten pounds, wouldn't you say, Mr. Macrae?"

It was a good thing tea had not yet been served. Nathaniel would have spluttered it all over his nice, clean shirt.

"I... I'm not sure."

Miss Sangford gave him a sidelong glance. "She didn't discuss the marquess's daughter and the unfortunate offspring with you?"

"I don't know what you mean!" Nathaniel's head began to pound again.

"How odd." Miss Sangford turned to her friend. "You were there, Olivia. Did she not say Mr. Macrae already knew the very story she had just shared with me? Quite a sordid little narration, wasn't it? And yet Mr. Macrae had already known a part of it before she told him the rest. How very resourceful, Mr. Macrae."

Miss Sangford's face was perfectly serene, but her words were arrows shot at close range. *Thwack! Thwack! Thwack!* They all hit their target. And Nathaniel's defenses were down.

For the first time, he could picture her as Lord Howell had described her. Ruthless. Scheming. Dangerous. And yet... She had the right to protect herself, didn't she? If she had discovered that he had been snooping in her personal business, it must have been a terrible shock. Why should she not confront him?

"I didn't follow a word of that," his mother said suddenly. "It sounds like so much gossip. And I am not partial to gossip." The pout of disapproval, paired with hooded eyes, told Nathaniel that Miss Sangford was losing favor with her. That would not do. He may not wish to have his mother foist a young lady upon him, but their guest should not be judged unfairly.

"I think there has been a misunderstanding," he said quickly. "I remember the conversation now. Not really gossip, was it, ladies? A sad story, to be sure, but then we all have secrets, don't we, Mother?"

He shot his mother a meaningful look.

She stared at him blankly. Then realization dawned.

"Oh. Er... of course." Her convivial smile was once again bestowed on their guests. "Tell me, Miss Sangford, do you think one might ask this Dubois personage if Nathaniel is safe from another attack?"

"I can answer for myself, Mother. And I can say with absolute certainty that my life is in my own hands."

"Your bandaged head suggests otherwise, sir," countered Miss Sangford. "Along with the scar near your eye. You are accumulating quite the collection of battle wounds. And I can't help from thinking it is my fault."

"*Your* fault, Miss Sangford?" Mrs. Macrae tilted her frowning brow at the young lady.

"Well, Mr. Macrae's eye was injured when he chased after the man in the park. And this nasty bump on the head came right after I was threatened..." She stopped, her eyes wide, her mouth frozen in mid-speech.

"What threat?" all three listeners asked in unison.

Miss Sangford sat in mute agony, biting her lip and twisting her skirt with her fingers. She no longer looked scheming or ruthless. In fact, she looked small and lost.

"I wasn't going to say anything. Certainly not to you, Mr. Macrae. My safety should not be your concern. Especially now that you know all about..." Miss Sangford ground to a halt again. She twisted to face Miss Bathurst. "And telling you, Olivia, would only have made you worry."

Nathaniel nodded. "So you told Madame Dubois."

His mother sat back. "Why would you not tell your father, Miss Sangford? Surely, he would want to protect you?"

The young lady grew quiet once more. She wove her fingers together and clenched them in her lap. "I cannot speak of it. Not yet."

"But he is your father!" Mrs. Macrae insisted.

Nathaniel reached out and touched his mother's arm. When she looked to him, he shook his head urgently, mouthing, *"Leave it."*

His mother continued to stare at him until she seemed to shake herself free and say, a little uncertainly, "Well, of course, it's none of my business... I suppose we are fortunate that this French woman has the sort of sway to offer you protection."

Miss Sangford looked fit to burst into tears. Her face was flushed, her lips pressed firmly together. She merely nodded in answer, as if unable to trust herself with speech.

Mercifully, the tea tray arrived. Nathaniel's mother set about pouring the light-filled liquid into cups and offering sugar, followed by a plate of biscuits. During this time, Miss Bathurst quietly mumbled something to Miss Sangford, who shook her head firmly and sat up a little straighter, chin higher, making an effort to pull herself together.

Nathaniel observed her closely, feeling wretched. He hadn't meant for her to discover that he knew about her past. Moreover, she must wonder what had put him on this path of discovery. She had hinted at the ten-pound payments. Had her father realized Nathaniel had been through his ledger? And what had convinced Madame Dubois to reveal all to Miss Sangford when she had been adamant it should be kept from her?

Honest, open conversation was needed. But how? By some unknown circumstance, it seemed Miss Bathurst had been elected as Miss Sangford's confidante, but Nathaniel did not wish to include his mother in this circle of secrecy. Not without Miss Sangford's permission. And he could not imagine her granting it.

A new and daring thought slid into his brain. Trust worked both ways. It was a huge risk. But one look at his hawk—who had tried to bite and claw and scratch at him because his shoulder was no longer a safe perch for her—now so small and frightened, and he was sure.

Including Miss Bathurst was another matter. However, if Miss Sangford trusted her with her own terrible secret, she must have been of sound character. He would just have to take his chances.

"Mother," he said in such a serious tone in the midst of their tea and biscuits that she looked up with a question upon her face. "Be so good as to close the door. What I have to say is not for the servants' ears."

Chapter Seventeen

 RS. MACRAE ROSE obligingly and closed the doors.

"What is this about?" she asked as she sat down again.

"They need to know, Mother."

"I do not understand. What is it they should know?"

"The truth about how I spend my time."

A long pause followed this statement. Mrs. Macrae looked very doubtful about her son's intentions. She turned her head and considered Irene.

"I see," she said. And then, "If you think it necessary."

He nodded. "There is a reason I do not usually speak of it, just as there a reason I must speak of it now."

He leaned forward, his forearms on his knees. "Miss Sangford, Miss Bathurst, what I am about to tell you has remained confidential so that what I do may be done with as little interference as possible."

Irene had no interest in the scandalous activities Mr. Macrae got up too, but she kept that to herself for now. However, if he thought that sharing the details of his debauchery would somehow show integrity, he was very much mistaken.

"For the past two years, I have been in the employ of Lord Howell as a criminal investigator."

Nothing on this good, green earth could have prepared Irene for that statement. Her mouth dropped open involuntarily and she was aware, in the corner of her eye, that Olivia was likewise agape.

"In order to gain the sort of information that solves such cases, I have frequented places and become acquainted with the type of people who are frowned upon by civilized society."

Irene understood now. "Like Madame Dubois."

"Yes. Like Madame Dubois." Mr. Macrae turned to his mother and stated bluntly, "She is one of *those* madams, Mother."

"Oh, I see." Mrs. Macrae nodded, as if such news were an everyday occurrence in her household. Which, Irene now realized, it was. Mrs. Macrae, however, had just come to a realization of her own. "Oh, my dear," she said to Irene, her eyebrows arched and her mouth a soft pout, "whatever were *you* doing mixing with the likes of her? To think that you would reach out to such a… a… *person* instead of your own father. What awful circumstance would drive you to such desperate action?"

"Mother," Mr. Macrae scolded gently, "we are discussing *my* affairs, not Miss Sangford's."

"Yes," said Mrs. Macrae, "but still…" She waved a hand toward Irene. "The poor girl."

A stern look silenced her. Well, almost. There was a brief muttering under her breath about just worrying for the dear child, but Mrs. Macrae's murmurs soon subsided and she said nothing more.

"As I was saying," Mr. Macrae continued with a longsuffering sigh, "my reputation as a rake and a scoundrel is grossly exaggerated but unavoidable. I cannot correct public opinion without revealing the reason why it is false. My informants must believe I am who I pretend to be if they are going to speak freely. Sadly, it means that even those I *wish* to befriend as a gentleman of good character must necessarily think me beneath them."

Oh, the irony! Irene wanted to laugh. A rueful laugh, to be sure, perhaps with even a hint of hysteria. For here she was, a product of greed and ambition, a bastard posing as a woman of society. Meanwhile, Mr. Macrae, supposedly unworthy of her father's consideration, was a true gentleman in character and deed, willing to carry the burden of a tainted reputation to serve his fellow man. If she didn't laugh, she would cry.

"I confess I am both relieved and ashamed, sir," she said.

"What shame could you possibly carry, Miss Sangford?" he asked, his head cocked to one side, his brows puckered.

"Oh, sir." She puffed out a laugh of disdain. "You know all too well. You and Miss Bathurst both."

Mr. Macrae looked across at Olivia and shrugged. "I see no signs of condescension upon the features of Miss Bathurst. Are you ashamed of Miss Sangford, Miss Bathurst?"

"No, indeed, Mr. Macrae, I am not!" Olivia spoke with such earnest conviction that she forgot to lower her voice, but nobody seemed to notice. Her alarm at the very suggestion that she should think less of her dear friend stood out so boldly upon her face, Irene could almost believe she was ready to put up fists to defend Irene's good name.

"Then what need have *any* of your friends to be ashamed of you?" Mr. Macrae wanted to know.

"You are a far better person than I," she answered, her voice reduced to the barest whisper.

"Oh, my dear, what is this?" Mrs. Macrae cried, rising from her chair and pulling a pretty lace handkerchief from the wrist of her fine muslin sleeve. "We can't have Nathaniel's dear friends think so little of themselves." She held out the handkerchief and Irene took it, tears that had been held back now flowing freely into its soft creases. "My son is an excellent judge of character, you know. There is no use in finding fault with yourself when he sees none. If the flaw was there, he would have seen it." She smiled with parental pride upon her only child.

Her kindness only made Irene's tears flow more hotly. If this lovely woman only knew! Then she would want nothing to do with her. Instead of her handkerchief Mrs. Macrae would be showing her the door.

"You know, Mother," said Mr. Macrae suddenly, "I do believe

a bit of fresh air would do my head the world of good. If Miss Bathurst would be so kind as to push the chair, I think we might tempt the ladies to visit the shrubbery. Didn't you say the blooms were early this year?"

"Oh, you clever boy!" Mrs. Macrae beamed. "That is exactly what we shall do." Without waiting for the approval of her guests, she marched across to the glass-paneled door and threw it open with great relish. "A perfect idea for a perfect day, Nathaniel. I shall send for more tea and some sandwiches and we shall dine prettily amid birdsong. What say you, ladies? Can you bear our company an hour longer? It is so rare that we have young people visiting. Nathaniel can hardly bring his informants home with him. And not all our friends have been as understanding about his "habits" as you appear to have been, even before he explained himself to you. I can see why Nathaniel has wanted to visit you more often."

"He has?" Utter astonishment had caused Irene to say this out loud. She could feel Olivia's knowing grin beaming across the back of her neck. Mr. Macrae, to her relief, made no comment.

Mrs. Macrae, however, was a different matter altogether.

"Oh, *yes*, dear! It was only his strong sense of propriety that kept him home." She caught her son's eye. "Oh, *do* stop glaring at me, Nathaniel. You've told her your most well-guarded secret. Do you think it will frighten her to know a lesser one? Miss Sangford must know that it is only your gentlemanly nature that has prevented you from enjoying a fuller friendship with her. And why shouldn't you? If Miss Sangford had attended our dances in years past, the two of you would have been friends long before."

A fresh wave of shame washed over Irene. Ah, yes, the dances she and her family had been too good for. They hadn't been bothered to mix with *those* sorts of people. Except now *she* was that sort of person. And she'd be only too grateful to be considered worthy to attend.

Guilt climbed into the mix of emotions. If Mrs. Macrae knew the truth about her, she would not be so welcoming. Although her own son hung about with the dregs of society, the lady could explain it away as his work. Then again, Irene was amazed his mother tolerated the idea that her son worked at all. It seemed to her that Mrs. Macrae must have been fundamentally good-hearted. Envy slipped in with the growing tumble of feelings that churned within her.

"I think, Mother," Mr. Macrae said very carefully, "you may be giving Miss Sangford the wrong idea. Your enthusiasm at having young ladies in our home may have caused a certain casualness in your statement. We would not want our guests to misunderstand what you mean by friendship."

Oh, yes, thank you, thought Irene. *Let me add disappointment to the rush of unwanted emotions I am experiencing.*

"Miss Sangford does not misunderstand me, do you, Miss Sangford? Your family has high aspirations for your match and Nathaniel has guaranteed himself ineligible. I could therefore only mean friendship in the most innocent sense."

The words were unambiguous, but Irene couldn't help noticing an undertone of rebuke. Poor Mrs. Macrae had no doubt realized that her son's choices would not easily win him a bride. No daughter-in-law, no grandbabies. And Mrs. Macrae seemed the sort who would dote on grandbabies.

Irene was starting to consider that Mr. Macrae might well have been a bachelor by choice. Perhaps his work served a double purpose: the satisfaction of catching criminals, and the means of keeping bothersome matches well away from him.

A tricky thought slid in through the back door of her mind. Mr. Macrae wasn't... No, surely not... There were definitely molly houses in the districts he frequented. Did he visit them under cover of his work? She didn't know much about such men, but she knew they existed, and that their activities were against the law. Was that yet another secret Mr. Macrae hid from the world? Was that why he could understand what it was to live in the shadow of the truth when that truth would ruin one's reputation, destroy one's life?

Irene very selfishly wished this wasn't the case. She wanted to admire him as a woman admired a man, to desire him and wish for him to desire her in return. And yet she found herself feeling suddenly and vigorously supportive of him. He had accepted her as she was, shown her kindness and respect. She wanted very much to offer him the same.

Then again, if he wasn't... *different*... did it even matter? He was never going to be hers. Her father had taken care of that.

If Irene could have walked, she would have plodded miserably behind the others, alone with her unhelpful thoughts. As it was, though, she was being pushed forward by the quietly attentive Miss Bathurst, who now leaned down and whispered in Irene's ear, "Methinks Mr. Macrae doth protest too much. He only fears you will think him forward, but I reckon he is very pleased to have you here."

Irene shook her head. She could not whisper back, for the necessary twisting of her body would draw attention to them.

"No, indeed," said Olivia, slowing down and allowing some distance to form between them and the Macraes. "It is only his mother's comments that annoy him. When she is not pushing the issue, his eyes are constantly upon you. I have seen that look. My cousin, who married for love, looked with that exact same expression upon his wife when they were courting. I believe Mr. Macrae has an earnest interest in you."

"You feel compelled to say these things as a friend," countered Irene stubbornly. She didn't want hope. Not when she had been let down in so many ways.

What a terrible lie! her brain shouted at her. *Of course you want hope! Hope in Mr. Macrae above all. Just look at him, all bandaged up because he chose to help you that day in the park. See the way he turns back to make sure you are managing, when he should be taking extra care not to stumble in his recovering state. There is not an iota of judgment in his eyes. It is as if he never spoke to Madame Dubois. What a man! What a...*

"Is everything all right, ladies?" Mrs. Macrae called from a distance away. She had stopped by a large viburnum with a profusion of blooms.

"We're coming," called Olivia, pushing the chair, and Irene within it, toward the pretty shady spot. High above, the boughs of an oak extended the shade, and invisible birds called out to each other cheerfully. A table and six chairs implied this was a favorite spot for the family to dine out of doors.

"I was thinking of a brief stroll." Their hostess indicated where the path continued. "I do not want Nathaniel to exert himself too much too soon. And Miss Bathurst cannot be expected to heave the chair around as if she were a footman. What say I let the staff know to prepare the table while you continue on this short, circular route?"

She did not wait for a response but strode off purposefully back to the house.

The moment his mother was out of sight, Mr. Macrae sat down and motioned the ladies to join him.

"Is it too much for you, Mr. Macrae?" asked Olivia. "We do not need to stay if you'd rather be resting."

"No, no. It is not that. I must speak with Miss Sangford urgently, and since you appear to be initiated into the inner circle, Miss Bathurst, I will include you in what I have to say."

"Oh! A declaration!" Olivia clapped her hands and dropped into the nearest chair. "Pretend I am not here. The two of you can say whatever is on your hearts. I shall be mum."

Mr. Macrae stared at Olivia in mortified silence. Irene imagined her own expression was identical to his: a deep blush, eyes that did not know quite where to look, and a mouth slightly agape.

"Olivia!" Irene hissed. "Don't say such things!'

"Oh, have I misunderstood?" Olivia asked. She angled her head at Mr. Macrae. "You're not going to tell her how you feel?"

"*Olivia!*" Irene wished she could sink into the ground. "What must Mr. Macrae think? I assure you, sir, I have no such expectations. Please tell us what is *really* on your mind."

The gentleman struggled to pull himself together. "Oh, I... Yes... The thing is..."

"Go on," urged Irene. "We're listening."

"I just thought you should know, in the interest of transparency..." He paused, uncertainty seemingly stealing his confidence.

"Yes?"

"When I met you, I was searching for the very man who thereafter alarmed your horse. He had been hired to murder someone, and I was trying to prevent him from succeeding."

"A hired killer!" Olivia breathed in awe. "We knew he was dangerous, wielding a knife like that. Do you know who hired him?"

"The same person who instructed him to offer me this battered head as a warning."

"And you know who that is?" Irene asked, wondering why he would tell them about his investigation.

"I do. And I know who two of his accomplices are. There may be a third, but I have yet to prove it. I want you to know that I am investigating this avenue. I want no more secrets between us. I need you to be able to trust me. Even when what I do seems intended to harm you."

Irene didn't like where this was going at all. Of course she wanted to believe in him. With her whole heart, she wanted it. So few people remained in her tiny circle of confidence. She could not bear to lose even one. But what he was saying sent warnings up and down her spine.

Who was this third person? Was it her mother? Madame Dubois had her hand in some interesting pies. But would she stoop to murder? Irene did not know her well enough to say with certainty that Madame Dubois was an honorable woman. Yet she felt it. Call it instinct. Perhaps she merely wished it so.

"Well," said Olivia, "are you going to tell us or not?"

Mr. Macrae swallowed hard. "We—that is to say, Lord Howell and I—have reason to believe the attempted assassination was motivated by money. The target was one of the leaders of the recent uprising. Men such as Cranbourn, Pratt, and Bligh are wealthy mill owners who stand to lose much if the workers down tools or, worse yet, force a change in Parliament that favors the workers rather than the mill owners. We know Cranbourn is the ringleader. But we are not certain how far this 'ring' extends."

"I know these names." Irene's voice was filled with dread. "My father does business with them. Mill business, among other things."

"I am so sorry, Miss Sangford. I desperately wish this task did not fall to me."

Irene believed him. She could see the pain behind his eyes. She did not feel it as he did. It should have hurt her more, discovering her father was a suspect. But she knew now what he was capable of. The man could be ruthless, calculating. He believed himself entitled to control the lives of others. Who could guess how far he would allow himself to go?

"I want to help," she heard herself say. It barely shocked her. Why should it? Nothing in her life was as it ought to have been.

"I could never ask that of you," Mr. Macrae said, his voice low and urgent.

"You didn't ask."

"Irene, think what you are saying!" Olivia cried. "You are talking about your father!"

"No, I am talking about the man who used my conception to further his own ambition," Irene said bitterly.

Approaching footfalls made all three of them shift into a pose of light conversation and force smiles upon their faces. "Oh, you are back already!" called Mrs. Macrae. "Did I really take that long?"

"We cut our walk short," said Mr. Macrae. "I grew tired. Thankfully, the ladies were understanding." He broadened his smile at them. Yet it was not the same open-hearted, all-encompassing smile that he had offered on previous occasions.

"Perhaps this is a sign that we should cut our visit short, too,"

Irene suggested. "I am satisfied that Mr. Macrae will heal fully, given time. But we will only hamper his recovery if he overexerts himself because of us."

"Nonsense!" said his mother, sitting down. "Thanks to you, he has hauled himself out of his room, made civilized conversation, and even taken a brief amble among the shrubbery. These are the things that truly heal us: fresh air and good company."

"Nevertheless," insisted Irene, "I feel he has done well and earned respite. There is such a notion as too much of a good thing. I should feel terrible if our visit should tire him so much that he has no energy left for what remains of the day."

Mrs. Macrae leaned with one hand upon her knee, the other gesturing in the air. "There, Nathaniel, what did I tell you? A true friend indeed! Miss Sangford, it makes a mother's heart glad to see someone carry her son's wellbeing in the forefront of their mind… and heart."

The last two syllables were added with obvious satisfaction, for Mrs. Macrae beamed at the two young folk as if she could see grandchildren on the horizon.

"So, we're not staying for the picnic, then." Olivia looked sadly at the empty table. "It seems a pity when the staff will already have begun to prepare it."

"We were only having sandwiches, Olivia," Irene reminded her. "Not cakes."

"Oh, no, my dear," corrected Mrs. Macrae. "You are mistaken. Our cook is as delighted to have guests as we are. She will be surprising us with a number of special treats. Of that, you can be sure."

"Oh." Olivia's eyes, head, and shoulders all drooped simultaneously.

"I suggest a compromise," said the ever-chivalrous gentleman. "I shall retire to my room, with thanks to Miss Sangford for her insight into my current limitations. You three ladies, however, shall continue to enjoy each other's company. If our guests are willing to accept these terms, that is."

Olivia sat up a little straighter, her eyes focused and pleading. Irene thought that she rather resembled a puppy, quivering with excitement. If Olivia had had a tail, Irene was sure she would have wagged it. How could she deny her friend this small pleasure? She could never repay Olivia for the loyalty she had shown when Irene no longer had anything to offer but herself. What was an hour of sandwiches and cake compared to such a gift?

"If Mrs. Macrae is content with just the two of us, Olivia and I would be delighted to stay," she said.

Irene was touched by the glow that lit up their hostess's face. She was starting to understand just how much Mr. Macrae's parents had sacrificed in supporting their son. Friends who had forsaken them. The unlikelihood of their only child making a suitable match. The absence of lively young people who should have been regular visitors with their son. And yet they had chosen to hold their heads high and take it all on the chin because they loved him and were proud of what he was doing.

Irene's heart twisted into a knot. What she wouldn't give to be part of a family like that! The Macraes exuded a warmth and acceptance she had never truly experienced within her own home. She wished she could know that these wonderful qualities would still be there if her hostess knew the truth about her. She felt such a fraud as they sipped tea and conversed pleasantly. More than once—as Mrs. Macrae turned bright eyes upon her and expressed gratitude that her son had friends who stood by him—Irene had wanted to blurt out her own truth. To say, *"See, I, too, am an outsider. But I am afraid to declare myself, and I choose to live a lie. Will you still have me?"*

Instead, she smiled and nodded and watched as Olivia sampled the treats with obvious delight. Irene was learning to appreciate the simple pleasures. And they had nothing to do with wealth or title.

No, they had to do with gray eyes that gazed at her unflinchingly. Arms that lifted her without apology, in whose strength she could nestle like the soft thing she had never allowed herself to be. A mouth whose butterfly curve called to hers, asking her to bring her own tender lips closer, to touch in silence, no words being necessary.

Instead, the ladies made small talk, nibbled the food delicately, and parted on very good terms with the promise to pick up where they had left off at the Sangford dinner in ten days. Irene assured Olivia she would be invited. Irene could not imagine surviving the dinner conversation without someone by her side who knew exactly how she felt.

Olivia had become a vital support. Irene hardly noticed the challenge of her friend's voice anymore. She simply knew that this was a voice that spoke up for her.

Their departure, as with their arrival, was a laborious affair. Cedric had carried Irene to the carriage before he and Barton wrestled the chair to the roof of the vehicle. There was much grunting and, Irene imagined, there would have been some cursing, too, if the ladies had not been present. She was very sorry to be the cause of such struggle, and told them so. Of course, they denied that it was much trouble. The grumbling subsided in the wake of her comment. She hoped it was because their efforts had been acknowledged. The servants had become her allies to a certain degree and Irene wished for them to see that she valued them.

The commotion caused a curtain to flick open in a window upstairs. A curious maid, perhaps? Or was it Mr. Macrae, attempting to rest and being disturbed by the noise? The window opened and a bandaged head leaned out.

"Safe journey, Miss Sangford!" the gentleman called down to her. A hand snuck out and waved.

Irene's heat skipped a beat. It had been such a small gesture, but it meant everything to her. She waved back, hoping not to seem too eager, though, of course, she was.

The carriage dipped as the groom and footman climbed up into their seats. The head and hand disappeared back inside the window.

Ten days to wait. A small eternity. But she would have this moment to cherish.

Irene sat back against the leather upholstery. Olivia folded her gloved hand around her friend's and squeezed it. "Just ten days to wait," she said, offering a smile of encouragement.

"But I will see you tomorrow, I hope," said Irene.

Olivia nodded. "I have some new ribbon. We can freshen our bonnets. I think you'll be stepping out on someone's arm very soon. We must make sure you are ready to look your best."

"I'm not stepping anywhere at all for a while yet," replied Irene. "And when I do, I don't think I deserve that particular arm."

Olivia patted her hand. "I think that is for the gentleman to decide."

They rode the rest of the way in comfortable silence, having had their fill of conversation at the home of the Macraes. Irene allowed herself to daydream a little. About a gentleman with sandy-blond hair and a smile that lit up her heart, whose arm she would give all the titles in the world to have wrapped around her.

CHAPTER EIGHTEEN

Wednesday, April 9th, 1817

A WEEK LATER, Nathaniel was back to his old self again, with just a tender spot that remained when he combed his hair. His mother reluctantly agreed that he was ready to return to the world beyond their estate. When he donned his hat late that afternoon, however, she stood by the door, wringing her hands and unable to keep the worry from showing.

"You will be careful, won't you?" she almost pleaded.

"I promise not to put myself in harm's way unnecessarily." He gave her a reassuring hug.

"They'll be watching to see if you've heeded their warning."

"Rest assured, I will be staying well out of the way of Cranbourn and his accomplices. Lord Howell's informant will follow up on anything I have missed. We have already identified the mastermind behind it all. It is only Albert Sangford who must be ruled out. And Howell's men have their eyes and ears upon his movements.

"*My* role will be to observe the talk among the workers. If more unrest is planned, Cranbourn and his ilk will not be done with their mischief in stopping it." His mother made as if to speak, and he hastily added, "Do not fret, Mother. I shall take care not to do anything that may arouse Cranbourn's suspicion. That includes avoiding Shelby's. As far as they are concerned, I have learned my lesson."

"I suppose I cannot ask for more." His mother sighed.

"For that matter," Nathaniel said as casually as possible, "it is best I avoid the Sangfords, too. At least until dinner next week. Since you are also invited, it will clearly be a social call to anyone watching. It would probably arouse more suspicion if I did *not* attend."

"Oh." His mother looked positively crestfallen. "So, you will not be calling on Miss Sangford, then, despite her obvious desire for you to do so?"

Nathaniel heaved a sigh of his own. "Mother, you really must stop trying to throw us together. It is very unkind to Miss Sangford."

"'Unkind'? How can it be unkind to encourage something that clearly already exists?"

"What do you mean?"

"Oh, you men! You rule the world but cannot see what is right in front of you! Miss Sangford has feelings for you. Strong enough for her to have reached out, hoping I would invite her here because she was that worried for you. I lost count of the number of times I caught her staring at you, only to look away quickly when she saw that I had observed her. She may be trying to hide it, but she is terrible at it. She is besotted with you, Nathaniel. The only unkind thing would be to ignore her."

"Her feelings aside," Nathaniel said with difficulty, because his mother's words had touched on his own unexplored emotions, "there is no point in encouraging her. Mr. Sangford would never approve of our match. I am, in that respect, *persona non grata*. The occasional visit and this forthcoming dinner have only been made possible because I have helped his daughter in a crisis. If he thought for one minute that I was looking to deepen my acquaintance with her, that would be the end of all contact."

"And you would hate that," his mother pointed out. "Because you love her."

It was not a question.

Nathaniel was about to protest, but the words died on his

lips. He had not allowed such thoughts to germinate in his mind. But they had sneaked into his heart, anyway. His feelings for Miss Sangford had cocooned themselves there, a seemingly harmless chrysalis readying itself to emerge a spectacular butterfly. He felt it now, pushing at him, asking to be set free, to enter the world and present itself to his beloved. The wings shivered in their folded state, wishing to unfurl and be magnificent, giving flight to what had once been a mere kernel of an idea.

Nathaniel shook his head like a wet dog. His injury complained at the sudden movement, and he ceased at once. "It cannot be," he said, more to himself than his mother.

"Because of her father?" Mrs. Macrae scoffed. "He can try his luck with his next daughter. Miss Sangford is approaching spinsterhood. He would likely be happy to have her find a husband who is at least wealthy if a title evades her."

"My reputation precludes such a possibility."

"It can be mended."

"But my work…"

"Nathaniel, are you telling me you would choose chasing criminals all over Munro to a life with Miss Sangford?"

His lips tightened. "I would prefer not to have to choose."

His mother was not to be discouraged. "There may come a time, my son, when you will have to. What if someone comes and snatches her up and you lose your chance with her?"

He lowered his eyes. "Then I would wish her well."

His mother sucked in her breath. "*Nathaniel Macrae*! I did not teach you to lie! Least of all to yourself!"

Nathaniel waved an agitated arm. "What would you have me *do*, Mother? My work has meaning. If I give it up for a woman, I should grow to resent her."

"You could do what other gentlemen do."

"Do you mean hunt? And lounge about at Shelby's?" Nathaniel puffed out a wry laugh. "Good grief, Mother! Do you know me at all?"

She turned her head away and raised a palm in protest. "Fine,

fine, spend your time in the back streets with your informants. But the day will come when you will want more. You may not see it now, but mark my words, it will happen. I only hope you remember how I tried to reason with you. May it comfort you when there is no one to warm your bed."

The bluntness of these words awoke Nathaniel's ire. His mother did not understand. She *enjoyed* the domesticity of life.

"I will take my chances." He huffed, plodding down the front stairs to where the groom stood waiting with his horse. He did not turn or tip his hat to his mother, but threw himself into the saddle and gave the stallion a swift nudge with his ankle to set his mount in motion.

"Women, Archer," he complained to his horse. "They are a bothersome bunch."

But his words fell flat on his own ears. How could he ever describe Miss Sangford as *bothersome*? Despite her own recent trials and challenges, she had proven herself gracious and kind. Lord Howell might say these were newer traits, but that only made her choice to learn and grow under difficult circumstances more commendable. Nathaniel had a world of respect for her.

As for love… He dared not even ponder his mother's words. Why give himself hope? He stood no chance. There was little point in desiring someone he could never call his own.

But he *did* desire her. *Oh*, yes! Her rosebud mouth. Her elegant form. The sensual curve of her neck. He had noticed a spot, just *there*, where her throat and collarbone met, where he yearned to place his lips and feel the smooth warmth of her skin.

Already, the heat rose within him. The mere thought of her was enough to drive him to distraction. If she had been here, now, he might very well have declared himself. But where would that lead?

Life, it seemed to Nathaniel, was unnecessarily complicated. In a simpler world, if people were lucky enough to find the one who made them feel this way, they would marry them in an instant. Well, certainly an instant after the banns were called.

There would be none of this fretting over the rules of engagement.

Ah, he thought scornfully, *the double meaning of that thought does not escape me.*

"After all, Archer old boy, love is a little like battle, isn't it?" He patted the horse's neck. "And nobody likes to lose."

He took his time riding to his destination. His head wasn't ready for a gallop just yet. Besides, he didn't have far to go. A favored gathering place for the disgruntled millworkers was a barn on the land of a sympathetic farmer called Harrison. He needed to see for himself how much active dissent was ongoing. If talk was still animated, then Cranbourn would be taking further steps to quell it.

The countryside showed itself verdant and velvety, almost mosslike in its moist growth. Recent heavy rains had been responsible for this profusion of green and had also kept the rebellious hearts at home. Today, however, the sun shone, warm and inviting, and a gathering, if one was wanted, would be in full swing.

A trail of villagers was winding toward the large, vaulted structure that was the ancient, wooden barn. Nathaniel slipped from Archer's back and led him off the path to a shady spot among some trees. He tied the reins to a sturdy branch, removed his hat, coat, cravat, and gloves and balanced these in the crook of a bough where it joined the trunk. Loosening his shirt at the collar and wrists, he rolled up his sleeves and ruffled his hair, wincing as he touched the lingering bruise too briskly.

It was the best he could do. He still looked every bit the gentleman, but those who knew him would simply laugh and say, *"Don't worry about 'im. He's just here because 'e's bored. 'E's harmless."* For good measure, he would splash a little liquor from his hip flask onto his shirt and enter the building with a well-practiced stagger. He would stumble and let himself fall into a pile of straw. That would give everyone a good laugh at "them stupid, rich toffs" and then they would forget about him. Maybe the odd brute would aim a kick at him. But they would let him stay, a ruined gentleman among them, while he listened and observed.

It didn't take long to gather that this was a different sort of meeting altogether. These weren't just millworkers. They were villagers from all walks of life. And the mood was angry. The talk was bitter, a hostility brewing that would necessarily flow into action.

Nathaniel soon realized why.

"Men of Munro! Let us be quiet for our speaker!" cried a voice into the crowd. It took a while to settle everyone, and there were many men to settle. Eventually, all heads turned toward a pile of hay stacked high enough to form a platform for the speaker to be seen by all.

A man of medium height and sinewy build climbed up onto the makeshift podium. He had a haunted look about him, as did those who had spent years of their life in the cells of Fleet Street. Some men were broken by such experiences. Some grew hardened. And a very few could not wait to inflict the sort of misery and pain upon others as had been doled out to them.

The speaker was such a man.

Even before he began to stir up his audience, Nathaniel's fingers involuntarily reached for the bruise on his head. For the man who was invoking the gathering to march on their masters was none other than the assailant from Munro Park.

CHAPTER NINETEEN

"GOOD AND HONEST folk of Munro," began the speaker. His voice was surprisingly soft. Nathaniel guessed it was to force his audience to quiet down and listen carefully. As it was, one could hear a pin drop in the vast space of the crowded barn.

"We have talked and planned, and our time has now come. How long have our masters forced the yoke of oppression upon our necks? Even our attempts to humbly ask for what is fair have been denied us. Our Regent ignores our pleas. Parliament makes laws that favor the rich. But we know, if every man had a vote, every man would have a voice."

The speaker was forced to pause as shouts of agreement echoed his words. When the noise lingered, he raised his arms and patted the air with his palms. "All right," he said in his barely audible voice. Neighbors started hushing each other, a sound that grew quickly and took a full minute to subside. The speaker continued, every eye once again upon him.

"You are not alone. As we speak, men gather in every corner of our great country. Thousands already wait for us to join them in London."

Another round of cheers, but this was brief and the speaker did not pause to wait for silence.

"This time, they will not treat us like dogs. No one will drag good men to London in irons. We will take what we have to defend ourselves and our cause. Whether it be a knife from your kitchen or shears from the farm. Some of you are heroes from the war against Napoleon. Perhaps you have a pike or a pistol. Bring them! Show them we mean business!"

"Yeah!" shouted more than a hundred voices, fists in the air.

Nathaniel did not move. Riled up like hounds in a pack, any one of these men might make an example of him. Men who would, on any other night, let him buy them a drink at the nearest watering hole and offer them a chance to speak of the sins of their employers. Decent men with families who only wanted a fair shake of it. Cowed men whose poverty and sorrows meant nothing to the so-called gentlemen who grew rich off their backs.

Nathaniel could understand their frustration, their hatred. He even agreed that things should change. But this speaker was not their friend. *His* pockets were already lined with thirty pieces of silver. He would lead them to march, armed with desperation and hope and an assortment of rusty weapons. He would guide them into the muzzles of the militia. And he would melt away from the ensuing chaos, returning to his master like the dog he was.

And there was nothing Nathaniel could do.

With every fiber of his being, he wanted to stand up, call out this man who would ruin their lives for the liar and manipulator he was—a murderer of men, whether slaying them one at a time or in marching masses.

But, if he did, Nathaniel's poor mother would be told they had found her son's corpse floating in the River Mersey. Or worse yet, they would bury him in the woods and his mother would not even have his body for the funeral.

Nathaniel might have considered this sacrifice worth the price if he had thought it would make a difference. But these simple folk were not themselves tonight. They had swallowed the poison that had been carefully brewed for them.

Oh, Cranbourn had been clever. Very clever indeed. Since he could not stop the riots, he would drive them beyond control.

The Crown would be forced to take drastic measures. Fear would spread beyond Munro to all of England's upper families. And what was the easiest solution? Would it be to give these families better wages, healthier living conditions? Heavens, no! After all, these men had brought their garden implements to attack the good men who upheld the law. Parliament could not reward such behavior. No, they would tighten restrictions, punish heavily, put that fear into the rebels instead. Soon the rioters would go back to a quiet day's work. And if they grumbled under their breath, well, the masses were always complaining about something, weren't they?

Nathaniel thought he might throw up.

He lay there, powerless, upon the straw as the men filed out. He imagined himself leaping up when the barn was empty and seeking out that vile Judas to wring his villainous neck. But when it was finally safe for Nathaniel to jump to his feet, there was no sign of the man.

"You all right there, me lad?"

The farmer stood in the doorway of the barn, his hand upon the lock. "You look like you've seen a ghost. The wrong sort of drink can do that to you. Best cure, I find, is another drink."

Nathaniel rushed toward him, eyes wide, hands flailing. "These men, Mr. Harrison, they're marching into a trap," he said urgently. "We've got to stop them somehow."

"There now." The farmer smiled to placate him. "The drink's gone and done your brain in. What march is this we're talking about?"

"You don't need to pretend. I know. I heard that man talk. I saw them swallow every lie he told them. Some will pay for it with their *lives,* Harrison. We can't let that happen."

"Are you talking about Mr. Richards? Ah, he was just giving the lads a chance to let off some steam. Nothing will come of it."

Nathaniel shook his head, ignoring the ache stirred by the movement. "You're wrong. So terribly wrong. I wager he has already warned the militia. And his master will warn the magistrate. It's all been planned, you see. It's all…"

Something in the farmer's stance shifted. The jovial smile slipped into a narrowing of the eyes. His shoulders squared as if in readiness for Nathaniel to pounce.

There was only one reason for such a change.

"Oh, merciful saints, you're one of them! You're one of Cranbourn's cronies!" Nathaniel tried to reason through the shock that had just hit him. "How much have they paid you? I can double the fee. You will not be able to live with yourself, Harrison. How will you look their families in the eye if these husbands and fathers are carted off to be hanged for treason? Think, man!"

"And what have they ever done for me?" Harrison wanted to know. "Nah, Mr. Macrae, it's every man for himself in this world."

Nathaniel curled his fists. "Then step out of my way, Harrison, before I lay your worthless body out on this floor."

"There'll be no need for that, Mr. Macrae," came the placid response. "You just sit yourself down on that comfy pile of straw. You're not going anywhere tonight."

Nathaniel lunged toward the treacherous farmer. He had scarcely taken one furious step when his arms flung forward as he lurched to a halt. Another man had joined Harrison in the doorway. In his hand was a knife, held with casual menace.

"Mr. Richards, I believe," said Nathaniel, straightening his back and keeping a close eye on the weapon.

"Ah, Mr. Macrae. You should have heeded my warning. Now what are we going to do with you?"

Nathaniel had the distinct impression that Mr. Richards knew exactly what he was going to do. The question was: could Nathaniel wrestle the knife from Richards's hand before it was plunged into his own belly?

"Shouldn't you be getting instructions from Cranbourn?" he asked, hoping to throw off the man's concentration. "I reckon he might not like you thinking for yourself. Besides, you're not the cleverest man in that regard, are you?"

Richards snarled. "Why, you little…" He took a step forward, knife shifting to readiness.

Harrison's arm blocked him. "I hate to say it, but Macrae's right. We can't kill a man like him without Cranbourn's say-so. Besides, you've got a small army to lead to their doom. We haven't time to be looking for a place to bury a body. We'll lock him in here for the night. Cranbourn can decide his fate in the morning."

Nathaniel considered taking them both on and making his escape. But Harrison was a big, burly fellow, toughened by years of toiling in the sun and rain alike. And Richards… Richards had murder in his eyes. The knife sat between whitened knuckles of hatred. Those years in debtors' prison would have embittered his heart toward any man of means. So-called gentlemen were the thieves who stole food from the mouths of the poor. It didn't matter that the Macraes were nothing like this. They represented the oppressors.

Nathaniel understood it all too well. Even though his family spent their money generously on the needy, these funds they were able to give had once been a harvest of oppression. Somewhere in their past, they had guilt on their hands. And Nathaniel's pretended reputation for debauchery only made him appear privileged and wasteful. Oh, yes, a man like Richards would loathe him profoundly.

Nathaniel lowered his fists and stood down. For the first time in his life, he felt truly powerless, his life in another's hands entirely. *This* was exactly what Cranbourn and his ilk were using to sway those villagers: the promise of a little self-determination. It would be the tastiest of all forbidden fruits for the humble folk who only knew hardship and poverty and humiliation.

Harrison must have sensed Nathaniel's submission because he pulled Richards away by the arm, a move that nearly cost him his hand.

"Don't touch me!" growled Richards, pointing the knife at his throat. "Cranbourn didn't say anything about not killing a farmer, especially one he owes money to. You'll be wanting to watch yourself."

Harrison threw his hands in the air. "Hold on now! I was only wanting to close and lock the door. We need to get going."

Richards cast an assessing eye around the barn. "Is there a way for him to get out?"

"The barn might be made of wood," answered Harrison, "but these beams have grown like stone over decades. If it can keep thieves out, it can keep one pretentious gentleman in."

"I don't like leaving him here unguarded. What if someone finds him?"

"Out here? Too far from the road for anyone to hear him shout. That's the advantage of farm life. No one to bother you."

This seemed to satisfy Richards. He withdrew from the doorway and allowed Harrison to shut the door.

Nathaniel could hear the padlock click shut. Light shone through the narrow gaps between the slats, briefly interrupted by the men's shadows as they moved on. Footfalls retreated.

He waited a few minutes to make sure they were gone. And then a few more to kick himself mentally for being such a fool. No one else knew where he was. He had planned to write a report to the viscount once he was home again. Too often he had made up his plans as he went along.

There was no one to stop the march. No one to warn them it was a trap. Not unless he found a way out of there. As for what would happen to him in the morning when Cranbourn had been informed… Well, best to focus on the here and now.

He paced the perimeter of the barn, looking for a weakness in the wooden framework or a tool to dig a hole beneath it. But there was nothing useful. No lever with which to pry the latch. Not even a loose nail with which to scrape patiently at a single slat in the hopes of breaking it.

It was not harvest season. There were no bales or equipment. With it being spring, the building had likely been cleaned up and the overwintering creatures like mice and spiders had been swept out. All that remained were a few piles of hay used for feed or perhaps as a spot where the chickens liked to roost.

Nathaniel sat down on the straw platform with his head in his hands. This was a very fine mess indeed. He wondered when someone might come looking for him. Probably only in the morning. That was the problem with cultivating a reputation as a reprobate. Staying out all night was considered the norm. By the time anyone realized he was missing rather than simply galivanting, he would likely be dead.

He wondered if he could ask for mercy for his horse. Poor Archer was still tied to the tree, though loosely. He could graze—even escape if he put his stubborn, equine mind to it. But he was not a restless animal and was used to waiting for his master at odd hours. If Richards came to kill him, Nathaniel would tell them where to find Archer and beg for them to set him free. After all, leaving him there to suffer would only provide proof that Nathaniel had been nearby when Archer was eventually discovered. Harrison would not want Nathaniel's disappearance to point toward his farm.

Having made plans for his horse gave Nathaniel a strange sense of calm. There was nothing more he could do now but wait. He might as well try to sleep. If he stood any chance of besting Richards when Cranbourn sent his lackey to kill him—and Nathaniel had no doubt that would be his plan—he must be clear-headed and ready to fight.

The strain of his misadventure had left Nathaniel hungry. He felt in his pockets for the monkey nuts he kept there as a treat for Archer. He had never actually tried one before. They weren't something he would ordinarily eat, but he had to keep his strength up. Archer seemed to like them, so how bad could they be?

He cracked the two-bulbed shell of one and tipped the duo of small nuts into his hand, rubbing them together gently between his fingers to remove the purplish-brown, paper-like skins.

Popping one into his mouth, he was pleasantly surprised. The taste was earthy and creamy. He chewed warily, but no strong aftertaste followed. Soon he had a small mound of empty shells on the ground in front of him and a slightly less plaintive belly.

Nathaniel rolled down his sleeves and lay back with his forearms crossed behind his head. Mercifully, the evening was not too cool. He was sorry now that he had left his coat and gloves with Archer, especially when he heard the first gentle patter of rain. The drops began to fall harder, continuing for some time so that hope sprouted in Nathaniel's mind that the march may have been cancelled.

But he knew these men. A flame had been lit in their hearts. A fire born of resentment and feeding off hope. It would not be doused by mere weather.

As the rain drummed harder against the solid roof of the barn, Nathaniel finally succumbed to sleep.

His next waking thought was many hours later, when what sounded like a gunshot rang through the air.

CHAPTER TWENTY

Thursday, April 10th, 1817

IRENE STARTLED AT a banging noise sounding from their front door.

She had been up and about since early morning, determined to learn to manage her crutches. A month into healing, her leg felt much better, and she figured, if she was careful, she could get about more easily if she could balance on the crutches without risking a fall.

However, she had not counted on the shock of the sudden urgent hammering and very nearly tumbled onto the sofa as her concentration was pulled out from under her.

A woman's voice protested at what must have been Hutchins's plea for her to calm herself. Even in its agitated state, it was a voice Irene recognized. But it didn't explain why Mrs. Macrae was so desperate to be let into the Sangford home.

Irene hobbled with clumsy determination toward the entrance. It wasn't yet a civilized hour for social calls, which meant that the only other person who came to see what was going on was Irene's father.

"What is going on here?" he demanded just as Irene came around the corner with halting steps.

"Mrs. Macrae," she said, a little out of breath with the effort, "what is the matter? Has something happened? Is Mr. Macrae all right?"

"Oh, Miss Sangford, thank goodness it's you." Mrs. Macrae sagged with relief. "I didn't know where else to go!"

"Come through," said Irene, limping toward the drawing room, where she lowered herself carefully into the nearest seat. "Hutchins, bring some of that strong tea for Mrs. Macrae. You know the one I mean. She looks as white as a sheet."

Irene's father trailed behind them. He must have guessed he was not needed, yet old habits dictated a show of interest from the host.

Mrs. Macrae perched rather than sat, her hands restlessly folding around each other in alternating motion.

"He didn't come home," she said. "He always comes home. We had an agreement. No matter what he got up to during the night, he would always be home before breakfast, even if it meant I found him stretched out upon his bed, fully clothed."

"I don't see what that has to do with…" Irene's father began to protest, but Irene shushed him at once.

"Have you asked Lord Howell? Mr. Macrae must surely report his movements to the viscount."

"Why on earth would he…?" her father tried again, only to be completely ignored.

"I did," said Mrs. Macrae, speaking to Irene as if Mr. Sangford's voice were mere background noise. "I sent a note to him first thing. But he said his informants had been looking into someone else and would have no idea what avenue of investigation Nathaniel might have been following until he reported his own findings today. Which he hasn't done."

"Excuse me," said Irene's father, a little more insistently this time, "what do you mean by 'investigation'?"

"Not now, Father! Mr. Macrae has gone missing. Can you not understand what is important here?"

Mrs. Macrae looked up at the confused man. "I am sorry to have barged into your home like this. I only came because I thought Miss Sangford was the one person who could help me."

"Why would…?" asked Mr. Sangford, but he gave up. Irene

did not even acknowledge him.

"I will do whatever I can," she said. "What do you need?"

"Well, you mentioned that woman who had helped you when… you know… you were not feeling safe." Mrs. Macrae eyed Irene's father warily. "She seemed to have useful contacts. I was hoping you could tell me where to find her so that I could appeal to her to help me search for my son. Something must have happened to him. He would not let me worry like this. It's simply not who he is."

"That is good thinking," Irene answered before twisting her head to the left. "Father, where is Madame Dubois's place of business?"

Mr. Sangford, who must have considered himself well and truly dismissed from the conversation at this point, now looked horrified to be included in it. He froze in a position that closely resembled a man caught *in flagrante delicto*. A position, Irene considered wryly, in which he had been caught before.

"Ma… Madame Dubois?" he stammered, no doubt trying to gather his thoughts and the remnants of calm that were left to him. "The name does not ring a bell."'

"This is not the time for niceties," scolded Irene. "We can discuss the details of your acquaintance later, but right now, we need an address. Time is of the essence!"

Her father stared in frozen silence. The implication had already been made that he knew the location of such an establishment and who ran it. His mind would have been churning with all sorts of insecurities about what Mrs. Macrae must have been thinking of him, not to mention several doubts as to what, exactly, Irene knew about his connection.

"Hutchins!" Irene called in exasperation. She did not want to involve him, but she hoped her father might be shamed into compliance.

The butler hurried into the room with as much grace as he could muster at high speed.

"Yes, Miss Sangford?"

"I will need a footman to help me to the Macrae carriage. If we have to visit every brothel in Munro to find Madame Dubois, so be it. But…" She threw a stern glare at her father. "If Mr. Macrae is harmed because we did not reach him in time, I will never, ever, *ever* forgive you."

"I know where she is," said Hutchins unexpectedly.

"You do?" Irene hoped she sounded convincingly surprised. "I would be grateful for an address, Hutchins."

He provided it at once and was turning to leave when Mr. Sangford—having apparently gathered himself—called out, "There is no need to fetch a footman, Hutchins. I will accompany Mrs. Macrae myself. And when I get back, you and I will discuss how it is that the head of my staff has knowledge of such places."

Irene turned on her father with quiet fury. "You leave Hutchins alone, Father. He has been nothing but loyal to this family. I will not see him punished for sharing private knowledge he could have kept to himself but offered up instead to help find Mr. Macrae. As for you going in my place, that is out of the question. Since you say you do not know Madame Dubois, I am the only one who can introduce Mrs. Macrae to her and vouch for her. Otherwise, Madame Dubois might be loath to divulge any information she has. As to why *I* know her, well that is a conversation for another day. Perhaps at dinner with the Macraes?"

If a sense of horror could have been personified, then the pale, stupefied face and half-step back of Mr. Sangford would have served the image well.

"There is no need…." He stopped and shook himself a little as if to steady his thoughts. "I will accompany you regardless. Two women of quality should not go unattended into such an establishment."

Oh, well done, Father, thought Irene. *You have managed to claim a heroic role for yourself. But I see you. I see your fear at what I might know. And you think that being present when my mother and I meet today will give you a clue. But I will give you no quarter. Not when you have chosen your own reputation over helping Mr. Macrae. I have yet to decide how much I hate you. But you no longer have even the remnant of my love.*

"That is very kind of you, Mr. Sangford," said Mrs. Macrae a little uncertainly. The unhappy dynamic between father and daughter was not subtle. But she did not have the luxury of questioning where her help was coming from. Nor, Irene imagined, did she care, as long as help came quickly and her son was found unharmed.

Irene reached for her crutches, pulling herself up and shuffling the supports in under her arms. She swing-stepped with the broken leg lifted away from the floor. Mrs. Macrae hovered anxiously beside her, while Irene's father hung back, no doubt aware his assistance was not wanted.

At the top of the front steps, Hutchins took the crutches from Irene while a footman lifted and carried her into the waiting carriage. The walking aids were passed to the Macraes' footman, who slid them in under his seat before helping his mistress up the carriage step and into the compartment, where she took up the open seat opposite Irene. Mr. Sangford sat next to his daughter, who did not acknowledge him at all.

Hutchins gave the address to the driver and stepped back. The mood being tense, and the Macrae servants being aware of the urgency of the matter, they set off at once at the highest speed that could be managed safely along the crowded streets of Munro. The deeper into town they got, however, the more the traffic slowed.

"This is bad even for our busy high street," said Mrs. Macrae, looking out the window anxiously when the carriage barely moved at all. "And the people look upset about something." She sat back and directed her focus at Irene's father. "You don't think we're heading into the midst of a riot, do you?"

"No, madam, I do not," Mr. Sangford said with far too much certainty for Irene's liking.

Lowering the glass pane, Irene called to a nearby street urchin, who rushed over at the prospect of a coin to be earned. "What's happening?" she asked. "Is there trouble brewing?"

"No, miss. Trouble's been and gone."

"Explain."

"Big crowd came through at dawn. 'Undreds of men. King's Own Dragoons were waiting for 'em. There was a right tousle. Many of 'em scattered, but I'd say at least fifty were grabbed an' dragged off. Heard someone say they'll be 'anged for treason. Got a lot of angry wives and mums 'ere, wiv a protest of their own. That's all I know." He paused, then cocked his head. "Got a tuppence for me? 'Aven't 'ad me breakfast yet. Nor supper before that."

Mrs. Macrae poked around in her reticule for her pin money, drawing out a sixpence and handing it to the boy. His eyes lit up and he ran off at once, weaving between the throng of bystanders while the Macrae coach could scarcely move an inch.

"Take us down a side road as soon as you are able," called Mrs. Macrae to the driver. "We'll make more progress along the back streets."

"If you're sure, ma'am," said the driver.

"I'm sure," she replied. "Besides," she murmured to Irene, "I don't know how long it will be before this crowd decides to make an example of us. Can't really blame them. They have so little as it is. But to have a loved one dragged off, never to see them again, is a terrible thing to bear. And this coach represents the people who take things from them. Whether it truly applies to us or not."

Irene's father wisely said nothing, but Irene sensed guilt even in his silence.

At this point, the footman hopped down from the back of the carriage and began to walk in front of the horses, firmly nudging people out of the way to create a space for the animals to squeeze through.

"Tell him to stop that!" Irene cried urgently. "This crowd is in no mood to be pushed around by a man in livery. They will trample him if..."

A brick of a fellow, built like a battering ram, blocked an arm that swung a broken bottle at the back of the unsuspecting footman's head. The jagged glass was wrenched from the assailant's grasp with so little effort, the wielder of the item widened his eyes at his own arm's ineffectiveness.

"You," said the brick-man to the footman, "get back up to your post." He leaned his head—perched on a neck so thick, it resembled the trunk of a tree—into the compartment and said, "You all right in there, Miss Sangford?"

"Er, yes," she answered. "Quite fine, thank you. May I ask...?"

"Best not to, miss. All you need to know is that Madame Dubois told me to watch out for you."

"Oh," Irene answered rather weakly. Madame Dubois had not exaggerated when she had described the sort of fellow who worked for her. "Er, thank you."

"You'll be wanting to turn here," he indicated, "and go past the tannery, then the butcher's. No one's there now. Half of Munro has been disrupted by the goings-on. Don't worry. I'll be around." And then that monstrous slab of muscle managed to disappear from view.

"You heard... the, er, *man*," Mrs. Macrae said to her driver. "Take it slow, but get us off the high street."

The driver didn't need to be told twice. Inch by inch, he drew the carriage away from the center of the road, the protestors grudgingly shifting. The occasional voice expressed recognition of whom the carriage belonged to. In most cases, the person would then make room more willingly.

Irene was impressed by the impact of the right sort of reputation. Her family could never hope to inspire such a response. The distinction they had sought for themselves would only engender animosity in a crowd like this. But the Macraes were famously welcoming to all, exactly the reason why the Sangfords had never attended their dances. The irony was not lost on her.

It seemed such a waste now. All those years of mixing with dull society that were deemed suitable. Dressing herself up, inside and out, as some desirable commodity deserving of superior attention. It meant nothing to her anymore. What she wouldn't give right now to have Mr. Macrae safely beside her, his kind, intelligent eyes focused on her, believing her worthy! *His* was the only approval she craved.

She pictured herself sitting with her hand in his, her head resting against his arm, his lips pressed gently against the crown of her head. In her mind, the world went about its business. But for them, time stood still. If Irene could have believed this were really possible, she would have given anything to claim it.

Instead, the carriage picked up speed, and Irene was reminded, with a nasty jolt of reality, that she did not even know where Mr. Macrae was, or whether he was safe, or, for that matter, alive.

This last thought brought a surge of nausea to her throat. The thought of never seeing him again—his perfect face, his tall, strong body, the heart that carried so much goodness—made her want to retch.

The carriage stopped so suddenly, Irene was almost sick involuntarily. She swallowed down the bile that had risen and fought the remnants of queasiness, hoping her skin had not acquired a greenish hue.

"This is the place, ma'am," called the driver, and sniffed. He would never have been called upon to bring his employers to such a place before. He was not some common hackney driver, that sniff declared.

The footman reappeared, no doubt happy to be alive and unscathed, to unfold the steps and lift Irene from the carriage. She grudgingly held on to her father's arm until the footman had brought her crutches. Then she led the way into the establishment as if she'd been there before. *That* would certainly make her father stop and think!

Brick-man was waiting in the doorway. Where had he materialized from? Irene could not fathom how such a giant of a man could move so silently and undetected. "The madam is waiting for you," he said, leading the way inside the brothel.

Madame Dubois rose quickly from behind the desk in her office as they entered the room.

Her mother.

The truth of it hit Irene differently this time. Already, Madame Dubois—Irene wished she knew her real name—had protected her with the ferocity of a mother tigress. And now, as they stood in her place of business, Irene could see the softening of the woman's face as she looked upon her daughter.

Irene likewise felt herself release some of the pain of her past. A sense of being loved, nay *cherished*, seeped into the crevices that had been hollowed out by rejection and disappointment.

Mother, she almost said, but she stopped herself in time. "Madame Dubois, forgive our intrusion and the company who has insisted on tagging along." She tilted her head at her father. "But we don't know who else might be able to help us. Mr. Macrae is missing, and we fear some misadventure has befallen him. We thought, with your special knowledge of many activities within Munro, you might have heard something or know whom to ask for information. Mrs. Macrae is obviously beside herself with worry."

Her mother scrunched a brief crease between her brows that told Irene how much that worry was shared by all. Then she snapped to attention and strode to the door. "Come in," she told whoever was standing there. Brick-man entered as silently as a cat, if a cat could ever be described as a small, moving building.

"You've been watching the Sangford house," she said rather than asked. "Did any suspicious characters appear as expected?"

"Sorry," said Irene's father, apparently still fully disconnected from the urgency of the matter at hand, "you were having our house watched?"

Madame Dubois nodded. "Irene… that is to say, Miss Sangford… had been threatened. I offered her protection."

Irene's father pointed an angry finger at her. "You have no authority over my family! She should have come to *me*. I am her father. I will see to her needs."

"If you had done so," said Madame Dubois through tight lips, "she would not have needed to come to me."

"Stop it, both of you!" If Irene could have stomped her foot, she would have. "We are wasting precious time." She turned to the watcher who had been assigned to protect her. "Did you see anyone or not?"

"I did. There was a man—medium height, lean build, scar through one eyebrow and eyes like a tortured animal—who came by several times. He hung about, sometimes for five minutes, sometimes an hour. I reckon he was keeping an eye out for you, Miss Sangford. But since he never crossed onto the property, I couldn't be sure. For all I knew, it was some fellow infatuated with one of the maids."

"That's the man from the park," said Irene grimly. "I'll never forget those eyes. He's the one who hurt Mr. Macrae before. Do you think he…?" Irene could not bring herself to finish the sentence.

"He hurt Macrae?" her father asked, his brows drawing together tightly.

"Took a heavy object to his skull," said the watcher. "Bad business."

"Why would he…?" But a furious glare from Irene shut her father up instantly.

"Lord Cranbourn!" she all but shouted. "*Your friend.* He ordered his man to do it as a warning."

"You know this?" Her father asked, his brow pleated with confusion.

"Yes, and much more besides. But none of that is relevant now." Irene turned to her mother. "Do you think Mr. Macrae might have crossed a line? Made them consider a warning no longer… sufficient?" She swallowed hard. She feared the answer, the question hanging in the air like the sword of Damocles.

"Me and the others," said the watcher to Madame Dubois, "we figured it might be worthwhile to follow that sinewy fellow, see if we could find out who he reports to. Then we could cut the head off the snake, so to speak."

"And did you?" his employer asked him.

"He went to Shelby's quite a few times. Used the servants' entrance. We couldn't follow him inside, but he either works there, meets someone there on the regular, or both."

"Anything else?"

"Trailed him to a farm once. Run by a man named Harrison. Several men were gathering there. Looked like some kind of meeting in the barn. But no one looked like they were in charge. Just a bunch of village folk who wanted to air their grievances. You know, the sort of crowd that would make politicians nervous."

"He could have been meeting his master at Shelby's," Irene suggested.

"But we can't confront anybody there," said Mrs. Macrae. "It's a gentleman's club. They won't allow us in."

"What about your husband?" Irene asked Mrs. Macrae.

"He's away on business. And just as well. Gentle-spirited though he is, he'd be stringing men up by their thumbs to make them talk if he were here."

"*You* could go," Madame Dubois said pointedly to Irene's father.

To Irene's chagrin, he shook his head.

"What possible reason could you have not to help the Macraes?" she demanded.

"I've withdrawn my membership," he said. "Too few real gentlemen to interact with," he offered as excuse.

It sounded like the sort of patronizing comment he might have been expected to make. But Irene wondered if there weren't more to it. Had he had a falling-out with Cranbourn? How involved was he in their dealings? Or was that a thing of the past?

There wasn't time to ponder this now, but if Mr. Macrae

returned safely, she would definitely be sharing this little detail about her father with him.

"What about the farm?" asked Mrs. Macrae. "If there was an uprising in the early hours, maybe they met there beforehand to organize themselves? It would be just the sort of thing Nathaniel would look into. Maybe he even followed this man like you did," she told the watcher.

"Why would your son involve himself in this business?" Mr. Sangford wanted to know.

"To protect your daughter," Madame Dubois said quickly. "He knew she was in danger from his assailant. Perhaps, like my men, he believed he could put a stop to it, once and for all."

"This seems as likely a place to start looking as any," said Irene. "Unless anybody else can think of another suggestion."

"Take two of my men," instructed Madame Dubois. "They might come in handy."

"We should take the ladies home first," said Irene's father. "This is not a suitable situation to put them in."

"Absolutely not!" cried Irene. "We will only be wild with worry if you leave us behind."

"And *I* would worry if you entered a dangerous situation," her father countered.

Irene hesitated. She knew her father cared for her in his own way, but she didn't have patience for his needs at the moment. "You'll just have to trust that these gentlemen can handle it," she said. "They've kept me safe thus far."

"But we don't know what we're walking into." He must have seen the stubborn set to her jaw, because he tried a different tack. "Besides, there isn't space in the carriage for us all."

"Oh, I think we'll manage. The footman can ride up front with the driver. This gentleman here can ride with us, if Mrs. Macrae will allow it, and the other fellow can ride in the footman's place. All nice and snug. See?"

"Fetch another of the men and get going," Madame Dubois told Brick-man before Irene's father had recovered from his most recent defeat. "And make sure you keep Miss Sangford safe. She is as much at risk as Mr. Macrae. If she is harmed, I'll have your guts for garters."

Irene did not question how her mother would exact this punishment. She only knew that the woman was not to be trifled with, especially, it seemed, where Irene was concerned. This knowledge offered her a strange sense of pride, a feeling of belonging where she was valued. It gave her a small degree of comfort as she worried for Mr. Macrae.

Hobbling out on her crutches, Irene was grateful not to be bound to the chair, even though she cherished its association with her handsome benefactor. Her independence was slowly returning. And if—no, *when*—Mr. Macrae was safely restored to them, she could be of greater use to him. She no longer linked her worth to marriage, but to having a better purpose. And what could be nobler than to help Mr. Macrae with his cases? She could not imagine a world without Nathaniel Macrae at the center of it. She would accept whatever form that was allowed to take.

As they all squeezed into their positions in and on the car-riage—Irene beside Mrs. Macrae and her father almost engulfed by Madame Dubois's man—a prayer rose up, unbidden, within her. She would happily give up everything—her father's name, the security of his home, her place in society—if only Mr. Macrae could be found and rescued. She repeated this pledge like a mantra as they made their way along the outskirts of Munro and edged into the countryside where the farmland began. She called to Mr. Macrae with her heart. *I am coming. Hang on.*

They turned into the long, dirt road that wound toward the farm buildings, trees stretching on either side of them, but not a soul to be seen. All appeared calm, even idyllic.

Until the morning stillness was broken as a sound like a gun-shot rang through the air. Somewhere, close by, a horse whinnied. Another bang. Then silence descended once more.

CHAPTER TWENTY-ONE

NATHANIEL SAT BOLT upright. He felt his chest. No bullet wound. Now that his brain had caught up with his pounding heart, he realized he felt no pain at all. In fact, he was still quite alone in the barn.

A very insistent whinny sounded through the slats. Another gunshot. Only, this time, Nathaniel realized it was no gunshot at all.

He rushed across to the locked door.

"Archer?" An answering nicker confirmed his guess.

"Archer, you got loose! You clever boy! How'd you find me, hey?"

The horse pawed the ground and blew out a bass-pitched, rumbling breath.

"Followed my scent, did you? Now, how are you with doors? Feel like kicking the lock off for me? You've certainly got a powerful hind leg. It nearly frightened the life out of me."

When no response followed, Nathaniel sighed. "I suppose you're hungry. Me too. I wouldn't mind having a good breakfast if it's going to be my last."

An amicable silence hung between them. Nathaniel slipped his fingertips between the slats and Archer snuffled at them with whiskery lips. It was difficult to comfort his horse when he was on the other side of the barn wall.

"Hang on," Nathaniel cried as realization hit him squarely between the eyes. "You're loose! Go *home*, Archer. Go get breakfast. If you arrive at the stables alone, Mother will think I've had a fall and come looking for me. And then she'll... Oh." His heart sank. "She'll have no idea where to even start." He pulled his fingers back and shoved them through his unbrushed hair, bits of straw falling to the ground as he did so. "Well, this is a fine mess I've gotten myself into."

If only he had something to write with. Something to use that might give his mother a clue as to where to find him.

His belly rumbled uncomfortably.

The hunger must have affected him more than he'd thought because Nathaniel could have sworn that, above the groans of his empty stomach, he was hearing the sound of carriage wheels. But that couldn't have been. Cranbourn wouldn't come in person. It would be too dangerous to implicate himself in any of the dirty work. No, it must have been a hallucination conjured up by his hungry belly and hopeful mind.

The tread of heavy wooden wheels grew louder. Nathaniel peered with one eye through the slats. There *was* a carriage! And it was getting closer. In fact, it had turned off the path to the farmer's cottage and was heading straight for the barn!

With a leaping heart, he recognized the driver and footman.

"I'm here!" he shouted, squeezing as much of his fingers through the gaps in the wall to wiggle at whoever might have been looking for him.

The vehicle pulled up right outside the door and emptied itself of a surprising number and variety of people, including—he could scarce believe it—Miss Sangford, who was calling for crutches and then driving herself forward at an impressive pace to keep up with his mother and... Mr. Sangford? The two burly bodyguards he already knew. He was almost surprised not to see Madame Dubois riding up on horseback like Joan of Arc. It certainly was a spectacle, even without that added image.

"Archer!" cried his mother. "Where is Nathaniel?"

"I'm here!" he shouted again. "Inside the barn. They locked me in here last night. Richards was coming back this morning once he had his orders."

"Is Richards the man who attacked you?" asked one of Dubois's men.

"Yes. And I expect him back any minute to kill me."

"You don't think they'd go that far, do you?" Mr. Sangford's voice wavered, though Nathaniel could not make out whether the hesitation indicated fear or concern.

"Let's just get him out of there," Miss Sangford urged. "We can discuss the details later. Richards might not come alone. And he will be armed."

Madame Dubois's man smiled and pulled back one side of his coat to reveal a pistol holstered in his belt. "Don't worry, miss. We've got that covered."

His partner reappeared, carrying a large hammer that nevertheless looked a little lost in his massive hands. "Stand back," he ordered.

Everyone, including Nathaniel, shuffled away from the door. The footman led Archer toward the carriage horses, which soothed the animal's restlessness somewhat.

With the space around the door cleared, the bodyguard hefted the hammer and swung a mighty blow at the lock. It made no pretense at fighting back but dropped from the door in submission to his strength. He slid the bolt back.

Nathaniel waited with as much self-control as he could muster for the man to remove his bulk from the doorway. Despite the spaciousness of the empty barn, the sensation of being locked in had been a deeply unpleasant one, and Nathaniel was eager to be out in the open air again.

He had barely taken his first step into the morning sun when his mother rushed forward and embraced him tightly. "You gave us such a scare! I thought I'd lost you." She gave a little sniffle. Stepping back quickly to dab at her nose with her handkerchief she turned to the only other lady present. "If it hadn't been for

Miss Sangford, I don't think we would have found you in time. Or perhaps ever." The sniffle became a sob and Nathaniel threw his arms around his mother, comforting her with his very-much-alive presence.

Over her shaking shoulders, he mouthed a silent *"Thank you"* to the woman to whom he owed his life. It might have been Madame Dubois's men who had brought their particular skills, but they would not have been here without Miss Sangford fetching them. The fact that her father was here also meant that she would have had to reveal at least a portion of her secret knowledge in front of him. She had paid a personal price to find him, and Nathaniel could never properly repay her. Not for his life, which she had saved, and not for the gift she had given his mother in rescuing him.

Whatever Lord Howell had once accused her of, Miss Sangford was no longer that same person. Her selflessness of character was more than equal to her elegant beauty. As she stood, calmly holding the space between them, Nathaniel knew that he loved her. He didn't want to fight it anymore. With his mother still held gently against his breast, he held out a hand to his heroine.

Miss Sangford's mouth opened. Her cheeks flushed. She stepped forward hesitantly, balanced carefully, and reached out her hand to his.

Nathaniel folded her knuckles to his lips and pressed upon them gratitude and relief and shameless affection. And the self-control that must have been holding her together gave way completely. She took his hand in both of hers and held it to her brow, deep, shuddering breaths escaping her usually restrained form.

His mother, even in the midst of her own strong feeling, recognized what was happening and drew Miss Sangford into the embrace between Nathaniel and herself. The crutches toppled to the ground, and Miss Sangford was compelled to lean her full weight against Nathaniel's shoulder.

A calm descended into Nathaniel's being. In this moment, all was right with the world.

"Ahem." Mr. Sangford coughed into his hand. "I don't wish to undermine the obvious happiness we all must feel at the fact that Mr. Macrae is alive and well. However, I believe there was mention of this man Richards coming to finish what he started. Since we do not know whether he will come alone, and whom he is willing to harm to preserve his own freedom, I suggest we take ourselves away from this place. I am sure Mr. Macrae would appreciate a hot bath and good breakfast. The rest can be dealt with in due course."

It was sound advice, and true, but Nathaniel couldn't help resenting Mr. Sangford in that instant. He grudgingly released Miss Sangford, who kept her eyes cast down until his mother collected her crutches and guided her back to the carriage with these words, "You must come to tea this afternoon, Miss Sangford. No need for a chaperone, unless you wish to bring your lady's maid for the ride over, as I will be present. I feel compelled to thank you properly. You will do this for me, won't you? Please?"

Miss Sangford nodded silently, but a shy smile transformed her usually regal expression. Nathaniel noticed that she was cupping one of her hands to her breast. The hand he had kissed. A smile of his own pulled his lips into a pout, which he hoped his mother did not see, as she was already plotting. For the first time, he did not mind.

"Are we to return these borrowed men to Madame Dubois?" Mr. Sangford asked of his daughter.

"We'll hang about your street a while longer, if it's all the same to you," said one. "Just until this Richards fellow is apprehended."

The recue party began to clamber back onto and inside the carriage.

"I'll be with you shortly," said Nathaniel. "I want to collect my hat and coat where I left them in the woods last night. Hopefully, the rain has not completely ruined them."

"We are not leaving without you," his mother said firmly. "No one is moving until you are alongside the carriage."

"Very well." Nathaniel would have tipped his hat to the driver, but that item was still waiting on the bough of a tree. Or so he hoped.

Leaping up onto Archer's back, Nathaniel hastened toward where he remembered leaving his horse the night before. It took a few minutes to locate the spot because none of the trees contained his belongings. Instead, he found them in a sad puddle at the base of a trunk. He dismounted and scooped up his coat, wringing it out as best he could before laying its bedraggled shape over Archer's neck.

His hat had not fared as well. It was soggy and misshapen, almost past the point of being salvaged, but Nathaniel planned to try, anyway. He dumped the gloves and cravat, muddy as they were, inside the beaver-felt top hat and clambered back onto his horse, balancing his hat between his thighs while he shortened the reins for firmer control.

He was just about to exit the edge of the woodland when he spotted someone walking along the track toward the farm. The person had not yet rounded the corner where they would be able to see the buildings—with the carriage waiting in front of them.

It was unlikely to be Harrison. That fellow was built like a man who worked the earth for a living. Besides, Nathaniel was pretty certain he would be on horseback. No, this man's stride—if his hunched tramping could be called that—resembled the now-familiar movements of Richards.

Nathaniel—hat forgotten as it tumbled once more to the ground—spurred Archer forward at a gallop, racing in a long, leaping motion toward the as-yet-unsuspecting man.

The thudding of hooves must have alerted Richards, for he swung about and faced the oncoming rider. His mouth dropped open when he recognized Nathaniel. He drew his knife and readied himself for a fight. But Nathaniel drove Archer hard, pounding the earth so that clods of mud sprang up behind them.

The furious approach of horse and rider robbed Richards of his armed confidence, as it was intended to do, and he began to stumble backward, finally turning and running up the lane, shouting for Harrison and weaving to avoid being trampled.

Nathaniel bore down on him with Archer, though he had no intention of letting his horse step on the man, only because it risked Archer stumbling and injuring himself. No, he drove Richards forward, herding him, so that any second now, he would come face to face with a carriage-load of witnesses and then it would be easier to arrest him without being stabbed in the process.

Indeed, Richards came to a grinding halt as Madame Dubois's men stepped into the path, each raising a pistol in mute expectation of Richards's full cooperation.

Nathaniel slid from Archer's back, and—with immense satisfaction—claimed the knife from the would-be killer's unresisting fingers. "I'll take that, thank you." He threw the knife into the ground at the feet of one of the men, who swiftly took possession of it while keeping his eye on Richards. "Anyone got a piece of rope, or even a length of ribbon we could use to tie this wretch up?"

"Got some rope in the boot beneath my feet," said the driver, reaching down to dig it out from the storage area and throwing the coiled length to Nathaniel.

Richards, unsurprisingly, was not happy about the turn of events. He fought as Nathaniel tried to bind his hands, but one of the bodyguards came forward and pinned his arms down so that no further struggle was possible.

"What do you want us to do with him?" asked the man holding the now-docile Richards.

"He needs to give evidence against his employer," said Nathaniel.

"Never going to happen," said Richards sulkily.

"We'll see about that. I imagine you won't want to be going to prison alone. Especially not if it's a gentleman you'll be allowing to escape justice."

"Won't they know he's not done the job, especially if it's you bringing the man in?" asked the bodyguard. "They might have a backup plan, if you catch my meaning."

"Hmm." Nathaniel rubbed his hand across his stubbled jaw. "That's a fair point. Then again, there's Harrison. I reckon he'd sing like a canary if we offer him a lesser punishment. He'd no doubt prefer a transport ship to the noose. They need farmers in the new territory of Terra Australis."

"Where is Harrison now?" he demanded of Richards.

Silence.

The carriage door swung open, and a gentleman descended the steps. Mr. Sangford strode across the grass and halted in front of the immobilized Richards.

"So, you're the man who threatened my daughter?"

"I don't know what you're talking about. Who are you?"

"I am Albert Sangford. And you have made my daughter's life a prison for the past month."

"Only following orders. And you know all about those. Don't you, Mr. Sangford?"

"I would never give an order for you to hurt my family!"

"But you might not care so much for a man by the name of Bill."

"Are you trying to implicate me in your master's sordid schemes?"

"If the shoe fits…"

"You know it jolly well doesn't!"

"I wouldn't know about that. My employer mentioned your name several times…"

"He can name me as much as he wants! That doesn't mean my dealings with whoever he is—if there even *were* any dealings—would have been anything more than simple business. You can't throw around insinuations and hope that I will buckle, Mr. Richards. I know who I am and what I stand for. And murder is not to my taste."

Richards shrugged. "That is not for me to say. But if you want your family safe, you should arrange that with my employer. I am not his only worker bee."

Mr. Sangford's eyes narrowed. "Are you threatening me?"

Richards grinned. "How can I harm you when I am in the custody of this fine…" He paused as he summed up the stature of his captor. "Barn of a man?" he finished.

Mr. Sangford leaned in toward the captive. "I warn you," he snarled, "if my family is endangered in any way…'"

"Nah, see," said Richards casually, "I never figured you for much of a family man. I reckon you're just trying to clear your name in front of these witnesses here. If I was you, I would…"

The flow of his words ended in a gurgle as Mr. Sangford wrapped his hands tightly about his neck. It was a short-lived attack, for the bodyguard holding on to Richards simply freed one arm and used it to pull Sangford and Richards apart. Both were panting, one for air, the other with rage.

"You tell them!" Sangford all but screamed. "You tell them it wasn't my idea!"

"That's not how I heard it," taunted Richards from the safe arms-length distance provided by his captor.

"It wasn't my idea," repeated Mr. Sangford to his small audience, his eyes wide with desperation. "You've got to believe me!"

"Mr. Sangford," Nathaniel asked, "do you know who Richards's employer is?"

"Of course not." But Sangford's tone had quietened, and Nathaniel couldn't help wondering how much Albert Sangford was hiding from them.

"If you know anything, it is better you tell us now. We will soon have his name and evidence against him."

"Irene implied it might be Cranbourn," mumbled Mr. Sangford.

"And *is* it the baron?"

"How should I know?"

"Sir," Nathaniel said with some frustration, "you do realize that if you are guilty in any way, it will ruin your family. But if you were forced to cooperate, well... a case may be made to exonerate you."

"It will be his word against mine," said Sangford, his mood thoroughly low now. "Who would believe me over a man of title, especially if his friends back him up?"

"Do you mean Pratt and Bligh?" Nathaniel inquired.

Mr. Sangford's face blanched. "So, you know."

"I know enough. If you tell me everything, I can help you."

"Nothing's going to help him," said Richards suddenly, "and he knows it."

"Be quiet, you," said Dubois's man.

"He's right," said Sangford miserably. "I cannot protect my family if I speak up."

"And what of the family of Bill O'Neal?" demanded Nathaniel. "Or anyone else who gets in their way? What about all those men who will hang for treason because Richards here convinced them to take up arms and bring down the Crown's wrath upon simple folk? It won't end here, either. The next time they want to manipulate a situation in their favor, they might come knocking on your door again. And you won't be able to say 'no' because you fear for your family. The best way to end this is for them to pay for their crimes."

Mr. Sangford said nothing. He appeared to be considering Nathaniel's words. He looked back at the carriage where his daughter sat, likely under strict instructions to stay safely out of sight.

He seemed to have made up his mind because his roving eyes focused and he straightened up with a deep sigh.

"Lend me your horse," he said to Nathaniel.

"What do you want to do?" Nathaniel asked, taken aback.

"I want to fetch something at home that will resolve this issue once and for all."

"Evidence?"

"I need to do this before Cranbourn finds out you have his

man. He mustn't have any warning."

Something felt off to Nathaniel, but he couldn't put his finger on it.

"My mother would happily have her driver take you home," he countered.

"The coach is already too full. Somebody would have to stay behind if you are taking this man in." He indicated with his chin toward Richards. "And I'd rather not have a murderous criminal on the same coach as your mother and my daughter. If I go, I can sound the alarm and send my own coach to transport you and Richards and Madame Dubois's men. Meanwhile, Mrs. Macrae can take Irene home with her. I'm sure they would be a comfort to each other. It has been quite the morning."

Nathaniel could not fault Mr. Sangford's reasoning, but his scalp prickled a warning he could not ignore. "I could just as easily fetch the constables myself. Cranbourn would have no warning."

Sangford shook his head. "You underestimate him. I will not have him harm my family to try to ensure my silence. The sight of you will be all the warning he needs. You must allow me the upper hand. I have to catch him off-guard, before he has a chance to make plans." When Nathaniel hesitated, Mr. Sangford quickly added, "I was under the impression you cared for my daughter. Will you not let me protect her?"

When he put it like that, Nathaniel knew he had no argument against the man. "Here," he said, handing the reins to Sangford, "You will have no trouble with Archer. I only ask that he be given food and rest at your stables. It's been a long night for him."

"Gladly," said Mr. Sangford, swinging himself hurriedly into Archer's saddle. "I will send my coach to fetch you. You will have to allow some time for it to be readied and then to reach you. I suggest you make yourselves comfortable in the barn. The wait could take an hour."

"A sound suggestion, sir," said Madame Dubois's man. He tightened his grip on Richards and began marching him toward the entrance of the barn, keeping his bulk between the criminal and the carriage so that Richards could not peer inside and make unsettling remarks at the women.

Nathaniel remained where he was, watching the figure of Mr. Sangford ride off on his horse. He could not shake the feeling that he had missed something. It bothered him that he had no answer to satisfy his misgivings.

He might have stood there for some time if not for Dubois's second man.

"Are you joining us in the barn, Mr. Macrae? If you want to sit in the carriage with the ladies, we can watch him just fine on our own."

"I've no doubt you can. And thank you. I think my mother will derive comfort from having her eyes firmly upon me after her terrible worry this morning."

"No problem at all," said the man, who strode toward the barn with legs resembling the thickness of a well-bred bull.

Nathaniel made his way toward the waiting carriage, its door still open from Mr. Sangford's departure. He would certainly like to offer his mother the relief of his presence. And, if in so doing, he also enjoyed the proximity of Miss Sangford… Ah, yes, the day would definitely be looking up.

CHAPTER TWENTY-TWO

SEVERAL HOURS LATER, Irene returned home and found the house in chaos. Servants were rushing about. Her travel chest was open in her upstairs room, and Finnegan was packing her lady's belongings at a furious pace.

"What on earth…?" she cried as the footman set her down on the edge of her bed, which was covered in garments. Irene could not tell if these dresses had been rejected in favor of others or whether these were the ones that had been selected to be packed.

"Mr. Sangford said to prepare for a lengthy stay, miss. I did my best without you here. I hope I chose right."

"Fetch Hutchins," Irene told the footman as he was about to leave. "At once!" To the flustered lady's maid, she said, "You can stop what you're doing, Finnegan. I am not going anywhere."

"But Mr. Sangford said…"

"My father does not decide for me whether I travel or not. To start with, my leg is in no condition to be jostled about on a long journey. And furthermore, I have not been informed of any such travel plans. I am of age and cannot be dragged off as if I were in some Gothic drama. Kindly return my things to where they belong."

Finnegan stood undecided. Irene's father employed her and could undo that arrangement at a moment's notice. But Irene was not someone to be trifled with. If she refused to leave, it was better to be on her side and stay where a lady's maid was needed.

"You heard me," said Irene when her maid hesitated. "I'm not leaving. Whatever my father has gotten into his head has nothing to do with me."

Finnegan began to hang up the dresses that lay strewn upon the bed. Perhaps she hoped to avoid actually unpacking anything until Irene's father had been consulted.

In the background, Irene heard Amelia wailing, "But, *Mother!*" The rest of the argument was muffled, except for a bitter cry of, "You think *I* want this?" It seemed to Irene that the two women were no more enamored with the sudden departure than she was. The sound of running feet and a hasty cry of "Coming, Mrs. Sangford!" told Irene that all the servants were on high alert. Her stepmother would take out any of the frustrations her husband had caused on the staff. For them, it would be a very long day, poor things.

Hutchins came puffing up the stairs from wherever he had been ordering the servants to complete their master's urgent instructions. Irene felt sorry for him. His position had once come with implied dignity. This was not the way a butler wanted to run the household.

"Miss Sangford," he said before stopping to catch his breath. "How may I be of service?"

"Oh, don't be obtuse, Hutchins," Irene answered irritably. "Tell me what madness had entered my father's head."

"I cannot speak for the master's thoughts," said the butler, "but I can repeat what instruction he has given me."

"Get on with it, then," Irene demanded.

"After you all left this morning for the…" He eyed Finnegan and cleared his throat. "The, er, lady you wished to visit, you were gone for some time."

"I know that, Hutchins. I was there."

"Yes, of course. But Mr. Sangford returned alone at about noon…"

"'*Noon*'? What was he doing all that time? He must have left us an hour before that. He should have been home long before."

"I think he may have been to the bank, miss, because the gentleman from Rothchild's came to see him just now, apparently 'as per earlier arrangement.'"

"And now we're packing? Where is it we're supposed to be going?"

"Abroad, miss. To the German Kingdom of Hanover. I understand you have relatives there."

"Well, yes, distant ones whom I have never met. And we're leaving today?"

"Er, within the hour, I believe. That is why Mr. Sangford sent for you to return from the Macraes. He is in a meeting at present. The plan is to leave as soon as he is done."

Irene's spine prickled. "With whom is he meeting?"

"Lord Cranbourn, Mr. Pratt, and Mr. Bligh. Possibly they will manage his financial interests while you are all away, being long-time associates."

Irene's veins turned to ice. "Hutchins, I want you to fetch the footman back. I need to go downstairs. And tell him to have my crutches waiting when I get there. Be quick about it!"

"Miss?"

"Do it, Hutchins. Do it *now!*"

Hutchins hesitated for but the briefest second before Irene's command prodded him into action. He spun around on his heel and marched quickly out the door.

Irene turned to Finnegan and waved her hand at the clutter of the room in its state of mid-pack. "I have an urgent matter to attend to," she said. "But I want this sorted before I get back."

Finnegan bowed her head obediently, but Irene could tell the situation caused her lady's maid considerable distress.

You don't understand the half of it, thought Irene grimly.

Within a few short minutes, Irene had been transported downstairs and stood balanced on her crutches outside her father's study. She knocked loudly. Conversation within paused, but no one came to open the door. Irene tried the handle. It was locked. She knocked again. "Father," she called.

"Not now, Irene," came a muffled answer through the door.

She banged with her fist. "Father, I must speak with you!"

"I said, '*Not now!*'" came the agitated answer.

Irene was about to pound once more upon the frustratingly closed door, when a voice behind her made her jolt with shock.

"What is this nonsense I hear that you are staying?" Her stepmother demanded to know.

Irene shuffled around to face the irate woman. "Why would I leave?" she replied, in no mood to be dealing with her.

"Because your father has decided it. You can hardly stay here by yourself."

"I don't see why not. I would have Finnegan to tend to me. And Hutchins will run things. Unless the entire household is going with you."

"All of this is being done *for you*, you foolish girl! He would ruin us to protect you."

"What do you mean? How is this trip going to ruin us?"

Her stepmother merely shook her head. "He should have left you with your mother all those years ago." The hatred lay shallow in the older woman's eyes.

"Ah," said Irene with some satisfaction, "honesty at last."

Mrs. Sangford's lips twisted into a sneer. "Your father said you had probably learned some of the truth, if not all. I am glad of it. The pretense all these years has been a thorn in my side. As have you."

"Then again," said Irene, her eyes latched on to her stepmother's with some ferocity, "how much pretense has there really been? You have always treated me as a lesser daughter."

"Was it not enough that I treated you as a daughter at all?"

"You had a choice. I did not."

"Did I? Then you have underestimated your father's role in how it happened."

Irene was taken aback. "What do you mean? When, exactly, did you learn of my existence? He must have told you immediately, if I was to be passed off as your daughter."

"You do not give him enough credit. He plans everything to flow with his will."

Irene's legs grew weak. Had no one been spared in the unhappiness of her existence? "I need to sit down," she announced, a little shakily. She half-swung, half-lurched into the library and lowered herself into a deep-seated, upholstered chair.

Mrs. Sangford stood in the doorway. "I don't have time for this. There is much to be done."

Irene lifted her head, heavy with churning thoughts. "You're not coming back to Munro, are you?"

"No. *We* aren't."

"Then tell me. You owe me that much. I need to know how I came to live with him and not my mother."

"He can tell you everything on the way to the docks. We can't miss the boat."

"I'm not leaving."

Mrs. Sangford's sudden movement made Irene flinch. Her stepmother bore down on her, finger wagging. "You selfish, ungrateful child!" she cried. "For you, he will uproot his whole life, *our* lives, and you will say 'no'?"

"If he is running from something, I want no part of it."

"But you are at the very heart of it." Mrs. Sangford flailed an arm. "If not for you, and his desire to keep you safe, none of this would be necessary."

"If my father is running from something, it is of his own making," Irene replied coolly.

"That may be so, but he will not abandon you, even now when he believes you know his secrets."

Irene's jaw clenched. "Do not make him out to be some sort of saint. He used my mother and abandoned her. I was only acquired as a pawn to gain that precious connection to a title he has craved his whole life. And now, if I am to understand you, he married *you* to create a fiction within which I could be bartered without shame. It was a home without love." Irene shook her head slowly. "He used us all. And you would have me be grateful." A wry laugh punctuated her breath. "I think not."

"I have made my peace," Mrs. Sangford said, her voice low.

"Then you won't mind telling me how it came to be that you raised me." Irene pressed her. "After today, you will never have to see me again. But you owe me that much."

"'Owe' you?" Her stepmother laughed. "I have sacrificed enough."

Irene grew quiet. "It could have been different," she said softly. "You could have taken pity on me. I was only a baby. If you had found a way to love me…"

"'Love' you?" the woman spat out the words. "When I realized he had only married me to claim you? Oh, your father was clever. He took himself abroad when it all went awry with your mother. He actively searched for someone who was on holiday there, who would know nothing of his dalliance with the marquess's daughter. I was swept off my feet. And, when he asked for my hand, I agreed immediately. We were married within the month, under an Italian sky. I thought it all so romantic. Then he bundled me back to England, to a private cottage, where we lived like eloped lovers. I thought he was so in love with me that he wanted me all to himself. But he was waiting for you to be born. And when you were, we returned to Munro with 'our' daughter. It was the first I knew of you. And I had no power to reject what he had arranged."

Irene had no words. And yet something had to be said. "I'm sorry," she offered weakly. For what else was there? She understood now. They had never been given a chance. They were all merely puppets while her father pulled the strings.

And yet he wanted to protect her. That was what he had said. Did he really love her, then, after all? Was it mixed in so well with everything else that he could no longer separate affection and manipulation?

The door of the study opened. Pratt and Bligh exited, passing the doorway of the library as they went. Their faces were ashen, their shoulders cowed. They caught sight of Irene and her stepmother and hurried faster, as if afraid that being seen would extract a heavy price.

The study door snapped shut.

Voices rose within the closed room. A shout. The sudden blast of gunfire. A sharp cry. A pause. A thud.

And the entire household descended upon the scene.

CHAPTER TWENTY-THREE

"MOVE ASIDE!" IRENE shouted, her voice pitched high. She tried to push through the press of servants who had gathered more quickly than she could move. Her heart thudded in her ears, fear driving her to shout again. "Move, I said!"

The staff began to shuffle and make room for her as their own shock was overridden by the forcefulness of her command.

Everyone froze when the study door opened cautiously and Irene's father stepped out, shutting the door behind him. He frowned at the assembly waiting for him.

"What are you all doing here? You should be packing."

"We heard what sounded like a shot being fired, sir," said Hutchins.

"Oh, that," Mr. Sangford said with remarkable composure. "I was loading my pistol for the journey. You never know what you'll have to deal with when you travel, especially in unfamiliar territories. It misfired. Nothing to worry about."

"I heard a thud," Irene pointed out.

"Er… I had a bit of a shock and dropped the weapon. That is all it was."

"And Lord Cranbourn. Is he all right?"

"Cranbourn?" The frown returned and deepened. "The meeting is over. They have all left."

That didn't sound right to Irene. She had not seen the baron leave with the other two gentlemen. Was it possible she had missed him? Maybe when she'd had her back to the doorway? She was sure she had not heard the study door open and close except when Messrs. Pratt and Blight had left. But she had been upset. She could not be sure of anything.

There was one way to find out.

"Can I talk to you now, Father? In private?" She made to enter the study.

"We don't have time for this," he said sternly. "We are leaving in a matter of minutes. In fact," he said to the assembled staff, "why are you standing around? It's time to load up the coach. Whatever isn't packed already must remain behind."

"But, Father," wailed Amelia, who had come to stand beside her mother now that the servants were no longer crowding the corridor, "I can't possibly leave all those dresses! Some of them have only just been made and I haven't even had a chance to wear them yet!"

Mr. Sangford ignored her. Instead, he turned to his wife and said quietly, so that the departing servants did not overhear, "Make sure to take all the jewels, and anything of value that is small enough to fit in a valise. Quickly now, Dorothea. Our time here is done."

Mrs. Sangford nodded, but Amelia, who had heard the instruction, pointed accusingly at Irene.

"Why does *she* get to just stand there? Why aren't you chasing *her* to pack her things?"

Mrs. Sangford grabbed her roughly by the arm, an action that provoked a loud *"ow"* as Amelia shook herself free. She looked at her mother as if she had sprouted horns. "You *hurt* me!" came the indignant claim.

Amelia turned to her father for support, but his stern glare caused her ire to wilt. When her mother once again took her by the arm—rather more sedately this time—she allowed herself to be led meekly, a sight Irene thought she would carry with her for the rest of her life.

Alone in the passage, Mr. Sangford looked upon his eldest daughter, who stood as resolute as she could while hunched over her crutches for support.

"I suppose we should get Cedric to help you into the carriage. I am sorry for the rush. I trust Finnegan has packed all you need."

"Why *is* there such a rush, Father? You have mentioned nothing of this journey before."

He smiled unconvincingly. "I thought it would be good to get away for a while, shake off all this nonsense with Cranbourn and Richards. I would prefer an environment where you can feel safe until Cranbourn is tried and found guilty."

"And then we will return?"

"Of course!"

Irene cocked her head and gave him a sidelong glance. "Why would you lie to me about this, Father?"

"I am not lying!"

Irene would have crossed her arms defiantly if she did not have to cling to the bothersome crutches. "You have lied to me my whole life. This would be no different. Your wife at least has had the good grace to spare me any further deception."

Her father opened his mouth and closed it again. His gaze flicked toward his study.

Irene narrowed her eyes. "Why did you meet with these men today if you knew them to be involved in criminal acts?"

Mr. Sangford straightened up and tugged at his lapels. "I wanted to give Pratt and Bligh an opportunity to confess, as they were only accomplices. It was Cranbourn whose thoughts had turned to violence."

"And you know all this because…"

Her father sighed. "You want the truth? Very well, you shall have it. For all the good it will do," he muttered.

He paused. Irene waited, wishing she could tap her foot at him to hurry up.

"It was *my* idea to disrupt the protests," he said matter-of-factly. He shrugged. "A mere counteroffensive. I was only trying to protect our investments. I intended no harm to come to anyone." His eyes darkened. "*That* was Cranbourn's contribution. And once he started down that path, I wanted nothing more to do with any of it."

"Why did you not report his plans to the constabulary?"

"It was too late. I was connected to the plot and everything that followed. Not only that, but Cranbourn threatened you, even your sister and your mother, if I did not cooperate."

"Stepmother," corrected Irene.

Her father paused. "Yes." He sighed. "Stepmother. Though she has been a mother to you all these years."

Irene opened her mouth to refute the accuracy of this statement, but he was already continuing his defense.

"I agreed to keep quiet but refrained from meeting with them any further. I did not want to have blood on my hands."

"But you *have*, Father," Irene told him bluntly. "You know the sort of man Cranbourn is, what he is capable of. By saying nothing, you allowed everything to happen as he arranged it. Innocent men are going to the gallows."

"But not me."

The appalling selfishness of the statement shook Irene to her very core.

She sucked in her breath and puffed it out in a wry laugh "That's what this is really about, isn't it? Everything else is just for show. It's the same with all you have ever done. You care so much what people think of you. You abandoned my mother because she could not give you the life you wanted. Then you kept me for yourself, robbing me of my mother, so that you could have another chance to enter that world again by pawning Amelia and me on the marriage market. Titled men only, isn't it, Father? Whatever it takes to give you more status and power and wealth. *Good grief*, you were even willing to abandon Mr. Macrae to his fate rather than to admit you knew the owner of a brothel! And now you flee the country to escape your consequences once again."

Mr. Sangford sneered. "Would you rather see me hang?"

"For trying to end the unrest? They would probably elect you to Parliament!"

"You forget. They will associate me with Cranbourn and his crimes."

"A good barrister could acquit you of such implications."

"It is too great a risk."

Once more, his eyes were diverted to the door of his study.

Something wasn't right. Irene felt it in her belly. And her father would never tell her the whole truth. He just didn't have it in him.

Before he could have time to react, Irene tightened her hold on one of her crutches and grasped the door handle with the other hand, twisting it and throwing the door open in one deft motion.

Nothing could have prepared her for the scene that met her startled eyes.

Cranbourn lay on the ground, his body sprawled unnaturally. Edges of pooled blood seeped from beneath his torso into the thick, woolen carpet. His hand was wrapped loosely around her father's letter opener, which was firmly planted in his belly at an upward angle, his fingers having released the murder weapon as strength waned with death.

"What have you done?" Irene barely had the breath to utter these words. The shock of seeing a body had knocked the wind clean out of her.

"He tried to shoot me. I was defending myself." Her father's voice was unemotional, as if this statement were enough to explain the horror of the act and the evidence he had intended to simply leave behind.

"You lied," said Irene. She shook her head. "I don't know why that surprises me."

"What did you want me to say? Nobody would have believed me." He reached out a hand and beckoned with curled fingers. "Come away now. We will close the door. It is time to go. There is nothing to be done here."

"'Nothing to be...'" The words trailed away as Irene's sight fell upon the pistol on her father's desk."

"That is your pistol."

"What of it?"

"Why would Lord Cranbourn try to shoot you with your own pistol?"

"I had it out to protect myself. I knew he'd be angry when Pratt and Bligh signed those confessions implicating him."

"Or you had it in your hand already," said Irene slowly, as the cogs turned in her mind. "You were forcing them to sign."

"They may have needed a little persuasion." His voice was cool. As though it didn't matter.

Her eyes followed the line of fire. No broken window. No scuff mark on the wall behind the desk where her father would have been standing. Her gaze lifted. There, in the ceiling, sat the bullet hole with the bullet imbedded within it.

With the slow speech of one thinking aloud, Irene reasoned, "If he had grabbed the pistol from you, and the shot went off in the air, no further shot following, you must have successfully wrenched the weapon free from him. Then why is he dead?"

"I told you." Her father sounded less certain now, as if the effort of making up the necessary lies were catching up with him. "He was wrestling with me for my pistol. I couldn't get it from him, so I lunged at him with my letter opener."

"You could have stabbed him in the arm. He would have dropped the weapon."

"It happened too fast."

"I think," said Irene, as the terrible reality began to sink in, "that you *meant* to shoot him. And when he stopped you, you stabbed him. You thrust the blade up into his heart to be sure the wound was mortal."

Mr. Sangford looked much more uncertain now. He shifted his weight onto the other foot, his hands restless at his sides. "Why would I do that? Cranbourn was going to hang, anyway."

"You said it yourself," said Irene, clarity descending upon her as all the pieces slotted into place. "You were afraid of what he might say in court. You probably wanted him to sign a confession too. But he was going to take you down with him. He was that sort of man, wasn't he?" She looked at the corpse of the monster who would gladly have ordered them all disposed of and shuddered.

"I did it for you." Her father wheedled, sticking to the story he had concocted to allow himself to commit this ghastly deed. "To keep you safe. He could still have arranged to harm us. He was a danger to us until that noose shut him up forever!"

Irene shook her head. She wasn't going to let him use her to justify murder. "We would have organized protection. My mother's men…"

"Look, this is pointless." Her father chopped at the air with a stiff wrist as he spoke. "An evil man is dead. You are safe. We are all safe. We will start again in Hanover, where our family name is respected. But we need to go *now*."

The magnitude of her father's indifference struggled to sink in. "You would leave the servants to deal with this." She indicated the bloody corpse.

"They are not my concern. You are. Come now. Time is of the essence."

"What will happen to them?"

"To whom?"

"The servants, Father. The staff who have served us faithfully for years."

"The house is a loss to me," he said in a disturbingly detached manner. "Some relative will claim it if it is not seized by the authorities. The servants will find other positions. They should not be your concern. It is time to leave Munro behind. There is nothing for you here anymore."

Irene looked at her father properly for the first time. He flinched a little under the raw judgment in her eyes. "You are wrong, Father, about so many things. I would venture to say you have been wrong about *everything*. Munro has what matters most to me. My mother. Mr. Macrae. Dear Miss Bathurst. Hutchins and these servants whom you would cast aside so callously. Each of them is worth more to me than you and your self-serving lies. Go ahead and leave. Don't look back. There is nothing for *you* here. I, on the other hand, intend to start truly living at last. A life you would not grant me. Go, by all means. You are not wanted."

Mr. Sangford stood motionless for what felt like an eternity. Irene began to tire, her crutches digging into her underarms and her half-healed leg starting to swell. But she would not stir. He must not see her falter. This man must know she could stand without him.

He blinked, and the spell was broken. Wordlessly, he turned his back to her, taking one step and then another until he was striding down the passage into a future that no longer contained her. He did not look back, nor did she hope he would.

As soon as he was out of sight, Irene staggered back to the library to claim the nearest chair. She massaged her swollen limb as best she could, listening all the while to the sounds of their departure. No further attempts were made to include her. The bustle shifted out of doors. Loud voices orchestrated the loading of chests and bags and, finally, people. The carriage, heavily laden, rumbled past the window and down the street, the sound of the exodus retreating into silence.

Irene placed her hands upon her knees and let out a slow breath, exhaling the past. She felt strangely peaceful. Her future, as uncertain as it was, now lay firmly in her own hands.

Then she remembered Cranbourn.

"Hutchins!" she shouted, unable to reach the bell pull from where she sat.

The butler appeared in a rather subdued state before her. "You called, Miss Sangford?"

"Hutchins. Dear Hutchins. You are going to see and hear some rather unpleasant things today, I'm afraid. But I am counting on you to see it through with me. I promise to be honest with you every step of the way and will listen to any advice you have to offer in dealing with all that must be done. Are you willing to stick by me?"

"Miss Sangford," said the butler solemnly, "it would be my honor."

"Thank you. I am immensely grateful to you." She drew in a deep breath. "Then we should begin by sending for Madame Dubois. Now that my father is gone, she is welcome. You should know, Hutchins, that she is the woman who gave birth to me. If that shocks you, I ask that you keep that opinion to yourself until matters have been dealt with. But I expect her to be treated as any other guest while I remain lady of this house, however brief that may be."

Hutchins's eyes grew round, but he simply swallowed his personal thoughts and said, "Yes, miss."

"You will also need to have Mr. Macrae fetched. And tell him to bring a constable and a doctor. We have a body in the study. My father, as it turns out, is a murderer. I shall not be protecting him from the consequences of his actions. If he is caught before he escapes abroad, so be it." Irene had said enough. Reporting her father's intended destination to the authorities was necessary. She just didn't have the heart to give him up entirely. Irene was not made of the same cold and ruthless stuff her father was. If and when he was arrested, that was his due. But helping them find him and hang him… Irene shuddered. No, she had done enough.

Hutchins stood with jaw open, seemingly unable to comprehend what he had been told or to bring himself to move.

"That is all for now," Irene said as calmly as possible, though she had started to tremble as the magnitude of the day's events began to settle upon her with its full weight. "I believe that is the worst of it." She clenched her hands into balls to try to keep from shaking. "As for the staff, I shall help each and every one of you find new positions. If my name no longer means anything, I shall rely on the goodness of Miss Bathurst and Mrs. Macrae to speak on your behalf. I give you my assurances in that regard."

Hutchins gave a quick bow of the head. "Very good, miss. And when I have made these arrangements, I shall have some tea sent to you."

"The strong kind?" She offered a half-smile, her lips twitching as she fought for self-control.

"The strong kind," he answered warmly.

"Perhaps the servants would be thirsty too," she suggested.

"Yes, miss. Most kind of you to think of them. Strong tea for everyone, then."

"Thank you, Hutchins." Her voice grew small, and her chin began to quiver.

The butler cast his gaze upon the floor. "If you will excuse me…"

Irene nodded silently.

After Hutchins left the room, Irene allowed the fullness of her emotions to surface freely. Disappointment, betrayal, fear—these roared up through her throat in convulsive sobs. She uttered a primal groan, born of a place so deep, she had not known it existed until now. Her lips pulled back to release the full extent of her heartbreak. All pretense, all claim to dignity, was gone.

She grieved for being denied the mother she should have had. And for the years wasted following the example of a father who had only sought his own interests. She wept until the wracking of her body subsided and she entered a strange pool of calm.

At first, she only felt numb, her head dull and thick. It was scarce an improvement to the intensity of her tears, for it seemed to her she had lost all sense of self.

Irene's face was uncomfortably hot, her nose stuffy even after she had blown it soundly several times. She eyed her crutches. She was in no mood to struggle with them, but she must learn to care for herself.

Pulling herself upright, she steered her legs carefully through to the drawing room and out through the French doors. A light breeze began to cool her skin at once. The touch was gentle, soothing, like a mother's love. Irene took a few deep, nourishing breaths. The garden was awash with the scents of a myriad blooms.

She settled herself onto the bench that Mr. Macrae had carried her to before, on a day that seemed like a lifetime ago. Irene wished he were here now, not to go through the motions of a murder inquiry, but to sit with her, letting the sun warm their faces, speaking easily—or not at all, as the mood dictated.

She had told him she would help with the investigation into her father. And she had kept that promise. What she wanted now was simple kindness. Tenderness. *His* kindness. *His* tenderness. Irene wanted to shed the disappointments and lost opportunities like a skin that had grown too tight for her. To stretch her vulnerable new self and grow into the fullness of her potential. And she wanted to do this with Nathaniel Macrae.

If he would have her.

CHAPTER TWENTY-FOUR

NATHANIEL CURSED EVERY minute that passed before he could get to Miss Sangford. He was grateful she had felt she could count on him. But that meant doing as she had asked, making sure a constable and doctor were duly informed of the situation at the Sangford home. And that took time.

The thought of her abandoned in the house with the body of Lord Cranbourn, forced to deal with her father's crimes and an uncertain future, made him want to push the whole world aside and rush straight to her. If there were ever a time when reputation and propriety meant nothing at all, it was now. Nathaniel was not going to have anyone dictate whether or not it was appropriate to comfort her, or stand up for her, or personally throttle her father for her.

It was abhorrent to think of Miss Sangford tarred with her father's vile brush. Never in his wildest imaginings had Nathaniel believed the man capable of murder. The investigation had suggested Sangford's involvement in a plot, even an arranged assassination, but not murder with his own two hands.

If Sangford was captured before he left English shores, he would hang. That much was certain. As such, Nathaniel was relieved that elements of the information given him were too vague to act upon with impetus. For example, he did not know where the fleeing family was headed. And by the time he had gathered that information, there was a good chance the fiend would have gotten away. Depending on which country he fled to, he might have escaped for good.

There was a strong measure of relief in this outcome. Nathaniel could not bear the thought of Miss Sangford carrying the burden of her father's death upon her shoulders. She had reported him. If caught, he would surely be found guilty. There was only one suitable punishment for the caliber of his wicked deed. Though none of it was Miss Sangford's fault by any means, Nathaniel worried that she would feel somehow responsible for the just penalty her father would receive. After all, she was not the cold creature that he was. Truly, it was a miracle she was not. And he loved her all the more for it.

As he drew up to the mews beside the Sangford house, he leaped from Archer's back, tossing the reins over the saddle and calling toward the stables for someone to tend to his horse. He did not knock at the front door, but marched straight in. Hurrying from room to room, he called out, "Miss Sangford, I am here!" until her refined tones called back, "We are in the garden!"

'We.'

Nathaniel did not pause, but he lost a little momentum. He had pictured himself swooping in and taking Miss Sangford in his arms, soothing her and stroking her dark locks, speaking soft, nurturing words into her shattered heart. But someone was here already. Perhaps Miss Bathurst. Even in the presence of this supportive friend, Nathaniel felt a certain moderation was required in his actions, and he was bitterly disappointed.

As he entered the lush display of the garden through the French doors, Madame Dubois rose and released Miss Sangford's hand, which she had been holding in both of hers.

"Ah, Mr. Macrae," she said, smiling down at her daughter. "If you have come, then all is well now. I shall leave you two to talk. I think the need for a chaperone is a little superfluous under the circumstances. I shall see if I can be of use with the staff. A firm hand offering direction might give them a sense of order. If nothing else, they will feel less spare."

Nathaniel nodded and made to take her seat, but as Madame Dubois passed him, she squeezed his wrist and said in a low voice, "You have my blessing." It was not the sort of comment he was expecting under the circumstances, and yet it was oddly comforting.

Now that he was here, in the presence of his beloved—how strange it felt to use that word, and yet how right—he was reminded once again how much she resembled a fragile bird. With her broken leg still confining her movements, and her eyes glistening with recent tears, she looked for all the world like a hatchling who must be scooped up and returned to her nest. But her nest was gone, washed away by the storms of life.

Then she smiled. It began shyly at first, then warmed and widened. Her eyes, too, though wet with grief, carried a new confidence. She reached out her arm, her fingers lengthening until all of her was leaning forward, beckoning him closer.

His hesitation melted away. He rushed toward her and curled his fingers around hers, bringing her hand to his cheek and pressing a kiss into her palm. Her free hand cupped his face, her smile wobbling as tears fell afresh.

"I don't deserve this," she said, her voice a whisper.

"No," said Nathaniel, waving his arm toward the house behind him. "You didn't deserve *that*. But you are free of it all. And I will take care of you as you ought to have been cared for."

"I have some money of my own," she said suddenly. "My mother put it aside for me. You don't have to take pity on me."

Nathaniel's head jerked back. "Is that what you think this is? Does this feel like pity to you, woman?" His voice grew husky. "My heart is fit to burst with the love I have for you. I would carry you off and make you mine right now, but there has been enough chaos in your world of late. We will do this properly. No half measures."

She shook her head. "It doesn't matter what we want. Your parents would never accept me in your life now that my name is attached to the evil my father has done. Even if I keep my origins a secret, this deed makes me a pariah in the eyes of society."

"It is not society who wants to marry you," Nathaniel said, his eyes refusing to release her own.

"You do not know what you are saying." Miss Sangford finally wrenched her gaze from his. "It is impossible."

"Miss Sangford," he began with some frustration, then he gathered himself, softening his tone. "Irene…" Her head lifted. "I have fought these feelings ever since I met you, to no avail. Do you think it matters who birthed you or whether your father is on the wrong side of the law? It is *you* I love. Not some idea of you. Not a pretty package with a bow. *You*. Brave, beautiful you!"

"Mr. Macrae." Her voice had grown solemn, her mouth stern. "You move among the shadowy elements of society. Yet you are not truly one of them. You may still enter a gentleman's home if he chooses it. Just as there are men who visit my mother's establishment while keeping their status in the *ton*. There are rules that can be bent. But marrying me would smash them to pieces. It would be unfair to your poor, dear mother if her son were ruined because of me."

Nathaniel could not help himself. The guffaw escaped his throat before he could stop it. The look of abject horror on Miss Sangford's face cut it short, but he was forced to suck his lips between his teeth to stop himself from smiling.

"I fail to see the humor in what I have said," Miss Sangford pointed out.

"I'm terribly sorry. I meant no disrespect. It's just that, well, it wasn't that long ago that my mother wished I would marry the new kitchen maid. You might as well know she's desperate for grandchildren. And I am unlikely to provide her with any, thanks to the infamy my work has attached to me. No family of consequence will have me."

"So wed an honest kitchen maid," said Miss Sangford plainly, though her heart clearly wasn't in it.

"Don't want one," said Nathaniel, still grinning. "And my

mother already likes you. If I tell her you've said 'yes,' she won't be able to call the banns fast enough."

"Don't be ridiculous," Miss Sangford scolded, but she sat a little taller and her cheeks took on a faint blush.

His smile wrinkled with mischief. "We could even have the wedding at Madame Dubois's, and my mother would attend it."

Miss Sangford crossed her arms and scowled. "Oh, now you are just being ridiculous!"

"The real question is," Nathaniel continued, suddenly serious, "whether someone of your genteel upbringing could live with a husband who shamelessly visits all sorts of places of ill repute, coming home sometimes at dawn, smelling of a tannery or a dockyard or a woman's perfume, without doubting me or willing me to stay home at night."

"Perhaps," Miss Sangford said, lifting her head higher, "I could accompany you."

Nathaniel looked eagerly at his wonderful Irene. "Two of a kind, then?" he asked. "A duet of detectives?"

"I don't see why not," she answered. "What have I got to lose? We have already solved our first case together. And I would rather be digging up clues with you than waiting up for you to come home. I certainly have no future as a lady anymore. I might as well find a good use for my time."

"Ah, the secrets you will charm from the lips of unsuspecting gentlemen…"

Irene rolled her eyes. "More likely, they will confess from the sheer terror of what a Sangford might do."

"But you will be a Macrae, my dearest. And we are a witty, charming, likeable bunch. You will fit right in."

Someone cleared their throat near the French doors. They both looked up at Hutchins, whose ruddy cheeks suggested he must have had some *very* strong tea.

"The doctor is here, Mr. Macrae. He wishes to see the…er…"

"I'll be right there." Nathaniel grudgingly stood. The constable would be here soon. Until then, however, he was the nearest thing to the law in the house. Besides, Lord Howell would want a detailed report on everything that had transpired. He couldn't slack off now, no matter how much Irene Sangford drew him to her.

She must have read his mind, for she nodded encouragement to him. "I'm not going anywhere. I trust that you will see everything is dealt with properly. People are going to talk, but I would prefer if there was a healthy dose of accuracy in their gossip. That will make it easier to endure."

"When I return, we will resume our conversation about the future."

"Let us lay the past to rest first." Irene gave an involuntary shudder. "You may feel less inclined to talk about matters of the heart when you have been inside the study."

Nathaniel remembered, too late, that Irene had stood at the very place the murder had been committed. For all her poise and grace, a part of her must have been revulsed at the memory. "I'm sorry. I have grown calloused by my own experiences. I should have considered the impact of what you have seen. Would you rather I refrained from speaking of my hopes for our future while the coroner and the magistrate are busy with this case? I do not want to make light of all you have been through."

"Perhaps that is best. For now."

The added phrase gave Nathaniel hope that he had not over-stepped the mark completely. "I will wait for you to decide when the time is right," he said.

"Thank you, Mr. Macrae."

Nathaniel wanted so much to offer her the use of his first name. Seeing the word shaped by her tender mouth, knowing her tongue had formed it, was the sweetest expectation. But he dared not mention it. He had already rushed in like a wildebeest from the African plains, declaring himself without any thought to her circumstances. What must she think of him?

And yet... she smiled up at him. She had pondered marriage with him. Nothing seemed to frighten her anymore. Still, her wings were new and untested. He must give her time to grow stronger and shake this day from her as completely as possible.

Nathaniel resisted the urge to leave a kiss upon her milky brow. If he exercised patience, the time for kisses would come soon enough.

He entered the house, pausing as he remembered how she had reached for him when he had arrived, cupping his face in her hand. Nathaniel touched his cheek reverently, savoring the memory. Then he mentally tucked it into his heart. Unpleasant business lay ahead, and he would not taint the mental image of her with such matters.

Behind him sat Miss Sangford. *Irene*. He could feel her eyes upon his back. It grew warm and he hastened deeper into the house to escape the effects of her presence.

Soon, though. Soon.

Until then, he would be counting the hours.

CHAPTER TWENTY-FIVE

Monday, May 12th, 1817

THE BOARDING HOUSE was respectable and clean, but a far cry from what Irene had grown accustomed to. Still, she would never go back. Even now, she struggled to shake off the horror of what had happened at her father's house. She did not know if a new owner had been found. Nor did she care. There had been very few happy memories there, even before her father's heinous act.

She missed the servants, though. Not so much for the convenience of lifestyle they offered her, but for the company they had provided daily and which was now lost. Irene especially missed Hutchins, who had been willing to sacrifice his position to help find Mr. Macrae and who had put aside any personal reservations to help her when it had all gone so horribly wrong.

The only thing that made the loss of the loyal servants bearable was the knowledge that Mrs. Macrae had managed to find each and every one of them a new position. Hutchins, in fact, had taken on the role of under-butler at the Macrae residence. Although it was a step down for him, their own butler was approaching retirement, and who better to step into the role at that time than the man who had helped to save the young master's life?

Where the rest had shifted to, she did not know, but she trusted Mrs. Macrae to have done right by them. Indeed, if Mrs.

Macrae had had her way, Irene would have been currently be safely ensconced in one of their guest rooms. Irene, however, had put her foot down squarely. There was enough talk. She did not need to add "hussy" to the legion of names she had already been called.

The coroner's inquest had been swiftly handled, the evidence damning. By some small miracle, the case had been assigned to the next assize court, which was held within a month of the terrible climax of events. Since the high court judges did their circuit of the larger towns only a few times a year, this was a blessing indeed. Irene could not imagine the case lingering on and on for months. She wanted to be done with it.

Her father, of course, had managed his escape skillfully. However, his life in Hanover had come to nought. The Prince Regent had not considered their vague familial connection sufficient reason to tolerate his actions in England and her father had been forced to flee once again. His whereabouts were currently unknown, while his wife and Amelia remained in Hanover, no doubt having to protest the terrible "lies" being spread about them in England. Certainly, the days of seeking a husband with a title for Amelia were over.

Irene found it hard to pity any of them. If there had been kindness in her life, perhaps she… No matter. She would survive. They would simply have to do the same.

On the day the court was held, Irene did not attend. She did not wish to bear the humiliation that should have been her father's. Instead, she chose this day to send for Mr. Sunderland the surgeon to remove her "cast," as he had called it. She had waited an extra week to be sure all was mended. Her leg certainly felt much stronger, and the swelling was greatly reduced, such that the cast wiggled a bit as she moved. On this day, the courts would set her free of the past. What better occasion to reclaim her ability to walk?

"Now," said Mr. Sunderland as he carefully cut through the length of the cast and slipped it from her leg, "let us see how well it has healed. Will you allow me to palpitate the area to determine its condition?"

Irene nodded. Nervous excitement built up as he touched her leg with firm movements. She was relieved to discover that no pain accompanied his touch of discovery.

"Hmm, the bone is sound. Since you only had a fracture and not a complete break, it has set well. You will find, however, that the muscle has atrophied somewhat from disuse. You will remedy that with time. As movement resumes, the swelling will also subside. All in all, another two months should do it. It is imperative that you return to activity gradually. Limit your walking to flat surfaces and use your crutches for the next fortnight. I shall call on you again at that time. If you heed my advice, your recovery will continue as smoothly as it has until now."

Irene immediately reached for her crutches and pulled herself up. The partially healed leg did indeed feel weak and fragile without its protective cast. She slowly lowered her foot to the ground and stood, shifting her weight gingerly to center. It was a small feat… and yet such an accomplishment! "I shall walk you to the door," she said, feeling very pleased with her new ability, limited though it was. She stepped cautiously from the small sitting room, where the landlady allowed her lodgers to receive guests, and followed the surgeon to the front door.

As he swung it open, lifting his hat to bid Irene good day, they discovered a well-dressed woman on the step, her hand poised to knock.

"Madame Dubois!" Irene's surprise creased into a smile. "Do come in! I must show you my leg!" She promptly lifted her skirt to reveal a limb devoid of cast.

Mr. Sunderland, who had but minutes before been handling that same leg with professional hands, now blushed and all but fled the house, bidding them a hasty adieu before hurrying down the street.

"He seems unlikely to be one of your customers." Irene

grinned as they slowly returned to the sitting room. "Since showing an ankle is enough to bring color to his cheeks."

"You'd be amazed," said her mother. "Some men just like to talk while someone soothes their brow. There are a lot of lonely men in a city this size."

Irene carefully lowered herself back into a chair and sighed with satisfaction. Her mother sat in the seat nearest to her. "I am grateful to find you in a buoyant mood," she said, causing Irene to lift an eyebrow.

"Oh? Have you brought bad news?"

"No, not bad, but weighty. I attended the trials of Pratt, Bligh, Richards, and Harrison. I thought you might wish to know the outcome."

"It is done already?"

"It surprised me too. But Mr. Macrae says these matters proceed quickly because the judges have many cases to hear before they move onto the next town in their circuit. I believe, between witness statements and the coroner's report, they were able to judge all four men simultaneously. The verdict was quick and decisive and delivered within the hour."

"Mr. Macrae was there?" asked Irene, ignoring all other details her mother had just shared.

"Of course. Many of the statements were his. He has been instrumental in bringing those men to justice. That is what he does, after all. Although he took great care to present himself as an incidental witness rather than an investigator. The success of his work rather depends on no one knowing that he does it."

"Was it awful? Were there many details of… you know…"

"Enough for a clear conviction. Three of the men are to be shipped off to the penal colony in Australia. Richards, who did most of the actual harm, will hang for it."

Irene did not want to ask the next question, but she knew she must. "And my father? What will become of him? He is guilty of the worst crime of all."

Her mother pursed her lips. "As long as he remains anonymous wherever he is, he will escape the consequences."

Irene toyed with her hands, agitation rising within her. "It's not right. He killed a man. He even planned it. I am sure of it."

"He ruined many a life long before he used a weapon for it," her mother said matter-of-factly. "One day, he will cross the wrong person. Let fate deal with him. You must set these matters in the past now, dearest. Your life is but beginning." She lowered her eyes coyly. "If I am not mistaken, Mr. Macrae will make certain it begins with him."

Irene felt her cheeks grow warm. Mr. Macrae had called upon her a handful of times in the past month, but always, he had heeded the promise he had made to push no further on the talk of marriage until the case had been heard and the legal matters closed. Irene had hoped that she would then be able to stop holding her breath, for she half-expected her father to be dragged back to England and brought to the gallows in a public place. He deserved it. She knew that. But she still bore his name. It felt as if the noose were around her own neck.

"Mother," she said suddenly, for they had agreed to allow themselves this honesty and intimacy of reference when in a private setting. "What was your father's name? I do not want to think of you constantly as Madame Dubois. It is not a true reflection of who you are."

Her mother looked at her sternly. "We are whatever we choose to be. You should know that. Otherwise, you would have been in Hanover now, pretending to be outraged at your circumstances."

"But you didn't choose this life," protested Irene. "Not really. Who were you when you were but a child, with all the innocence of those years?"

"I have not spoken that name for many years." Her mother looked off into the distance, as if she could see exactly where she had left that part of herself behind.

"Won't you tell me? I would like to know where I come from. I would like to know your real identity."

Her mother shifted her focus onto Irene. "You can claim nothing of that world," she said, her body stiff, her eyes cold.

"I don't want anything but to preserve your name. To let it hang upon the air once again as it is spoken. I desire nothing more. Only to give back what was taken from you so cruelly. We shall keep it between us. And one day—may it be many years hence—I shall have it written on your tombstone. And your family will never be able to take it away again."

Silence sat between them for what seemed like an eternity. Then, with a solemnity that lay heavily upon the words, Madame Dubois declared her true self. "I was Giselle de Vere, daughter of the Marquess of Northumberland." And then, with a sharp tang of bitterness, she added, "For all the good it did me."

"Giselle De Vere." Irene repeated the name with care, allowing the taste of each word to linger on her tongue. "It is a beautiful name, Mother."

"*You* have given me the name I most desired," answered the woman now called Madame Dubois.

"What is that?" Irene asked, confusion knitting her brows together.

"'Mother,'" came the answer, followed by a smile that surfaced from the heart. "I have waited three and twenty years for the privilege of hearing it said by you. And I would have waited three and twenty more. I am satisfied."

"*Oh!*" said Irene, drumming with little fists upon her knees. "This leg! I want to jump up and hug you, Mother, but you will have to fetch it from my arms."

"Gladly," came the answer. Irene's mother rose from her chair and leaned down gracefully, every inch a marquess's daughter. Once she had Irene in her embrace, however, all names were forgotten, and the two women held each other as if, in so doing, they anchored each other amidst life's storms.

A knock sounded on the door of the boarding house.

"Ah," said Irene's mother, straightening up, "that will be Mr. Macrae. "Let me open the door for him and then I will be on my way. Just remember to send me an invitation to the wedding," she teased. Gliding across the carpeted floor, she stopped, turned back, and dropped a wink over her shoulder before resuming her exit.

"Mr. Macrae!" she cried, flinging open the door and causing the young man, who stood waiting, hat in hand, to step back in alarm. "The answer is 'yes,'" she informed him. "Don't waste too much time asking the question." And she swept out the door and down the street to call a hackney.

Mr. Macrae entered the house with perhaps rather less poise than he had intended, flustered as he was by Madame Dubois's greeting. Irene pitied him at once.

"Don't mind my mother," she told him. "Come and sit. I have already heard the news about the trial. And I am content that justice has been served as best it could be under the circumstances. My father may have escaped, but the fear that he might one day be punished similarly will follow him wherever he goes. Not only that, but the whole country will soon know of these men's interference in stirring up the unrest. If that can lighten the sentence of the workers who were drawn into an unnecessary uprising, I shall be even more at peace."

"I am grateful that some of your worry has been diminished," said Mr. Macrae as he lifted his coattails to sit in the chair Irene's mother had vacated. "Hopefully now, with the papers reporting the facts of the case, people will rightly focus their criticism on those who are actually guilty and give you some grace."

Irene cast her eyes to the floor. "I find myself growing a thicker skin," she said. "I no longer feel the jab of their comments as fiercely. But I worry for Olivia, whose parents have joined the hue and cry against my family and want her to have nothing more to do with me." She shrugged. "I'm not sure they ever really liked the Sangfords much, anyway. Our parents had been using each other to promote their own daughters, and I no longer have the status to continue such an arrangement. Besides, it was not an arrangement founded on affection. Mary's silence toward me is proof of that. However, Olivia is still my friend. I only wish I knew how to proceed with our friendship now that it does not have her parents' blessing. She has sneaked in to see me twice already and written countless letters. I do so appreciate her loyalty, but I would not have her suffer for it."

"No doubt she has realized your friendship is a worthy prize. It is to her credit that she has such good sense."

"But she is still dependent upon her parents for everything. She should not cross them. Not for my sake."

"The heart wants what the heart wants," said Mr. Macrae, leaning closer to Irene. "I believe the same can be said of true friendship. You have offered her what no one else has. She will not easily give it up."

Irene tried to concentrate, but his lips were very distracting, especially now that they had drawn nearer. "She has already paid back any kindness I have shown tenfold. She must take care of her own needs now." *Ah, yes, needs.* She needed that mouth to stop speaking and press against hers, parting to let his warm tongue slip between her lips and…

Mr. Macrae flashed his charming smile, lighting up his gray eyes. "I believe that is exactly what she is doing."

"Pardon?" Irene was wrenched back into reality.

"Miss Bathurst is taking care of her needs, as you suggested. She needs *you*. You underestimate how important you are to her. You have that sort of effect on people."

Irene thought she should probably make some sort of protest against the compliment, but she *wanted* to have that effect, at least on Mr. Macrae. And then all thinking left her, for he stretched out his arm, slipping his hand over fingers and sliding his skin against hers, his thumb resting in the hollow of her wrist so that her pulse leaped into it. Her entire body rippled with glorious tension, growing pert and soft simultaneously.

"I was wondering," he said in a voice so low, he almost purred, "whether we could revisit a certain conversation."

"Hmm?" she managed to say, incapable of bringing words

past the desire in her throat.

"I confess it has been a challenge to wait a whole month." His gaze dropped to her hand, his fingers caressing it as he spoke. "But I promised to give you space. You needed time. And now I'm wondering, if you do not mind me asking, whether enough time has passed?" He lifted his hopeful eyes to hers, as though begging for the answer to be "yes."

Irene nodded slowly, then more emphatically.

"You are ready for me to repeat the question?"

Irene's throat was so tight with anticipation, she dared not speak, for her voice would be nothing but a squeak. Instead, her nodding became almost vigorous, and she clutched his hand as if to anchor herself in the headiness of the moment.

Mr. Macrae stepped down from the seat onto one knee, his hand still cradling hers. "Miss Sangford, nothing could make me happier than sharing my messy life with you. Would you be willing to cast aside all usual expectations and be my wife, knowing that I will love you completely and enthusiastically?"

Irene squeezed his hand and nodded, tears pricking at her eyes, her lips crushing into what she could only imagine was a most unattractive smile as she fought not to cry.

"Yes?" Nathaniel asked, wanting to be sure.

"Yes," Irene answered in a voice that was more a high-pitched groan than a happy declaration. It was possibly the most unconvincing "yes" in the long history of proposals, but Irene could not help that joyful tears and relief had overcome her.

And then he kissed her.

Swooping her up against his chest, he kissed her mouth, her eyes, the hollow beneath her ears, and then her lips again until laughter broke through the tears and breathlessness, and Irene was able to say, "Put me down, Nathaniel. My leg is still too weak to stand for long."

Instead, he bent down and tucked an arm beneath her, lifting her up to float in his strong embrace. Now his lips found hers once more, lingering, parting just enough for their breath to mingle, pushing forward hungrily so that their mouths opened to devour each other with a yearning that seemed unquenchable.

Irene clung to him, her fingers digging into the muscle behind his shoulders, her breasts pressed up against his manly chest. She wanted more, *more*!

Nathaniel groaned and drew his mouth from hers, leaving her reaching for it, only to feel bitter disappointment when he carefully lowered her back into her chair.

"I will have the banns called at once." His voice was husky and thick. "Until then, perhaps a chaperone is required."

"'A chaperone'?" Irene could not hide her dismay. "I am no longer a lady of the *ton*. There is no reputation to be salvaged. And you have called upon me here without me needing a chaperone before."

"*I* need the chaperone," he answered, his eyes aflame with desire. "I would have you, Irene. Here. Now. Completely. But I would have you treated with the respect you deserve."

Irene folded her arms. "What if I don't want it? What if I feel respected enough and just want to be closer to you? You would deny me?"

"You minx." He growled. "Do not try to reason with your brilliant mind, for you will persuade me. I am not that strong."

"In that case…" Irene grinned.

"In that case…" Nathaniel stood up. "I had best be going. I want to call on the vicar immediately. And my parents are awaiting your answer as eagerly as I did."

"They are?"

"Oh, yes! My mother is assigning an entire wing of the house to us and the brood of grandchildren she hopes we shall fill it with. And my father is back from his business trip, ready to battle whoever says anything against us. They love me quite fiercely for such gentle folk. And they are eager to love you as their daughter."

Irene grew quiet, her earlier playfulness forgotten. "I never thought I would be loved like that."

"Now you shall know it in abundance." Nathaniel paused thoughtfully. "We must find a way for your mother and Miss Bathurst to attend the wedding. I shall put my mind to it as soon as I have spoken to the vicar."

"My mother disguises herself very well when she dresses as a lady of society. No one guesses her true identity unless they have sampled of her 'wares.' And then they would not dare speak up and say they recognize her."

"Agreed. And she must come to the ball. My mother insists on delaying the dance until our wedding day. Since we will have so few guests at the ceremony, she has decided against a wedding breakfast. Instead, she wants to host the ball in honor of our nuptials."

"Is June not too warm for dancing? The guests will use any excuse, I think, not to attend when they know I am to be a part of the family."

"Those sorts of people have never attended in the past, either," Nathaniel pointed out.

Irene's cheeks burned with shame. *She* had been that sort of person.

"Would you mind if Lord and Lady Howell attended the dance?" Nathaniel asked suddenly. "I understand there has been some ill feeling between you in the past."

Irene's humiliation sank even deeper. She had truly done very little to be proud of. Until she had met Nathaniel. Now she hardly recognized herself.

"If they will accept my apology for past actions as sincere," she answered, "I would be grateful to deliver it in person. But I would not be surprised if they wanted nothing to do with me."

Nathaniel considered this. "We shall see. Though I can assure you, if they attend, all our other guests will do the same. Our family has been blessed to know a fair number of very reasonable people."

Irene nodded in acknowledgement of his words, but the mood had shifted and she no longer answered with her earlier excitement.

Nathaniel angled his head at her. "Have I raised a ticklish subject?"

Irene stared at her fingertips. "It is not your fault that my past bears so little merit."

"Then we shall strive to amend it."

Irene lifted her chin. "Just like that?"

"Just like that." Nathaniel stepped forward and knelt before her once again so that they might look upon each other without the difference in height. "Why dwell on things that no longer play a role in our lives?" He tucked a whisp of hair behind her ear. "In a few weeks, we shall start our life together. It will be a new beginning in every way. That is enough for me."

"Nathaniel…" Irene said the name tenderly, but with a hint of insecurity.

"Yes, darling Irene?"

"I do love you so."

And there it was. His broad smile. The one that spread from mouth to cheeks to eyes and wreathed his entire face in joy. "As I do you," he answered.

The certainty of his utterance wrapped around her heart, binding its wounds. They had already begun to heal, like the fracture in her leg. *One day,* she thought to herself, *I shall be able to stand strongly again, inside and out. And when life rears at me and throws me off, this man will carry me safely home. I shall never again be afraid to fall.*

CHAPTER TWENTY-SIX

Monday, June 2nd, 1817

MR. AND MRS. Nathaniel Macrae arrived home, newly married, to the applause of the servants lined up at the end of the drive. Hutchins was there, grinning broadly as if he were the father of the bride—a reality Irene would have been mightily pleased with, had it been possible.

A new face stepped forward shyly.

"My dear," said Mrs. Macrae to Irene, "this is Patterson, your new lady's maid. Every woman of substance should have one, don't you agree?"

Nathaniel's mother had no doubt chosen her words with care, and Irene hugged herself that she was blessed with such a thoughtful mother-in-law. Until a few months ago, she had hoped for little more than marriage with a title and the barest of civilities. Now, however, she was nestled within the bosom of a family who truly understood what *being* a family meant.

"Thank you, Mother." Irene placed a kiss upon the woman's cheek.

The older Mrs. Macrae beamed. "You are most welcome. How is your leg? Would you like a footman to help you upstairs? Patterson can help you settle in your new room."

"I will manage, thank you," Irene answered. "I am much stronger now."

"Besides," said Nathaniel, puffing out his chest, "if anyone is going to be picking my wife up into their arms, it's going to be me."

"In that case…" Irene smiled coyly. "I feel positively weak and helpless. You should definitely help me to my room."

"Er… should I still help you with your things, ma'am?" Patterson asked.

Nathaniel answered, but his eyes were riveted upon Irene. "I think I shall be able to make my wife comfortable on my own, thank you, Patterson."

"Yes, sir." Patterson blushed right down into her white lace collar.

The senior Mrs. Macrae shooed the servants back into the house before taking her husband by the arm and suggesting they retire to the drawing room. The new couple was left standing on the steps, alone.

"I wonder who's going to undress me now?" Irene teased.

"It would be my pleasure." Nathaniel did not wait any longer. Lifting his wife into his powerful arms, he paced across the foyer, staggered somewhat up the stairs, and kicked the bedroom door open with the toe of his shoe.

"You can put me down now," said Irene.

"Yes, my lady." He bowed, but before he straightened, he reached under the hem of her dress and slipped her silk shoes from her feet. "I will need instruction for the fiddly buttons and ribbons," he murmured, "if I am to remove the rest."

Irene wished the heat that arose in her could simply disintegrate the clothing from her body. Instead, Nathaniel painstakingly undid the many fastenings, slipping each layer from her until all that remained was her slip.

"My turn," she whispered, shifting his coat from his shoulders. She loosened his cravat, pulling his shirt over his head, his smooth chest warm under the spread of her fingers. The buttons of his trousers resisted her hasty attempts to undo them, and Nathaniel put his hands over her own, guiding them to complete the task.

Passing footfalls in the passage echoed louder than expected, making Nathaniel spin around. "I forgot to close the door," he muttered, crossing the rug. "There," he said, satisfied. "Shut and locked." He turned back to Irene, unfastening the last of his trouser buttons as he strode toward her.

"Now," he said, as he leaned down to kiss her neck, "where were we?"

WHEN NATHANIEL APPEARED in the family ballroom with his wife upon his arm that evening, he knew he was the happiest man alive.

Irene was radiant in a white, silk gown with a fine, red tulle overlay and black-and-gold embroidery all along the hem and bodice. Nathaniel would not normally have noticed such details, but the dress was a gift from his mother, and she had drawn attention to every element of the design.

What Nathaniel *did* notice was the way his wife gazed up at him without reservation. Any bashfulness she might have had was now a thing of the past. She was his, from the tip of her elegant nose to the slender feet that stood her contentedly by his side.

His body still buzzed with the memory of their earlier intimacy. "It is unfortunate that married couples are not encouraged to dance together," he said a little wistfully, thinking of the long night that lay ahead.

"I would not be able to join in with such energetic dances as the jigs and reels, anyway," answered Irene. "But maybe you can save a waltz for me."

"A waltz?" Nathaniel pretended to be shocked. "Why, Mrs. Macrae, you surprise me! Such an intimate set of steps. What will people think?"

Irene reached up and whispered into his ear. "They will think we have danced like that before."

Her warm breath and even warmer insinuation made Nathaniel grateful that the doors and windows had been flung open and that a pleasant breeze drifted through the ballroom.

"The Viscount and Viscountess Howell," announced the footman on duty.

"Oh," said Irene, all playfulness vanishing from her voice.

"Shall we welcome them together?" Nathaniel asked. "I think the night will be far more enjoyable when this uncertainty has passed."

"Or it might be ruined by his inability to forgive me," Irene replied.

"They came to our wedding. I think he has given you the benefit of the doubt."

"His lordship only came to see if he should speak up and spare you."

Nathaniel shrugged. "Since he did not, and we are, in fact, wed, he must have seen enough to satisfy him."

While they had stood debating thus, the lord and lady in question had made their way across the room and now greeted the guests of honor warmly.

"Mr. and Mrs. Macrae." The viscountess smiled with open sincerity. "What a perfect way to celebrate your beautiful day! If I may add, it is a delight to see how well suited you are! My husband, in fact, remarked on that very thing."

Nathaniel could see the visible relief as tension drained from Irene's previously tight features. "My wife and I thank you for your kind words, Lady Howell. And for joining us tonight. You will be well aware of the marked effect of your presence. We appreciate you wielding your influence in our favor. My wife, in particular, values your willingness to see past what others might not."

Lord Howell, never a man known to waste words, answered bluntly. "I had my reservations, Mrs. Macrae. You will understand if I was slow in believing any change possible. Indeed, I discouraged Nathaniel from pursuing his fascination with you. But I can now say that I have never been more pleased to be so utterly wrong in my assumptions. My congratulations to you both."

Irene gasped.

Nathaniel smiled at his wife. "I am glad to hear you say that, your lordship. As it happens, Irene and I were thinking she might be of use in our future inv..."

Irene tapped him on the arm. She pointed with a finger to the air as if wanting him to listen. "It's a waltz," she whispered.

Nathaniel heard the melodic strains of the violin, saw the eagerness in his wife's upturned face. "Ah, forgive me, Lord Howell. I have promised this dance to the woman who stole my heart."

The viscount granted them a benign smile. "At least this is one theft that is easily solved."

But he was already forgotten. Nathaniel had slipped his hand around Irene's waist, pulling her firmly to him, his hand extended to receive hers. Rising up on their toes, they stepped into the graceful rhythm of the music, their eyes upon each other, the rest of the world fading into the background.

Gliding and spinning, they revolved around each other, pivoting around the axis of their hearts.

Later, much later, when they stumbled, exhausted, into bed, curling up in each other's embrace, their hearts continued to beat a steady pulse of contentment. They slept the undisturbed sleep of lovers who feared nothing. For they had everything they would ever need and more in the person whom they loved.

Acknowledgements

I will never grow tired of thanking my mom for her enthusiastic support of all my projects throughout my life. I know exactly how much of a privilege this is. It is especially meaningful to me that I can talk for hours (and I do!) about my latest manuscript and she will lend a genuinely interested ear. Thank you, Mamma, from the bottom of my heart.

To my hubby, who boasts about me to everyone when, in fact, *he* is so amazing at what *he* does, thank you for being my cheerleader. And for not letting me quit. Every step I take forward has been supported by you.

To my editor, Amy McNulty, a gifted author in her own right, thank you for expecting high standards of me. You help me shake off that dreaded imposter syndrome we authors so often have by holding up the goalposts and then helping me reach them.

To Regina Scott, Caroline Warfield, Alina K. Field, and the Bluestocking Belles, fellow authors who hardly knew me but offered support and encouragement and took me under their wing, my deepest thanks. There are few things more heartwarming than the unexpected kindness of generous souls. I promise to pay it forward.

To my readers, whether you be family, friends, or complete strangers, I wonder if you really know how special you are? Every person who reads a book is telling that author that they have done a good thing, that they have made something worth spending your valuable time on. Certainly, every time *I* see one of your enthusiastic reviews, I jump up from the computer and do a little victory lap through the house. I definitely phone a loved one (see above) and gush about how that has made my whole week. You make a difference. Thank you.

About the Author

Elizabeth Donne writes sweet Regency romance, a natural outpouring of a lifelong love affair with English literature.

She has spent most of her life in Cape Town, South Africa. In 2015, she moved to Iowa with her husband, their two children, two cats, and their African bush dog. When she's not writing, or discovering the secret wonders of the Midwest, she is enthusiastically introducing her visitors to the joys of drinking *rooibos* tea. With a biscuit, of course.